UNEARTHED

First published 2013 by Jurassic London
SW8 1XN, Great Britain

www.jurassic-london.com

978-0-9576462-8-5 (Trade)
978-0-9573475-9-5 (eBook)

Cover by Garen Ewing
www.garenewing.co.uk

2

eBook conversion by handebooks.co.uk

UNEARTHED

In partnership with
The Egypt Exploration Society

Edited by
John J Johnston &
Jared Shurin

For Bram Stoker

CONTENTS

Going Forth by Night   I
John J Johnston, Egypt Exploration Society

The Mummy's Foot   35
Théophile Gautier

Some Words With a Mummy   49
Edgar Allan Poe

Lost in a Pyramid   67
Louisa May Alcott

The Ring of Thoth   79
Arthur Conan Doyle

Lot No. 249   97
Arthur Conan Doyle

The Unseen Man's Story   131
Julian Hawthorne

A Professor of Egyptology   149
Guy Boothby

The Block of Bronze   169
Herbert Crotzer

The Story of Baelbrow   185
E. and H. Heron

The Vanished Mummy   199
Charles Bump

The Death-Bridal of Nitocris   209
George Griffiths

Contributors

About the Egypt Exploration Society

GOING FORTH BY NIGHT

Having provided an introduction to *The Book of the Dead*, Jurassic London's companion volume to *Unearthed*, it is a very real pleasure to have the opportunity of introducing these classic and in certain cases, somewhat less than classic, mummy stories to a new audience.

In writing this overview of mummy fiction, I have not endeavored to be comprehensive, there are entire books out there covering bibliographic information in considerable detail[1] but, instead, to simply provide some context for the tales contained in *Unearthed* and, where necessary, to comment on trends and influences within this important and often overlooked sub-genre of fantastic fiction.

Since long before Napoleon's Egyptian campaign opened the country and its wonders to the West, Egypt, of all cultures of the ancient world has held a peculiar fascination for the wider world. There has always been a small trade in Egyptian antiquities and mummies in particular, sufficient to allow European monarchs in the 16th and 17th centuries to imbibe, absorb and otherwise ingest powdered Egyptian mummy in the hope of extending their lives and increasing their majestic powers.

The trading and importation of mummies from Egypt, across the Mediterranean to Europe, gave rise to what appears to be the earliest recorded modern example of a supernatural tale relating to Egypt's mummified dead. In his 1699 publication, *Traité des Embaumements Selon les Anciens et les Modernes*, Louis Penicher relates an incident whereby the spirits of two mummies being, thus exported by ship, appeared before a priest, who happened to be on board, in "the form of a young man, dressed in a long robe of golden flax, dotted with hieroglyphic emblems from head to toe and covered with gold and precious stones. He had black curly hair and even a short beard and wore a gold medallion pendant on a neck chain, decorated with an ibis and

---

1   Frost, B J. *The Essential Guide to Mummy Literature*. Plymouth, Scarecrow Press.

several other characters[2]," after which, we are informed, the mummies, were summarily ditched overboard.

Away from the world of apparitions, the first scientific unrolling of a mummy appears to have taken place in London in December 1763, being conducted by chemist and physician John Hadley and the Hunter brothers before the German anatomist, Friedrich Blumenbach, almost thirty years later, in a fit of what may only be described as mummymania, tore his way through a number of human and animal mummies in private collections and even the British Museum, during a trip to London in 1792.

The flood-gates really opened, though, with Napoleon's 1798 expedition, after which Europe was in the grip of Egyptomania, as described in an 1805 letter to the London *Morning Chronicle*, which protested, "since this accursed Egyptian style came into fashion... my eldest boy rides on a sphinx instead of a rocking-horse, my youngest has a papboat in the shape of a crocodile, and my husband has built a watercloset in the shape of a pyramid, and has his shirts marked with a lotus."

Ancient Egypt was to be seen throughout Europe in the design of buildings, in private salons, and increasingly in public exhibitions. The rigid monumentality of much Egyptian sculpture arriving in Europe during this period was often seen as alien and barbaric – it provided something of a thrill for the sensation-seeking middle classes, who had grown bored with the elegant lines and perfect marble bodies of "improving" Greek sculpture and then, of course, quite apart from the art, there were the mummies...

The mortuary beliefs of the ancient Egyptians allowed amazed Europeans to gaze with a mixture of horror and wonder on the faces of those who had, no doubt, witnessed the Biblical exodus, marvelled at Joseph's multi-coloured coat and shared a divan with Cleopatra. Egypt's connection with Biblical tales was, certainly, a draw to many, but, far more were enticed by fantasies surrounding the arcane exoticism of this land of ancient knowledge and therianthropic deities and, frankly, the eroticism of lithe and dusky bodies, barely concealed by perfumed and diaphanous clothing. For, in the public imagination, as we shall see, the exotic and erotic often went hand in hand.

The reality, however, most usually encountered at public mummy unrollings in England, often presided over by the anatomist Thomas Pettigrew

---

2   Author's translation from the French.

(1791-1865) was somewhat less than erotic. Pettigrew, Professor of Anatomy at Charing Cross Hospital had made a lucrative and fashionable sideline for himself through the public unrolling of Egyptian mummies, particularly so after the publication of his *A History of Egyptian Mummies* in 1834. A serious and dedicated scientist and antiquarian, "Mummy" Pettigrew, as he became known, was, nonetheless, a considerable showman, whose initial experiments in the field had been attended by the great and the good of European society. Having removed the last of a mummy's bandages, and, often, the top of its head in order to show the empty skull within – the brain had been removed through the nasal canal – Pettigrew would stand the denuded mummy upon its feet in order that they could share the rapturous applause from the audience. What began as serious, scientific enquiry descended, quite rapidly, into grotesque exploitation of the dead with Pettigrew performing to crowds of up to six hundred in venues such as Exeter Hall on The Strand.

By the mid-nineteenth century, no society party was truly complete without an unrolling. The mummies were expensive, as were the celebrated scholars and anatomists who unrolled them: the Duke and Duchess of Sutherland hosted two such events at Stafford (now Lancaster) House in July 1873 and 1875.

Ultimately, however, the anticipation of an unrolling was far more thrilling than the resultant reality of a desiccated corpse, a handful of faience amulets and a bundle of linen bandages, consequently, this is the point where the literary mummy really comes into its own.

Mummy fiction in the modern world begins, as such things often do, with a whimper rather than a bang. Jane Webb's *The Mummy! A Tale of the Twenty-second Century*, published in 1827, is not at all what one might expect, and involves the resurrection, in the year 2127, of Cheops (Khufu), builder of the Great Pyramid, through galvanism, during an overhead thunderstorm – the book was published only nine years after Mary Shelley's *Frankenstein*, with which it has a number of similarities. In the event, Cheops is a rather amiable individual, whose influence tends to enrich the lives of those he encounters and the book is something of an amalgam of early science-fiction morality tale and Swift's *Gulliver's Travels*, with high-speed hot air balloon being the preferred mode of transport in Webb's vision of the future. Indeed, such is

Webb's fascination with the world she has created that it is not until page 219 that Cheops' eyes finally open, "shining with supernatural lustre."

Webb's book was sufficiently popular for a second edition to be published the following year, and for her future husband, John Loudon, the horticulturalist, to be desirous of meeting the book's author, so entranced was he by her futuristic concept of a "steam-powered digging machine."

With "La Pied de Momie," reprinted in this collection as "The Mummy's Foot," the poet, dramatist, critic, and novelist Théophile Gautier turned his attention to ancient Egypt, emboldened, no doubt, by the burgeoning trade in antiquities being carried out in Paris at the time. First published in the September 1840 edition of the French literary magazine *Musée des Familles: Lectures du soir*, this tale capitalizes on the aforementioned erotic aspects of the Egyptomania, particularly evident in the form of small desk ornaments, prevalent during the later nineteenth century, showing an exquisitely detailed painted bronze mummy coffin with removable lid, which contained, not, as one might expect, a mummy, but, instead, a tiny, finely patinaed bronze of a female nude, adorned with Egyptianising jewelry and hair ornamentation. It is a feature, not entirely peculiar to France but, which would, nevertheless, be revisited by Gautier in his 1858 novel *Le Roman de La Momie* and Georges Méliès' 1899 short film, *Cléopâtre*, in which an archaeologist, excavating a tomb, horrifyingly hacks up and burns the mummy he has discovered, in order to resurrect a beautiful and alluring woman. This element of Egyptological fiction would reach its apogee in Bram Stoker's 1903 novel *The Jewel of Seven Stars*, which presents the dormant but perfectly preserved and still beautiful mummy of the malevolent Queen Tera.

It is worth noting the ease with which the story's protagonist purchases the eponymous appendage and the fact that he does so not with any great academic purpose beyond the acquisition of a unique paperweight. He is a young man-about-town, not an Egyptologist.

Before moving away from the somewhat necrophilic tendencies of this tale, a perfectly reasonable question may linger, why a foot? Surely a hand may have been more palatable? The obvious reason seems to be that Gautier was obsessed by the ballet and, in particular, by the Italian ballerina, Carlotta Grisi, for whom he co-wrote the libretto of *Giselle*, first performed by her only eight months after the publication of "The Mummy's Foot."

"The Mummy's Foot" has rarely been out of print since its initial publication, and was translated into English for presentation in the American *Harpers New Monthly Magazine* in April 1871. One wonders whether Gautier's story provided the inspiration for the peculiar incident in Chapter IX of H Rider Haggard's 1886 novel, *She: A History of Adventure*, in which the archaeologist, Holly, is gifted a mummified but perfectly preserved "shapely little foot."

The next literary attempt to resurrect Egypt's ancient dead appeared in the April 1845 edition of *The American Whig Review* and could not be more different in style or intent. Entitled "Some Words with a Mummy", and written by the celebrated Edgar Allan Poe, it is also included in the current collection. Written with his tongue firmly in his cheek – Poe's mummy, revived, again, through galvanism, is named "Allamistakeo" and is decidedly sniffy about the so-called advances of nineteenth century technology. It is an amusing tale with an unexpectedly macabre conclusion. However, it also contains a few sideswipes at George Robins Gliddon, who appears in the tale as one of the mummy's more specious revivers. Devon-born Gliddon had grown up in Alexandria and became, by 1832, American Vice-Consul to Egypt. On a trip back to the United States he agreed to assist the anthropologist Samuel Morton, whose primary aim was to endeavour to prove the intellectual superiority of white men, by collecting skulls from Egypt and scouring the ancient monuments for appropriate evidence. In the process, Gliddon, somehow, developed a career lecturing on Egyptology and, emboldened by Pettigrew's work in England, became famous for the public unrolling of mummies. He toured the United States with his gaudy show and in 1850, proceeded, before a packed audience of some two thousand of Boston's leading citizens, to unroll the mummy of what he confidently described as a young priestess.

Gliddon's careers as both showman and errant Egyptologist were effectively over when the unwrapped mummy was revealed to be most decidedly male. It is particularly pleasing, therefore, to note that Poe had not only identified Gliddon as a charlatan some five years beforehand but also had the wit to immortalise him as such in this tale.

Although Poe's tale is an early entry in the canon of mummy fiction, his treatment of the subject could not really be described as influential. However, more than a century and a half later, Luc Besson's film, *Les Aventures extraordinaires d'Adèle Blanc-Sec* (France, 2010) specifically references

"Some Words with a Mummy" through the sneeze with which the mummy of Patmosis awakes, and in his discussion of the advanced technologies of ancient Egypt: Patmosis, is not, as Adele supposed, a physician but is, in fact, a nuclear physicist! Whilst the latter reference may be attributed to Jacques Tardi's original *bande dessinée, Momies en folie* (1978), Besson, as the film's screenwriter and director, must be responsible for the former.

Our next tale is Louisa May Alcott's "Lost in a Pyramid" published in the premier issue of *The New World* magazine, dated 16 January 1869. In addition to her more famously "wholesome" works, Alcott had written a number of thrillers prior to "Lost in a Pyramid", which is likely to have been written around the time that she sent her manuscript of *Good Wives*, the sequel to *Little Women*, to her publisher. The story was long forgotten until the late Dominic Montserrat resurrected it from the stacks of the Library of Congress for the publication *KMT: A Modern Journal of Ancient Egypt* in 1998, since when, it has been anthologised on a number of occasions. The premise of the tale comes from the belief, prevalent at the time, that seeds found in Egyptian tombs were still capable of germination, thousands of years after their interment. This may relate to the "corn mummies," frequently found in Egyptian tombs where the seeds of cereals were planted in a tray, shaped in the outline of the god Osiris, filled with rich, moist Nile silt, which would induce the seeds to germinate in the days following the sealing of the tomb, acting as a physical symbol of the deceased's rebirth after death.

While the tale provides yet another example of a female mummy, this one is not only appropriately desiccated but is of a powerful sorceress and, therefore, a precursor of Stoker's Tera. Alcott also incorporates the first instance of a curse: a form, which would develop increasing popularity in the canon of mummy fiction. The appropriateness of the Egyptologist's name, Dr Niles, is amusing, however, it has been suggested by Montserrat that Alcott deliberately used the name of the editor at her publishing house, Thomas Niles, because she "had not wanted to write the book [*Little Women*] and found the task very uninspiring."[3]

The aforementioned novel *She: A History of Adventure* by H Rider Haggard is not, in itself a mummy story. However, Haggard's tale of an immortal

---

3   Montserrat, D. 1998. "Louise May Alcott & The Mummy's Curse" in *KMT: A Journal of Modern Egyptology* 9/2: 70-85.

and powerful princess with Egyptian connections, her lost and reincarnated love, and a desert expedition to the legendary city of Kôr, guided by an ancient and inscribed potsherd, contains not only many of the trappings of a mummy tale but would also go on to influence many of the tales which would succeed it, not least in the thorny problem of reincarnation.

The concept of reincarnation was unknown to the ancient Egyptians and would have filled them with horror. For them, there was but one life, followed by eternity in the afterlife... if one was lucky and took the necessary precautions. Their belief in the permanence of *one* earthly body was, essentially, the driving notion behind the entire mortuary belief system and practice. It was the reason for preservation and mummification of the body after death, which still required food offerings to be brought to the tomb; in the event that these should cease, as they surely did after more than a couple of generations, the food buried with the deceased could, magically, suffice, as would the scenes of food and in its production carved and painted on the tomb walls. It was a pragmatically Egyptian "belt and braces" idea, which sought to counter every eventuality. Even the destruction of the body, (the Egyptians were only too well aware of the threat from tomb robbers) could be, similarly, addressed through the provision of two and three dimensional representations of the deceased, marked with his or her name. The mortuary sculptures, which are so admired for their artistic beauty and precision, in museums and galleries today were not art for art's sake, they could provide shelter for the soul of the deceased.

Nevertheless, rightly or wrongly, reincarnation has become one of the tropes of mummy fiction, both literary and cinematic, partly due to Haggard's novel, partly due to the comparative complexity of Egyptian religious beliefs and partly due to the large numbers of British who served and worked in India during this period and who consequently, encountered and developed some understanding of Hindu mortuary beliefs.

Haggard, himself, is worthy of mention in the context of nineteenth century Egyptomania. He owned and, apparently, kept in his study, the mummy and wooden coffin of a gentleman named Nesmin, son of Ankh-Hapy, from the Ptolemaic cemetery at Akhmim. The mummy and coffin are now on display in the Liverpool World Museum. In addition, however, Haggard was much given to wearing rings from the fingers of mummies and was an invited attendee at one of the last, great mummy unrollings in the United Kingdom. Held in the

Botanic Lecture Theatre of University College London on 15 December 1889, the event was presided over by Ernest Wallis Budge of the British Museum and attended by a great many amateur Egyptologists of the day. In addition to Haggard, the painters Edward Poynter and Lawrence Alma Tadema, whose works often had Egyptological themes, watched as Budge hacked away at the wrappings of one Bak-Ran, before distributing portions of the bandages to an appreciative audience. Interestingly, no invitation appears to have been made to Amelia Edwards or any of the Officers of the Egypt Exploration Fund (later Society). Flinders Petrie, who would not be made Edwards Professor of Egyptology at UCL until 1892, following Amelia's death, appears to have been conveniently out of the country. Press reports of both the event and the calibre of its esteemed invitees were published in newspapers from New Zealand to the United States but it would be the penultimate such public unrolling in the United Kingdom and was evidently a monumental sacrifice on the altar of Budge's overweening vanity. Happily, Nesmin is, today, in excellent condition, never having been subjected to the indignity of such a spectacle.

In order to explain the change in public attitudes, which had occurred before the UCL unrolling, it is worth going back some eight years to 1881, when the so-called "royal mummy cache" was uncovered: many of the great kings of the New Kingdom, and their queens, had been removed from their tombs in the Valley of the Kings by priests during the XXI Dynasty, in order to protect them from tomb robbers, and placed in a largely inaccessible mountain cavern at Deir el Bahri, where they had lain undisturbed for millennia until a local family, the Abdel Rassouls, had begun to trade in the jewels and objects buried there. When Émile Brugsch and his assistant, Ahmed Kamal eventually entered the cache on 6 July 1881 they discovered forty mummies, including those with an almost legendary status in the public imagination. These events are stunningly and moving retold in Shadi Abdel Salam's classic of Egyptian cinema *Al Momia* or *The Night of Counting the Years* (1969). Over the next years as the royal mummies were steadily unwrapped, *privately* and scientifically, at the Bulaq Museum in Cairo, and published, it became possible, for the first time, to gaze upon the faces of these once mighty rulers, to see the hereditary over-bite of Tuthmosis III, the inscrutable beauty of Seti I, and the aquiline imperiousness of the long-lived Ramesses II. Their photographs and detailed etchings appeared in newspapers and periodicals throughout the world, subtly changing the public's perception of the mummy. These were no longer bandaged and leathery unknowns, whose names and titles explained little of their history, these were individuals whose names were famous and were an integral part of the history not only of Egypt but the world.

While the public appetite for mummies remained unquenched, it found new forms of expression and consumption, consequently, mummy fiction, initially through serialised novels and short stories in periodicals, became an increasing element of "popular culture" for the educated masses of the period.

This collection's next tale "The Ring of Thoth", by Arthur Conan Doyle, is a major contribution to the sub-genre of mummy fiction. Published in the January 1890 edition of the literary periodical, *The Cornhill Magazine*, whilst the unrolling of Bak-Ran at UCL would still have been current and, with two successful Sherlock Holmes novels under his belt, Doyle created a tale of considerable atmosphere and, as it transpired, influence.

The use of the god Thoth in a supernatural literary context was not new. Thoth was the ibis-headed god of writing. Sometimes appearing as a cynocephalus baboon, Thoth was, to the Egyptians, also responsible for the many secrets relating to the written word. Spells and magical incantations were dependent upon writing and the hieroglyphs, themselves, held great and intrinsic power for the Egyptians. In the earliest tale of a living mummy, dating from Egypt's Ptolemaic Period (332 – 31 BC) the son of Rameses II, Setne Khamewase[4] enters the tomb of the great sorcerer Naneferkaptah in order to find the Scroll of Thoth, a collection of powerful spells. The undead sorcerer is not, of course, a bandaged desiccated corpse but a young, virile, and apparently normal human being. However in order to obtain the information he requires, Khamwase must compete against the sorcerer in the board game senet, which no doubt goes some way to proving the elegance and sophistication of this particular ambulant mummy.

As Doyle references the ring of the god Thoth, John L Balderston's screenplay for Boris Karloff's *The Mummy* (US, Karl Freund, 1932) would revert to the Scroll of Thoth, in which are "set down the magic words by which Isis raised Osiris from the dead." However, this is not Doyle's only influence upon Freund's film: Jack P Pierce's make-up for Imhotep's turn as the archaeologist,

---

4   The historical Khamwase is often referred to as the first Egyptologist on account of his apparent fascination with the kingdom's ancient monuments, having undertaken a number of restoration projects.

Ardath Bey, closely follows Doyle's description of Sosra, "Over the temple and cheek-bone it was as glazed and as shiny as varnished parchment. There was no suggestion of pores. One could not fancy a drop of moisture upon that arid surface. From brow to chin, however, it was cross-hatched by a million delicate wrinkles, which shot and interlaced as though Nature in some Maori mood had tried how wild and intricate a pattern she could devise" and even the lengthy close-ups of Karloff's eyes, of which there are many, conform to Doyle's description of Sosra's orbs, "They were vitreous, with a misty dry shininess, such as Smith had never seen in a human head before."

Similarly, Imhotep's night-time visits to the mummy of his long-dead beloved after the closure of the museum echo Sosra's *modus operandi*. However, like Haggard's Ayesha, Sosra[5] is an immortal being, he has never died nor been mummified, as such, even at this early and important point in the canon of mummy literature, there appears to be some confusion about what does and does not constitute a "mummy."

Most significantly, Doyle, here, entirely eschews the supernatural: Sosra's immortality is entirely alchemical. This appears to be an important consideration for Doyle, perhaps for reasons, which will become evident.

Two years later, in the September 1892 edition of *Harpers New Monthly Magazine,* Doyle's story, "Lot No. 249", crystallised the conception of the living mummy and it is essentially Doyle's visualisation of the Egyptian revenant in this tale, which continues, to this day, to haunt popular culture.

During the period between his two mummy fictions, Doyle and his family had returned from Vienna and set up a medical practice on Wimpole Street and home in 23 Montague Place, mere steps from the rear entrance of the British Museum. The proximity of the museum's display of Egyptian mummies is surely too great a coincidence, although I have little doubt that the legion of serious Doyle scholars throughout the world may suggest otherwise.

Doyle was a fascinatingly contradictory character: a medical man and the creator of fiction's greatest rational mind and yet, in his private life, he was deeply interested in the occult and would go on to become a committed and voluble spiritualist, lending credence to the celebrated case of the Cottingley Fairies in 1920. As such, I was disappointed to discover earlier this year, whilst

---

5   The character's name is almost certainly a corruption of Sarastro, the Priest of Isis from Mozart's opera, *The Magic Flute* (1791).

preparing a lecture on Egyptological Bloomsbury and its various personalities, that the creator of two such important pieces of mummy fiction, the famously open-minded Doyle, held such lamentable views regarding the beliefs and practices of the ancient Egyptians.

Writing of his 1896 visit to Egypt in his autobiography, *Memories and Adventures* Doyle says:

> "The race seems to have petrified and how they could do so without being destroyed by some more virile nation is hard to understand. Their arts seem to have been high but their reasoning power in many ways contemptible. The recent discovery of the king's tomb near Thebes – I write this in 1924 – shows how wonderful were their decorations and the amenities of their lives. But consider the tomb itself. What a degraded intelligence does it not show! The idea that the body, the old outworn greatcoat, which was once wrapped round the soul should, at any cost be preserved is the last word in materialism. And the hundred baskets of provisions to feed the soul upon its journey! I can never believe that a people with such ideas could be other than emasculated in their minds – the fate of every nation comes under the rule of a priesthood."

These rather blinkered comments are evidently driven by a stubbornly Imperialist attitude which surfaces a few pages earlier in the memoires where Doyle overlays Egypt's British protectorate, which lasted from 1882-1953, rather crassly, upon the entire 7,000 year history of the Nile valley, with the line, "of all the singular experiences of this most venerable land, surely this rebuilding at the hands of a little group of bustling, clear-headed Anglo-Saxons is the most extraordinary."

Nevertheless, Doyle's partially unwrapped mummy, stalking the country lanes of Oxford in order to perform the bidding of an occult practitioner, is a powerful image and one which would provide substantial inspiration both for the Universal mummy cycle of the 1940s and two of Hammer's four mummy films, between 1959 and 1966. These are the films which have cemented the concept of the mummy in the public consciousness as a murderous and somewhat mindless bandaged automaton.

In addition, it may be worth commenting that "Lot No. 249" may have provided inspiration for the writer and academic MR James, the first of whose short stories, "Canon Alberic's Scrapbook" and "Lost Hearts" were read in October 1893[6] and whose work would go on to include many tales of the uncanny with an archaeological or antiquarian basis, although lacking the Egyptological trappings. In his "Casting the Runes," the villain, Karswell, dispenses death via ancient sorcery and appears to have been inspired by Doyle's Bellingham.

In 1893, Julian Hawthorne, son of the celebrated American novelist Nathaniel, published "The Unseen Man's Story" within the collection *Six Cent Sam's*. It is presented as part of an overarching structure entitled *The Symposium*, in which, following a sumptuous Christmas meal, Sam's guests are encouraged to relate tales of their experiences or those of others, they have encountered.

The tale presents a reincarnated Egyptian and, for the period, a grislier than usual grasp of embalming practises. Like so many of the other tales presented, "The Unseen Man's Story" contains a hallucinatory visit to the ancient world and it seems apparent that these frequent historical digressions, which are evident in more than half of the tales presented are intended as rather more than mere window-dressing. This is an opportunity for the authors to expand their palettes in order to bring the colour, splendour and atmosphere of ancient Egypt into a modern setting. There is also a continuing hint of the aforementioned eroticism in these scenes with diaphanously attired princesses, priestesses and handmaidens disporting themselves in a very un-Victorian manner. The "flashback" scene is, therefore a vital element in these tales and that tradition has been transmitted to the cinema; the majority of mummy films will contain at least one such scene for very similar reasons. Terence Fisher's *The Mummy* (UK, 1959), in addition to a lengthy flashback to ancient Egypt, retains its "Egyptian" atmosphere, despite being set for the majority of its running time in Engerfield[7], 1898, through the use of numerous flashbacks to the events in the gorgeously crafted and lit tomb of the Princess Ananka.

---

6   James, a member of the Cambridge Chitchat Society, would read his tales aloud to the assembled company at their late evening meetings to the accompaniment of coffee, snuff and anchovy toast.

7   The name of the film's fictional rural locale is almost certainly a contraction of "England's verdant fields," which the camera pans across as the title card "Engerfield" appears.

It should be noted that neither of Doyle's mummy tales contains a scene exhibiting the wonders of Egypt, probably for the reasons already discussed; Sosra simply relates his memory of events, the reader is not transported there and the nameless mummy of "Lot No. 249" is given no back-story worth relating. He is an instrument of Bellingham's will, not a character in his own right.

Whilst Doyle's tales set out the tropes of mummy fiction, Australian, Guy Boothby's "A Professor of Egyptology", first published in the 10 December 1894 edition of *The Graphic*, uses the concept of yet another immortal Egyptian in modern disguise and a lost love embellished with a *fin de siècle* Cairo setting and a healthy dose of reincarnation. Balderston's screenplay for Karl Freund's *The Mummy* (US, 1932) owes Boothby's tale at least as much as it does "The Ring of Thoth."

During his brief thirty-eight years, Boothby was a prolific writer and is primarily known today for his Doctor Nikola series, written between 1895 and 1901 in which the elegantly charming but utterly amoral Nikola's search for the secret of immortality provided inspiration for a plethora of subsequent fictional villains, not least Sax Rohmer's diabolical chemist, Dr Fu Manchu[8] and the screen incarnation of Ian Fleming's Ernst Stavro Blofeld, complete with feline companion.

In 1897, Bram Stoker's *Dracula* was published and, in many ways, changed the concept of the Gothic novel with its potent blend of blood drinking and aberrant sexuality unleashed in contemporary England by the arrival of an ancient horror from the east. Whilst the novel thrilled and horrified its Victorian readers, it was, at the time of its original publication, outsold by Richard Marsh's *The Beetle*, published in the same year. Addressing many of the same themes as *Dracula*, Marsh's novel tells the story of the arrival in London of an immortal, sex-changing ancient priest of the goddess Isis, who can transform herself/himself into a gigantic carnivorous scarab beetle, in pursuit of a British politician. Despite being reprinted fifteen times in the first fourteen years since its publication, *The Beetle* lacked the endurance exhibited by Stoker's *magnum opus*.

The novel is relatively light on Egyptological elements and references to ancient religious practices are either opaque or fudged:

---

8   *The Mystery of Doctor Fu Manchu* was first published in serial form in 1912.

"'Can you tell me what were the exact tenets of the worshippers of Isis?"

"Neither I nor any man, – with scientific certainty. As you know, she had a brother; the cult of Osiris and Isis was one and the same. What, precisely, were its dogmas, or its practices, or anything about it, none, now, can tell. The Papyri, hieroglyphics, and so on, which remain are very far from being exhaustive, and our knowledge of those which do remain, is still less so."

Furthermore, with the exception of the immortality of the beetle/priest creature, described as a "child of Isis," the tropes usually associated with Egyptian fantastic literature are largely avoided.

Nevertheless, the shot in the arm supplied to Gothic fiction by both *The Beetle* and *Dracula* produced some interesting progeny and the debt owed to these novels by the next two tales in this collection, Herbert W Crotzer's "The Block of Bronze" (1898) and E and H Heron's "The Story of Baelbrow" (1898) is evident.

"The Block of Bronze", published in the March 1898 edition of *The Black Cat* magazine is presented in *Unearthed* for the first time since its initial publication. As such, whilst it cannot be described as a lost tale, it is certainly little known.

Published in Boston, Massachusetts, *The Black Cat* was, according to its editorial "devoted exclusively to original, unusual, fascinating stories." Although many of its writers are, today, unknown, it published a number of Clark Ashton Smith's early stories and helped to launch the career of Jack London in 1899 by purchasing his second story, "A Thousand Deaths", for the not inconsiderable sum of $40.[9] Although we have no idea how much Crotzer received for his tale, it is perhaps, indicative of the way in which *The Black Cat* operated, that "The Block of Bronze" was accompanied by four other tales of variable interest, including, as advertised on the cover, in large letters, the "$500 prize story, *The Heart of God*" by the otherwise unknown Jeanne E Wood.

---

9   Hendricks, K. 1966. *Jack London: Master Craftsman of the Short Story*. Utah State University Faculty Honor Lectures. 3.

As to the author of this particular tale, it seems likely that he was a newspaper man, connected with the periodical *Crotzer's Centennial and Journal of the Exposition*, published in order to commemorate the United States' first World's Fair in Philadelphia, from 10 May – 10 November 1876, for the anniversary of the signing of the Declaration of Independence.

He would also appear to have edited a Vineland newspaper called *The Record*, published from 1884 by Alex M Taylor.[10] There is also evidence of a William Herbert Crotzer, born 1851, who died in Philadelphia on 13 January 1898 and it is entirely possible, therefore, that he did not live to see "The Block of Bronze" published. It would certainly explain the absence of subsequent tales from Crotzer's pen.

That is not to say that "The Block of Bronze" is especially well written, however, it does present some novel and interesting ideas, not least the involvement of the dwarf characters, both ancient and contemporary. According to the archaeology and mortuary texts of Egypt, dwarves would appear to have held an important place in the Egyptian court and one is particularly reminded of the charming painted limestone statue of the high-ranking courtier Seneb, now in the Cairo Museum. Seneb, whose name means 'health' and undoubtedly gives some indication of his parents' anxiety at the time of his birth, is represented sitting, with crossed legs on a dais, next to his normally proportioned wife. Two of their three children, a boy and a girl, stand in front of the dais, taking the position, which would normally have been reserved, in such a sculpture, for the legs of a full-sized individual. Seneb's mastaba tomb, in which the sculpture was excavated, was discovered by Hermann Junker in 1926 and showed him to have been an individual of considerable wealth.

The god Bes, is usually depicted as a dwarf with an always frontally rendered, somewhat leonine face and lolling tongue. It is entirely possible that images of this deity inspired Crotzer's savage dwarf mummy. However, in spite of his fearful visage, often suggested as predecessor of archaic representations of the gorgon in Greek art, Bes was an apotropaic deity, most frequently associated with the protection of pregnant women and children.

Most amusingly, while the name of the archaeologist, Edward Van Zant, may have been inspired by Stoker's Dutch savant, Abraham Van Helsing, it

---

10   http://digital.library.unt.edu/ark:/67531/metadc9241/m1/498 <Accessed 24 September 2013>

also, unwittingly, anticipates Edward Van Sloan, the American actor who would play both Van Helsing in *Dracula* (US, Tod Browning, 1931) and the similarly heroic Egyptologist, Muller, in Freund's *The Mummy* (US, 1932).

Combining elements popular at the time such as mesmerism and remote viewing, together with hidden secrets, and a ferociously aggressive resurrected mummy, I hope you will agree that "The Block of Bronze" is long overdue excavation and reappraisal.

Our second tale from 1898, published the following month in *Pearson's Magazine* of London, is "The Story of Baelbrow" by E & H Heron. These authors are considerably less mysterious than Mr Crotzer. This was the *nom de plume* of Hesketh Vernon Hesketh-Prichard and his mother, Kate Ryall Prichard. Born into a British military family, in Uttar Pradesh, India, Hesketh-Prichard had trained as a solicitor, although a love of travel and adventure rather interfered with the possibility of any subsequent legal career. Hesketh-Prichard would later be sent on exploratory trips for the recently launched *Daily Express* newspaper, hunting the giant prehistoric ground sloth in Patagonia and being the first to record voodoo practices in Haiti.

Having published his first short story in *Cornhill Magazine* in 1896, *Pearson's* commissioned him to write a series of ghost stories and the mother and son writing team created the occult detective Flaxman Low. The stories, presented as factual in the introduction to the first, "The Story of the Spaniards, Hammersmith"[11], indicated public taste for such sensationalist fiction at the time and, whilst Flaxman Low, "who [had] devoted his life to the study of psychical phenomena"[12] was a short-lived supernatural Holmes manqué, drawing inspiration from Joseph Sheridan Le Fanu's rather more passive Martin Hesselius, the concept of such a figure would inspire William Hope Hodgson's more enduring tales of Carnaki, the ghost-finder, amongst others.

The story has, with its somewhat claustrophobic setting in an isolated ancestral pile, considerable atmosphere and the concept of displaying mummies in such private museums during the nineteenth century is fairly well attested throughout the length and breadth of the United Kingdom, from Trematon Castle in Cornwall to Dunrobin Castle in Sutherland. However, there is

---

11   Heron, E and H. "The Story of the Spaniards, Hammersmith." Pearson's Magazine, January 1898.

12   Heron, E and H. "The Story of Saddler's Croft." Pearson's Magazine, February 1899.

much in common with Augustus Hare's much-contested report of a vampire at Croglin Grange in Cumbria[13], originally written in 1896 but not published until 1900, in which an allegedly authentic revenant is described as "brown, withered, shriveled, mummified but quite entire." Perhaps the Prichards were inspired by this legendary tale, or perhaps, Hare's "authentic" report was inspired by the Prichards'. It seems unlikely that we will ever know the truth.

"Baelbrow" is an interesting concoction of Egyptian mummy story and vampire tale, making a determined effort to relocate Stoker's villains to the desolate places of the British Isles and, audaciously, claiming a far older, pre-Christian lineage for their mummy-possessing vampire than Stoker's already ancient Count. It is a pity, nevertheless, that the Prichards did not leave their vampire's origins squarely in ancient Egypt. One cannot help but feel that they missed a trick, which would not be capitalized upon until the 1980s, after which time vampiric ancient Egyptians became rather *de rigueur* in both literature and film.

The final mummy story of note from 1898 was Guy Boothby's novel *Pharos, the Egyptian*, published, initially in *The Windsor Magazine*, between June and December of that year. This was something of a return to earlier literary efforts with heady doses of both reincarnation and immortality: Ptahmes – whose soul now inhabits another body, that of the immortal Pharos, while his mummified corpse remains in the possession of a young Englishman – had been an Egyptian sorcerer, cursed to eternal wandering by the gods of Egypt when he signally failed to prevent the Biblical Moses from unleashing the ten Hebraic plagues upon the Egyptian populace. *Pharos* is, therefore, one of the first mummy stories to explicitly connect with Biblical events, although by the time of Stephen Sommers' *The Mummy* (US, 1999) the two would have become virtually inseparable.

In 1903 Bram Stoker published *The Jewel of Seven Stars*, the tale of Tera, a powerful seven-fingered ancient Egyptian sorceress who plots her resurrection in Victorian London, utilising the archaeological team who excavated her tomb and the beautiful daughter of the expedition's leader, Margaret Trelawny, who is her identical double. Though Tera's mummy remains prone throughout, her presence in the novel, particularly through her periodic possession of

---

13   Hare, A. J. C. 1900. *The Story of My Life*. London, George Allen: 203-208.

Margaret, born in England at the instant of the tomb's discovery in Egypt, is palpable.

I recently had the good fortune to be taken around the Hull Museum to see amongst their many other fascinating objects, including life-size replicas of numerous artefacts from Tutankhamun's tomb, loving recreated for the 1924 British Empire Exhibition, the famous "Whitby Mummy," which had until 1935 been displayed in the museum of that historically beautiful little coastal town. The fully wrapped mummy and its coffin date from some time shortly before Alexander the Great ousted the Persians from Egypt and belonged to a male priest from Akhmim – the gentleman's masculinity is evident from the false beard, affixed to the chin of his anthropoid coffin and in no way could either mummy or coffin be described as "feminine."

Nevertheless, a story has built up around this mummy and coffin, exhibited as they were in Bram Stoker's regular holiday destination, featuring so prominently in *Dracula*, that the mortal remains of this unnamed priest had provided the inspiration for Stoker's subsequent 1903 novel *The Jewel of Seven Stars*. This seems to be highly unlikely for, although Stoker's working notes reveal the gestation period for *Dracula* to be some seven years, it seems, in the circumstances, that the impetus for the later book began much earlier in Stoker's life.

Born in the little town of Clontarf, just on the outskirts of Dublin, Stoker had been a somewhat sickly child, however, as a robust adolescent, he attended Trinity College Dublin, where, initially through his positions within the University Philosophical Society, he became acquainted with Sir William Wilde, the noted ocular surgeon and keen amateur Egyptologist.

As the years passed Stoker became a regular visitor to the Wildes' home at Merrion Square, where Sir William kept a collection of artefacts from his visit to Egypt in 1837. As described, in his two volume work, *Narrative of a Voyage to Madeira, Tenerife and along the Shores of the Mediterranean*, published in 1839 and subsequently in an enlarged and revised edition in 1844, Sir William was something of an amateur Egyptologist, visiting not only the Giza pyramids but numerous cemeteries at the nearby sites of Dashur and Saqqara, where he encountered an anthropoid coffin "of great beauty and perfection [which] evidently belonged to a person of distinction,"[14] and, as a physician, was

14   Wilde, W. 1844. *Narrative of a Voyage to Madeira, Tenerife and along the Shores of the Mediterranean*. Dublin: William Curry Junior. 255.

much taken with the accompanying mummy, which showed signs of physical deformity and had been badly broken into pieces by treasure hunting tourists the previous day. It seems likely that these would have been the mummified fragments and possibly the coffin, which returned with him to Dublin and which were displayed with pride to the young Bram Stoker.

It is not difficult to imagine the effect that Sir William's tales of sleeping the night in a tomb with a coffin lid as his pillow, scrambling over rock-faces to study hieroglyphic inscriptions and examining the structure of mummy wrappings in the minutest detail, might have had on the imagination of the young Stoker.

Wilde's son, the more famous Oscar, who had unsuccessfully wooed Florence Balcome, the future Mrs Stoker, habitually wore a lapis lazuli – more likely faience – swivelling scarab ring,[15] although whether this came from his father's collection is unknown. It is also reported that many of his bright, young adherents affected similar jewellery.

In all the circumstances, I think that one needs look no further than the centre of Dublin for Stoker's initial Egyptological inspiration.

Egyptologically, Stoker's tale of a malign queen awaiting resurrection in *fin de siècle* England is no closer to historical Egypt than was his envisioning of Transylvania. It is undoubtedly well-researched but the pieces do not fit comfortably. However, certain elements are, or have since proved to be, spot on.

The eponymous seven stars, evident in the scarab ring, represent the constellation commonly known as "the Plough." To the Egyptians, erudite astronomers, this was the *khepesh*, and represented the foreleg of a bull, a form taken by Seth, the god of chaos in his interminable battle with his nephew Horus. Seth used the leg to blind Horus in one eye, after which, it was severed by the other gods and cast into the sky, where it could do no further harm. As a deadly weapon, therefore, it also provided the name and shape of a particularly savage Egyptian sword. However, in that duality, so frequently evident in Egyptian culture, the foreleg of a bull-calf is one of the implements used in the "Opening of the Mouth" ceremony, wherein the coffin of the deceased, containing the mummy, is placed upright and stimulated to live again. It is vital

---

15   Gide, André. 1905. *Oscar Wilde, A Study from the French.* Translated by Stuart Mason. Oxford: Holywell Press. 58.

for spiritual resurrection in the afterlife and, therefore, entirely appropriate for Tera's plans of physical resurrection in the real world.

The jewel itself is described in the novel as coming from an "aerolite," which fell from the heavens at the time of Tera's birth. Stoker is fully aware that rubies were unknown in ancient Egypt and, consequently, this ring is hewn from the heart of a meteorite. Since the novel's publication, an Italian scholar, in 1996,[16] identified the yellow-green glass scarab in the centre of one of the pectorals found on the mummy of Tutankhamun as being of meteoritic glass, created when a meteorite slammed into the desert sand and fused it into glass, in a manner, which was far beyond Egyptian technology of the period. Similarly, analysis has shown that the iron dagger found on the boy-king's mummy, together with a number of beads from other, unrelated burials[17] were formed from iron extracted from meteorites which had plummeted to earth.

Stoker's description of Tera's mummy is worth quoting at some length, for it is a description which could equally serve for one of Dracula's vampire brides and her facial features correspond to those of the Count, himself:

"We all stood awed at the beauty of the figure which, save for the face cloth, now lay completely nude before us. Mr. Trelawny bent over, and with hands that trembled slightly, raised this linen cloth which was of the same fineness as the robe. As he stood back and the whole glorious beauty of the Queen was revealed, I felt a rush of shame sweep over me. It was not right that we should be there, gazing with irreverent eyes on such unclad beauty: it was indecent; it was almost sacrilegious! And yet the white wonder of that beautiful form was something to dream of. It was not like death at all; it was like a statue carven in ivory by the hand of a Praxiteles. There was nothing of that horrible shrinkage which death seems to effect in a moment. There was none of the wrinkled toughness, which seems to be a leading characteristic of most mummies. There was not the shrunken attenuation of a body dried in the sand, as I had seen before in museums. All the pores of the body seemed to

16   http://news.bbc.co.uk/1/hi/5196362.stm <Accessed 25 September 2013>.

17   http://www.huffingtonpost.com/2013/06/01/egyptian-jewelry-space-iron-meteorite_n_3349054.html <Accessed 25 September 2013>

have been preserved in some wonderful way. The flesh was full and round, as in a living person; and the skin was as smooth as satin. The color seemed extraordinary. It was like ivory, new ivory; except where the right arm, with shattered, bloodstained wrist and missing hand had lain bare to exposure in the sarcophagus for so many tens of centuries.

With a womanly impulse; with a mouth that drooped with pity, with eyes that flashed with anger, and cheeks that flamed, Margaret threw over the body the beautiful robe which lay across her arm. Only the face was then to be seen. This was more startling even than the body, for it seemed not dead, but alive. The eyelids were closed; but the long, black, curling lashes lay over on the cheeks. The nostrils, set in grave pride, seemed to have the repose which, when it is seen in life, is greater than the repose of death. The full, red lips, though the mouth was not open, showed the tiniest white line of pearly teeth within. Her hair, glorious in quantity and glossy black as the raven's wing, was piled in great masses over the white forehead, on which a few curling tresses strayed like tendrils."

As a novel, *The Jewel of Seven Stars* is considerably less accomplished than *Dracula*, and there are many similarities between the two, not only in the description of Tera. Nevertheless it has not only an unsettlingly claustrophobic atmosphere – most of the novel is set in the confines of Professor Trelawny's antiquity packed Kensington Park Road (sic) mansion – but also a strangely dreamlike and liminal quality. It stands as possibly the single great work of mummy fiction even though Tera never once steps beyond the confines of her coffin.

Relocating to the caves of Cornwall for its conclusion, the novel ends, unusually for one of Stoker's novels, in tragedy, and it was not until its 1912 reprint that the dénouement was reworked, whether by Stoker or his editors, allowing Ross and Margaret Trelawny to live happily ever after.

Of the final tales presented in this collection, Charles Weathers Bump's "The Vanished Mummy", is a straightforward crime mystery, presented here as an example of the ways in which authors have drawn upon mummies, as objects of intrinsic financial and academic worth, in order to lend colour and atmosphere to their tales. Whether Bump does so successfully in this tale remains to be seen, however, the mystery, itself, is unlikely to have stretched even the prosaic Inspector Lestrade, let alone the great sleuth.

Published as the penultimate offering in Bump's 1906 collection, *The Mermaid of Druid Lake and Other Stories* the tale sits at an uneasy mid-point between the quirkily atmospheric crime stories of Poe and Doyle and the so-called Golden Age of crime fiction. Bump's detective is both bright *and* polite, but distinctly anodyne: American crime fiction was still a long way from being hard-bitten.

Nevertheless, it is an early entry in a sub-genre of mummy fiction (a sub-sub-genre?) which includes Christie's "The Adventure of the Egyptian Tomb" from 1924 and *The Mystery of the Whispering Mummy* by Robert Arthur Junior from 1965.

The last piece in the collection is not a work of short fiction but an edited version of the second and third chapters from George Griffith's 1906 novel, *The Mummy and Miss Nitocris: A Phantasy of the Fourth Dimension*. The piece stands very well on its own as an example of an ancient Egyptian revenge story. Within the overarching plot, Professor Marmion's dream of ancient Egypt, included here, is ultimately revealed to be his own memory from a previous life. Published only three years after Stoker's *The Jewel of Seven Stars*, there are a number of obvious similarities with that novel, not least the physical resemblance of the heroine, the improbably named Nitocris Marmion, to the long dead Egyptian queen, which is in the possession of her Egyptologist father.

However, Griffith's plot is far more convoluted, involving trans-dimensional travel, the reincarnation of numerous ancient Egyptians in turn-of-the-century Europe, and the threat of international war. It is a decidedly mixed bag and the archaic dialogue in the portion included in this collection is, at best, creaky. It does reminds me of undergraduate discussions about conventions for the translation of ancient texts with my professor at Liverpool University, A F Shore, to whom the usage of "thee" and "thou" was anathema, being too reminiscent of Frankie Howerd's 1970s comedy series "Up Pompeii," and so, I'm afraid, it seems to me today. Sadly George Griffith's knowledge of trans-dimensional travel had imparted no foresight of this British comedy genius and, as such his overtly "Biblical" language was deemed authentically ancient in 1906.

It is worth noting that the Egyptian Pharaoh-Queen Nitocris has a long and ignoble tradition in Egyptological fiction, which may be traced to Volume II of *The Histories* of Herodotos, a Greek writer who lived between c. 484 and 425 BC. He described how Nitocris lured her enemies to a banquet in an underground chamber, where she had them drowned in the waters of the Nile. Although frequently referred to as the "father of history," Herodotos made little effort to differentiate between history, folklore, and the telling of a good tale, consequently, among the, admittedly, valuable information he provides about Egypt and her neighbours, there is a great deal that should be treated with circumspection. For many years scholars believed that Nitocris may have been a Graecized version of the name Neith-Ikret and attempted to fit her reign into the Turin king-list as the last ruler of the VI Dynasty. Recent research[18] appears to show, however, that this cartouche was a misreading and misplacing of the name of a later male ruler and, as such Nitocris has been, once more, expunged from the historical record.

Herodotos' tale went on, however, to inspire *The Vengeance of Nitocris*, the first work of sixteen-year-old Thomas Lanier Williams, published in the August 1928 edition of W*eird Tales*. In addition to Herodotos' version of events, it seems highly likely that the author had also encountered Griffith's novel. Williams would go to make a career from similarly wronged and distraught female characters, after adopting the sobriquet "Tennessee."

And so in the opening years of the twentieth century our anthology reaches its conclusion. However, this was very far from being the end of mummy fiction, which was just beginning to get into its somewhat shambling stride.

Sax Rohmer published a number of mummy-related tales in both short and long form over his career, beginning with the distinctly un-supernatural "The Mysterious Mummy," published under his own name of Arthur Sarsfield Ward in 1903, he followed this with "The Case of the Headless Mummies" in 1913, "The Cat" (1914), "The Death Ring of Sneferu" (1917), "The Whispering Mummy" (1918) and "The Mummy that Walked" in 1938, certain of which involved elements of the supernatural, while others held the

---

18   Ryholt, K. 2000. "The Late Old Kingdom in the Turin King-list and the Identity of Nitorcris." *Zeitschrift für ägyptische*. 127: 91.

promise of such, until the devious criminal mastermind was revealed, using Egyptological trappings as a cover for his nefarious plans. In 1920 and 1928 Rohmer published two novels, respectively *The Green Eyes of Bast* and *She Who Sleeps: A Romance of New York and the Nile* but sadly neither of these live up to the promise of their titles or the atmosphere of Egyptological menace Rohmer creates.

More fascinatingly, a great deal of apparently extraneous Egyptianalia finds its way into Rohmer's novels and short stories of the Chinese "devil doctor," Fu Manchu, between 1913 and 1959. Rejuvenating himself with various elixirs across the series, Fu Manchu had been described as having a face "saving the indescribable evil of its expression, [that] was identical with that of Seti, the mighty Pharaoh who lies in the Cairo Museum" before, in Rohmer's final novel, *Emperor Fu Manchu*, it is suggested that the insidious leader of the Si-Fan, had, in fact, been, all along, an ancient Egyptian, staving off death through the use of his miraculous *elixir vitae*. It was a strange and somewhat unsatisfying conclusion to a series of some charm and ingenuity. However, completed just months before the seventy-six year old Rohmer's death, it may well have included an element of literary wish fulfillment.

Mummies, immortal, and reincarnated ancient Egyptians continued to appear spasmodically in popular fiction until Sunday, 26 November 1922, when Howard Carter breached the second doorway leading to the largely intact tomb of Tutankhamun in the Valley of the Kings. The feverish press speculation regarding the tomb contents ensured that Egyptian mummies would be *de rigueur* for the next two years. When Lord Carnarvon, the excavation's financial backer and one of the first, along with Carter, to enter the tomb fell ill and, subsequently, died, ancient curses were added to the mix. On this occasion, it was the world's press which was purveying these Egyptological fictions, desperate to report something regarding the tomb but hitherto, largely prevented by the exclusive deal struck between Carnarvon and *The Times* newspaper. Mediums, writers, and other "commentators" leapt with something akin to glee onto the curse bandwagon with Doyle stating that "an evil elemental may have caused Lord Carnarvon's fatal illness[19]," while Haggard sought to scotch what he viewed as unhealthy supernatural rumblings.

---

19   Luckhurst, R. 2012. *The Mummy's Curse: The True Story of a Dark Fantasy.* Oxford: Oxford University Press. 10.

The involvement of the somewhat disgruntled former Egyptologist Arthur Weigall, who had worked with Carter and had developed a close friendship with Alan Gardiner, the philologist called in to examine any texts discovered in the tomb, cannot be overstated. Weigall had suffered something of a breakdown in 1911 and, leaving the academic Egyptological community, found himself covering the non-story from the sidelines, for the *Daily Mail*. Some chance remarks and the publication of a best-selling book in 1924 entitled *Tutankhamen and other Essays*, which suggested supernatural explanations for Carnarvon's death and several other excavation incidents, did nothing to dispel the myth. Rapidly, the stories regarding the opening of the tomb developed their own momentum with tales of Carter's canary being swallowed by a cobra and the finding of a tablet in the tomb stating "Death shall come on swift wings to whoever touches the tomb of a Pharaoh." However, reality, as is often the case, was considerably more mundane and Carnarvon, who had contracted blood poising from an infected mosquito bite had not been in the best physical shape when he had first visited Egypt twenty years earlier. Whilst stories of the fates of those only tangentially connected to the tomb proliferated and, still do, to an extent, the vast majority of those working on and intimately associated with the tomb lived long, productive and curse-free lives.

The cultural effect of the discovery of Tutankhamun's tomb was two fold. Firstly, Egyptian designs heavily influenced the nascent Art Deco style, which proliferated throughout Europe and the United States – everything from hairstyles and fashion, to architecture, to interior décor and even dance music, was given an ancient Egyptian spin.[20]

Secondly, cinema turned its attention to Egypt, once more – suddenly the very name Tutankhamun represented potentially big business and it was only with considerable effort that the director Cecil B DeMille was convinced not to make Tutankhamun the Pharaoh in his original feature film of *The Ten Commandments* (US, 1923).

Universal, having successfully produced "talkie" versions of both *Dracula*, starring Bela Lugosi and *Frankenstein* (US, James Whale, 1931) released *The Mummy* in 1932 to a somewhat lukewarm response. As has already been noted, the script, by John L Balderston, one of the reporters who

---

20   Humbert, J-M et al (Eds). 1994. *Egyptomania: Egypt in Western Art, 1730-1930*. Ottawa: National Gallery of Canada. 506-551.

had waited with mounting frustration outside the entrance to Tutankhamun's tomb, was, to a great extent, based upon the somewhat genteel and rather dated mummy tales of the turn of the century. Apart from the startling make-up provided by Jack P Pierce to transform Karloff into the mummy of Imhotep, *The Mummy* tended to lack the visceral shocks which the other Universal horrors delivered and which the 1930s picture-going audience craved, being more obviously a Gothic romance with the luminous-eyed Zita Johann being a reincarnation of the Princess Ankhesenamon, reenacting scenes of trance-like somnambulism, which appear to have been directly lifted from Boothby's "A Professor of Egyptology." Universal laid the mummy to rest once more, but only for six years, when a rerelease caught the public imagination more effectively.

After this, the mummy would go on to become an effective, albeit limited, additional character to Universal's pantheon of horror with former Western star, Tom Tyler taking over mummy duties from Karloff in *The Mummy's Hand* (US, Christy Cabanne, 1940). The film, whilst recycling flashback scenes from *The Mummy*, is not a sequel but, in modern parlance, a reboot. Retaining the central theme of reincarnation of a lost love, which by now had become an important and accepted element of mummy fiction, Imhotep has become Kharis and spends the whole film as a shambling, bandaged mummy, rather than transforming into the striking but more recognizably human Egyptologist, Ardath Bey. Indeed, Kharis shambles considerably more than previously, with a withered arm and dragging foot making the mummy a more physically grotesque but somewhat less feasible threat. In a further change, borrowed directly from Doyle's tales, the mummy is given a controlling occult figure, here the actor George Zucco, as Andoheb, who could provide the otherwise mute mummy with not only motivation but also the expositional dialogue, otherwise lacking, and the mummy is revived and controlled by alchemical means, through the administration of infusions of tana leaves of varying strengths. Each of these new precepts would hold true in the ensuing series of films.

The Mummy's Tomb (US, Harold Young, 1942) now starred Lon Chaney Jr as Kharis. However this film, essentially a rehash of *Hand*, was cheaply produced, as evidenced by Chaney's rubber mummy mask and the relocation of events to Massachusetts, thereby limiting the need for expensive props or sets. Nevertheless the series continued with *The Mummy's Ghost* (US, Reginald

Le Borg, 1944) and *The Mummy's Curse* (US, Leslie Goodwins, 1944), each tawdrier than the last. One interesting element is introduced at the conclusion of *Ghost*, whereby the modern character of Amina Monsori, is not only revealed to be the reincarnation of the Princess Ananka but actually transforms into a mummy-like figure as she sinks to her doom in the waters of a Massachusetts swamp. Although regaining her youthful beauty in the sequel, the character of Amina has now been entirely subsumed by the personality of Ananka, so *The Mummy's Curse* has two mummies for the price of one, although the locale has changed, for no discernible reason, to Louisiana.

From 1922 to 1944, literary mummy fiction remained alive in the pulp magazines of the period. In the stories of H P Lovecraft, mummies had been transformed into something quite different, being interested less in the culture of ancient Egypt and far more in the ancient and eldritch civilization of his own imaginings. Being commissioned to ghost-write a story told in the first person by the famed escapologist and stage magician Harry Houdini, in "Imprisoned with the Pharaohs" (1924), Lovecraft imagines a pit beneath the Giza plateau where Nitocris, again, and Khafre or Khephren, builder of the second pyramid at Giza, both pay obeisance together with mummified monstrosities to the gigantic paw of a living creature which, Houdini realizes is the inspiration for the Great Sphinx. The tale is typically Lovecraftian and similar mummified non-human grotesques had already appeared in two of his other tales, "Arthur Jermyn" (1920) and "The Nameless City" (1921) although their connection to ancient Egypt is somewhat tenuous.

Perhaps more interestingly, the eponymous elder-god character of Lovecraft's 1920 story, "Nyarlathotep," at times, physically resembles an Egyptian king, while his name incorporates the Egyptian verb *hotep*, "to be satisfied". Whilst Lovecraft may simply have borrowed the word, it seems more probable that he is suggesting this vastly ancient, pan-dimensional creature has influenced the culture and language of ancient Egypt.

Some of the most interesting and imaginative pre-WWII mummy fiction was written by Chicago-born author Robert Bloch (1917-1994), today most frequently recognized as the writer of *Psycho*, upon which Alfred Hitchcock's 1960 film of the same name was based. This was, however, only one of thirty novels and literally hundreds of short stories produced by the incredibly creative writer. Known for his wickedly dark sense of humor and with a liking for twist endings, Bloch's writing career was encouraged by Lovecraft, with whom he had entered into correspondence as a youngster and encompassed screenwriting for film and television with episodes of *Star Trek*, horror films for British-based company Amicus, and an old-fashioned but rarely-seen TV Movie for Screen Gems entitled *The Cat Creature* (US, Curtis Harrington, 1973) involving an Egyptian mummy, the goddess Bast, a cursed amulet and feline lycanthropy.

In his short mummy fiction, all published in *Weird Tales*, Bloch typically approaches the standard tropes of the sub-genre in a series of new and disturbing ways. "The Brood of Bubastis," published in March 1937, is set in Cornwall and deals with mummified remains of the attempts by the priesthood of Bast to recreate their deity through the hybridization of humans and animals. "The Secret of Sebek," from November 1937 is set in New Orleans and involves a desecrated mummy and the vengeful crocodile god Sobek, while Bloch's April 1938 tale, "The Eyes of the Mummy" involves an Egyptological dig and a transference of souls.

"Beetles," from December 1938 is probably Bloch's most influential mummy tale, dealing with a stolen mummy which is protected by the scarab deity, Khepri, who controls hordes of flesh-devouring scarab beetles, evidently taking some slight inspiration from Richard Marsh's *The Beetle* but far more influentially providing a basis for Stephen Sommers' ravenous, burrowing scarabs in his 1999 *The Mummy*. Bloch's tale is surprisingly gruesome for its time. Like most of Bloch's short fiction, these tales, often anthologized, are worth rediscovering.

In 1955, Universal Studios gave the mummy one final outing, evidently impervious to the indignities already visited upon the character in the Chaney films, *Abbott and Costello Meet the Mummy* (US, Charles Lamont) sees the two failing slapstick comics – this was their penultimate film together and the last to utilize the "Abbott and Costello" prefix in the title – face Klaris (!), the mummy, portrayed by stuntman Eddie Parker in a distinctly vaudevillian idea of Egypt. In spite of some sterling support from Marie Windsor and Michael Ansara, the film is a long way from Karl Freund's conception of the same basic material bringing a close to not only Universal's mummy series but also their horror cycle in general. Following the law of diminishing returns, both artistically and fiscally, there was nowhere left for them to go.

It is all the more surprising, therefore, that only four years later, British company Hammer Films, should successfully re-launch the mummy, cinematically. This small independent production company with studios just outside the village of Bray in Berkshire and offices on Wardour Street had, almost by chance, stumbled into the business of producing Gothic horror, after the success of *The Quatermass Xperiment* (UK, Val Guest, 1956), their adaptation of Nigel Kneale's hugely popular television serial. Having produced, in fairly rapid succession, two superbly mounted colour adaptations of the novels *Frankenstein* and *Dracula* starring Peter Cushing and Christopher Lee, Universal, their American distributors, who had been saved from bankruptcy by *Dracula* (UK, Terence Fisher, 1958), opened their vaults and gave Hammer and their small band of professional, dedicated filmmakers free rein to remake any of their properties. Although the *Hound of the Baskervilles* (UK, Terence Fisher, 1958) was next, starring a meticulous Cushing as the great detective, Hammer turned their attention to the mummy properties in 1959, producing, quite possibly *the* classic film in the process.

Jimmy Sangster, Hammer's primary screenwriter for their Gothic horror output watched the Universal series of mummy films, which he synthesized into a new and original screenplay, retaining certain character names, specifically Kharis, Ananka, and Banning together with certain incidents, most notably scenes set around the swamp. There, the similarities end. In a tidying up of the concept, Isobel Banning (Yvonne Furneaux) looks like Ananka but is not a reincarnation and tana leaves are replaced by the Scroll of Life. Interestingly, Eddie Byrne's Inspector Mulrooney, makes a passing reference to Poe's "Some Words with a Mummy" in his dialogue.

Christopher Lee, acting only with his eyes and body, imbues his portrayal of Kharis with considerable pathos whilst presenting the mummy as an implacable foe bent on vengeance. His lean frame and the swiftness of his movements are strongly reminiscent of Doyle's nameless revenant in "Lot No. 249". Although hampered by being swathed in bandages and wearing a heavy, restricting make-up, his performance is not one, which could have been delivered by a stunt man.

Such was the success of *The Mummy* (UK, Terence Fisher, 1959) that Hammer produced a further, unrelated mummy film in 1963. *The Curse of the Mummy's Tomb* (UK, Michael Carreras, 1964) is closer in tone and, indeed look, to the later Universal series with Fred Clarke as a brash showman and a number of under-par performances. Nevertheless, there is a resurgence of the immortal ancient Egyptian, the mummy's sibling, who can only end his seemingly rather pleasant existence at the mummy's hand. The lack of originality in their names is deplorable: Ba and Ra, and, even at only eighty minutes, the film feels too long for the material.

One wonders whether Carreras, who not only directed but scripted *The Curse of the Mummy's Tomb* included Terence Morgan's immortal Egyptian because he was aware of the literary tradition or because he was involved the pre-production of an adaptation of Haggard's *She* (UK, Robert Day, 1965) for Hammer, at the time. The property had been rattling around the studio for some time as various writers searched for ways to approach the material. In the end, the material is well served by Hammer's approach, retaining many of the Egyptological elements from the book, as the earlier film adaptation of *She* (US, Lansing C Holden, 1935) had relocated the city of Kôr to icy wastes of the North Pole. Although considerably less complex than Haggard's book, the film is immensely entertaining and Ursula Andress makes for a suitably striking lead.

Hammer returned to the mummy theme with *The Mummy's Shroud* (UK, John Gilling, 1967), which, although largely dismissed by its writer/director is an incredibly effective iteration of the basic mummy concept with interesting visuals and an ambulant mummy drawn directly from a Roman Period specimen on display in the British Museum (EA.6704). Set in Egypt during the 1920s, and evidently informed by the discovery of Tutankhamun's tomb, the film also presents the mummy of a young prince, naturally desiccated by the sand and bearing a remarkable likeness to the burials known from Egypt's Predynastic Period.

Interestingly just four months before the release of The Mummy's Shroud, at a point when the BBC was particularly drawn to producing adaptations of Victorian and Edwardian literature, the series *Sir Arthur Conan Doyle* opened on 15 January 1967, with a straightforward adaptation of "Lot No. 249", here shortened to *Lot 249* (BBC, Richard Martin) by acclaimed television screenwriter John Hawkesworth. Sadly, the fifty-minute programme no longer exists in the BBC archives, so it is impossible to judge its effectiveness from the few extant stills. The unnamed mummy was portrayed by 6'7" actor Sonny

Caldinez, shortly before going on to play a number of similarly physically imposing roles in the BBC television series *Doctor Who*.

In 1971, Hammer began work on their adaptation of *The Jewel of Seven Stars*, here retitled *Blood from the Mummy's Tomb* (UK, Seth Holt, 1971) on the basis that studio Chairman, Sir James Carreras refused to believe in the marketability of the original title.

Although ITV had broadcast an adaptation of the novel on 23 February 1970 as the final instalment in their *Mystery and Imagination* series, under the title *The Curse of the Mummy* (ABC, Guy Verney), Hammer seemed curiously unaware of this earlier treatment or were, perhaps unconcerned by it. It is a curiously stagey piece of television, limited to largely three sets with some deeply unconvincing performances.

Hammer's adaptation updated the novel to the 1970s and opened it out considerably as the more explicitly malevolent spirit of Tera bloodily destroys the members of the archaeological expedition who discovered her tomb. Valerie Leon, at that time famous for a series of television advertisements for "Hai Karate" after-shave is effective as Margaret/Tera and Christopher Wicking's script efficiently points up the very un-Egyptian aspects of Tera's plan for physical resurrection. The film is largely dominated by James Villier's Corbeck, who manipulates Margaret and the other characters to his own ends. The film retains Stoker's destructively downbeat ending, although it adds a coda as Margaret or Tera, it is impossible to tell, is shown in a hospital bed, swathed in bandages, save for her eyes, and completely paralysed, unable to speak. It is a grimly appropriate ending.

The Jewel of Seven Stars would be remade just nine years later as *The Awakening* (UK, Mike Newall, 1980) with an enormous budget, allowing for filming in Egypt, including inside the Cairo Museum, however it is a distinctly lacklustre exercise.

Throughout this period mummy fiction was largely in the doldrums with few short stories or novels of interest until Anne Rice's *The Mummy or Rameses the Damned*, published in 1989. This is a sprawling tale, set in 1914, of alchemical immortality, lost love and the revived mummy of Queen Cleopatra. It is apparent that Rice has been heavily influenced by Victorian mummy fiction as among the novel's dedicatees are both Doyle and Haggard, with their respective Egyptological fictions name-checked. Although a best-seller, at the time of its release, the otherwise prolific Rice has yet to publish a sequel.

In 1994 Joe R Lansdale's novella *Bubba Ho-Tep* was published, pitting a soul-sucking Egyptian mummy against an aged Elvis Presley, now living out his days in a nursing home for the elderly. An admitted aficionado of mummy films, Lansdale, who briefly studied archaeology,[21] produced a quirky, funny, affectionate, and moving entry, which was filmed by Don Coscarelli in 2002 and has become something of a cult classic.

Between 1985 and 1999, R L Stine wrote a number of mummy tales intended for young adults, many of which were subsequently filmed for the very successful *Goosebumps* series of short television plays.

In 2000, Kim Newman's *Seven Stars* was published, which wove together a number of linked short stories set at various points in history, following the progress of Tera's meteoritic gemstone from ancient Egypt, where it had been responsible for unleashing the ten Biblical plagues of Egypt. Newman also employs the character of Margaret Trelawny, who is, by this point, fully possessed by the spirit of Tera in his highly engaging *Moriarty: The Hound of the D'Urbervilles* (2011).

However, since before the turn of the millennium mummies have been primarily based on screen, whether through a slew of "straight to video" features such as *Talos: The Mummy* (US, Russell Mulcahy, 1998) or a further insipid and unnecessary remake of *The Jewel of Seven Stars*, released in the same year and entitled *Legend of the Mummy* (US, Jeffrey Obrow, 1998), often referred to as *Bram Stoker's Legend of the Mummy*, in order to capitalize upon the Stoker name, which had regained something of its cachet following the surprising success of *Bram Stoker's Dracula* (US, Francis Ford Coppola, 1992). Starring Amy Locane as Margaret Trelawny, the film's most interesting element is the reuse of character actor Aubrey Morris in the same role, although the names have been altered, which he had essayed in *Blood From the Mummy's Tomb*, almost thirty years before.

However, the major onscreen mummy presence was felt in Stephen Sommers' films *The Mummy* and *The Mummy Returns* (US, 2001) in which Arnold Vosloo portrayed Imhotep, as a bare-chested, somewhat pugnacious

---

21   Lansdale, J R and D. Coscarelli. 2003. *Bubba Ho-Tep*. San Francisco: Night Shade Books. 4.

sorcerer, intent on world domination. The films were immensely popular with the cinema-going public, spawning a second sequel, *The Mummy: Tomb of the Dragon Emperor* (US, Rob Cohen, 2008) set in China as well as a spin-off series relating to the exploits of the Scorpion King. Far removed from their Karl Freund source material, the films heavily employed the concept of reincarnation and ancient Egyptian magic, allowing Imhotep to transform himself into billowing sandstorms and to control the weather. Although much had altered, the similarities to *Dracula*, evident from John L Balderston's 1932 screenplay had survived the transformation to somewhat gory action-adventure territory rather more successfully than either the character of Imhotep or the atmosphere evoked in Karl Freund's original. Certainly, there were mummies aplenty spread across Sommers' two films, however, their computer generated conceptualisation and apparent disposability reduced their screen presence considerably.

The films were a somewhat unfortunate return to the material for Universal and, at time of writing, press reports from Hollywood would seem to indicate that a further reboot of what is now termed Universal's "mummy franchise," is currently underway.

More happily, the mummies in *Night at the Museum* (US, Shawn Levy, 2006) and its sequel *Night at the Museum 2* (US, Shawn Levy, 2009) were a new and interesting take on the theme, Rami Malek revealing himself to be a charming and comely Akhmenrah under his wrappings, while, in the sequel, Hank Azaria's power-hungry villain, Kahmunrah, amusingly portrays him with a sepulchral English accent and a distinctly Karloffian lisp.

The final fictional mummies, I wish to mention appear in the aforementioned *Les Aventures extraordinaires d'Adèle Blanc-Sec* and show that CGI can be used to create convincing looking mummies, not least in that of Ramesses II, which looks marvelously similar to the king's actual mummy. The fact that the numerous mummies, appearing towards the films conclusion are granted something akin to rounded personalities, rather than being simple marauding monsters is distinctly refreshing as is the fact that Ramesses II is given one of the most amusing lines in the film.

As we enter the fifteenth year of this new century, one hundred and eighty-three years since the publication of Jane Webb's novel, it seems that the mummy remains a staple of popular fiction, having achieved the leap from printed page to cinema and television screen with rather more success than a number of his supernatural comrades, to become something of a cultural icon, instantly recognizable to children and adults alike, many of whom have never set foot inside a museum in order to encounter an actual mummified Egyptian. Whilst, perhaps, not as lively as at certain points in his literary and cinematic history, it is evident that life still stirs within the coffin, ready to spring forth again with renewed vigor in original and surprising forms.

I commend to you, then, this collection of nineteenth and early twentieth century mummy fiction. It is, as *Musée des Familles*, the publisher of our first offering would have had it, reading for the evening.

John J Johnston
West Dulwich
September 2013

THE MUMMY'S FOOT

THÉOPHILE GAUTIER

TRANSLATED BY LAFCADIO HEARN

I had entered, in an idle mood, the shop of one of those curiosity venders who are called *marchands* de *bric-à-brac* in that Parisian argot which is so perfectly unintelligible elsewhere in France.

You have doubtless glanced occasionally through the windows of some of these shops, which have become so numerous now that it is fashionable to buy antiquated furniture, and that every petty stockbroker thinks he must have his *chambre au moyen âge*.

There is one thing there which clings alike to the shop of the dealer in old iron, the ware-room of the tapestry maker, the laboratory of the chemist, and the studio of the painter: in all those gloomy dens where a furtive daylight filters in through the window-shutters the most manifestly ancient thing is dust. The cobwebs are more authentic than the gimp laces, and the old pear-tree furniture on exhibition is actually younger than the mahogany which arrived but yesterday from America.

The warehouse of my *bric-à-brac* dealer was a veritable Capharnaum. All ages and all nations seemed to have made their rendezvous there. An Etruscan lamp of red clay stood upon a Boule cabinet, with ebony panels, brightly striped by lines of inlaid brass; a duchess of the court of Louis XV nonchalantly extended her fawn-like feet under a massive table of the time of Louis XIII, with heavy spiral supports of oak, and carven designs of chimeras and foliage intermingled.

Upon the denticulated shelves of several sideboards glittered immense Japanese dishes with red and blue designs relieved by gilded hatching, side by side with enamelled works by Bernard Palissy, representing serpents, frogs, and lizards in relief.

From disembowelled cabinets escaped cascades of silver-lustrous Chinese silks and waves of tinsel, which an oblique sunbeam shot through with luminous beads, while portraits of every era, in frames more or less tarnished, smiled through their yellow varnish.

The striped breastplate of a damascened suit of Milanese armour glittered in one corner; loves and nymphs of porcelain, Chinese grotesques, vases of *céladon* and crackleware, Saxon and old Sèvres cups encumbered the shelves and nooks of the apartment.

The dealer followed me closely through the tortuous way contrived between the piles of furniture, warding off with his hand the hazardous sweep of my coat-skirts, watching my elbows with the uneasy attention of an antiquarian and a usurer.

It was a singular face, that of the merchant; an immense skull, polished like a knee, and surrounded by a thin aureole of white hair, which brought out the clear salmon tint of his complexion all the more strikingly, lent him a false aspect of patriarchal bonhomie, counteracted, however, by the scintillation of two little yellow eyes which trembled in their orbits like two louis-d'or upon quicksilver. The curve of his nose presented an aquiline silhouette, which suggested the Oriental or Jewish type. His hands – thin, slender, full of nerves which projected like strings upon the finger-board of a violin, and armed with claws like those on the terminations of bats' wings – shook with senile trembling; but those convulsively agitated hands became firmer than steel pincers or lobsters' claws when they lifted any precious article – an onyx cup, a Venetian glass, or a dish of Bohemian crystal. This strange old man had an aspect so thoroughly rabbinical and cabalistic that he would have been burnt on the mere testimony of his face three centuries ago.

"Will you not buy something from me today, sir? Here is a Malay kreese with a blade undulating like flame. Look at those grooves contrived for the blood to run along, those teeth set backward so as to tear out the entrails in withdrawing the weapon. It is a fine character of ferocious arm, and will look well in your collection. This two-handed sword is very beautiful. It is the work of Josepe de la Hera; and this *colichemarde* with its fenestrated guard – what a superb specimen of handicraft!"

"No; I have quite enough weapons and instruments of carnage. I want a small figure, something which will suit me as a paper-weight, for I cannot endure those trumpery bronzes which the stationers sell, and which may be found on everybody's desk."

The old gnome foraged among his ancient wares, and finally arranged before me some antique bronzes, so-called at least; fragments of malachite, little Hindoo or Chinese idols, a kind of poussah-toys in jade-stone, representing the incarnations of Brahma or Vishnoo, and wonderfully appropriate to the very undivine office of holding papers and letters in place.

I was hesitating between a porcelain dragon, all constellated with warts, its mouth formidable with bristling tusks and ranges of teeth, and an abominable little Mexican fetich, representing the god Vitziliputzili *au naturel*, when I caught sight of a charming foot, which I at first took for a fragment of some antique Venus.

It had those beautiful ruddy and tawny tints that lend to Florentine bronze that warm living look so much preferable to the gray-green aspect of common bronzes, which might easily be mistaken for statues in a state of putrefaction. Satiny gleams played over its rounded forms, doubtless polished by the amorous kisses of twenty centuries, for it seemed a Corinthian bronze, a work of the best era of art, perhaps moulded by Lysippus himself.

"That foot will be my choice," I said to the merchant, who regarded me with an ironical and saturnine air, and held out the object desired that I might examine it more fully.

I was surprised at its lightness. It was not a foot of metal, but in sooth a foot of flesh, an embalmed foot, a mummy's foot. On examining it still more closely the very grain of the skin, and the almost imperceptible lines impressed upon it by the texture of the bandages, became perceptible. The toes were slender and delicate, and terminated by perfectly formed nails, pure and transparent as agates. The great toe, slightly separated from the rest, afforded a happy contrast, in the antique style, to the position of the other toes, and lent it an aerial lightness – the grace of a bird's foot. The sole, scarcely streaked by a few almost imperceptible cross lines, afforded evidence that it had never touched the bare ground, and had only come in contact with the finest matting of Nile rushes and the softest carpets of panther skin.

"Ha, ha, you want the foot of the Princess Hermonthis!" exclaimed the merchant, with a strange giggle, fixing his owlish eyes upon me. "Ha, ha, ha! For a paper-weight! An original idea! – Artistic idea! – Old Pharaoh would certainly have been surprised had some one told him that the foot of his adored daughter would be used for a paper-weight after he had had a mountain of granite hollowed out as a receptacle for the triple coffin, painted and gilded, covered with hieroglyphics and beautiful paintings of the Judgment of Souls," continued the queer little merchant, half audibly, as though talking to himself.

"How much will you charge me for this mummy fragment?"

"Ah, the highest price I can get, for it is a superb piece. If I had the match of it you could not have it for less than five hundred francs. The daughter of a Pharaoh! Nothing is more rare."

"Assuredly that is not a common article, but still, how much do you want? In the first place let me warn you that all my wealth consists of just five louis. I can buy anything that costs five louis, but nothing dearer. You might search my vest pockets and most secret drawers without even finding one poor five-franc piece more."

"Five louis for the foot of the Princess Hermonthis! That is very little, very little indeed. "Tis an authentic foot," muttered the merchant, shaking his head, and imparting a peculiar rotary motion to his eyes. "Well, take it, and I will give you the bandages into the bargain," he added, wrapping the foot in an ancient damask rag. "Very fine? Real damask – Indian damask which has never been redyed. It is strong, and yet it is soft," he mumbled, stroking the frayed tissue with his fingers, through the trade-acquired habit which moved him to praise even an object of such little value that he himself deemed it only worth the giving away.

He poured the gold coins into a sort of mediaeval alms-purse hanging at his belt, repeating:

"The foot of the Princess Hermonthis to be used for a paper-weight!"

Then turning his phosphorescent eyes upon me, he exclaimed in a voice strident as the crying of a cat which has swallowed a fish-bone:

"Old Pharaoh will not be well pleased. He loved his daughter, the dear man!"

"You speak as if you were a contemporary of his. You are old enough, goodness knows! But you do not date back to the Pyramids of Egypt," I answered, laughingly, from the threshold.

I went home, delighted with my acquisition.

⚊∕⫫⚊

With the idea of putting it to profitable use as soon as possible, I placed the foot of the divine Princess Hermonthis upon a heap of papers scribbled over with verses, in themselves an undecipherable mosaic work of erasures; articles freshly begun; letters forgotten, and posted in the table drawer instead of the letter-box, an error to which absent-minded people are peculiarly liable. The effect was charming, bizarre, and romantic.

Well satisfied with this embellishment, I went out with the gravity and pride becoming one who feels that he has the ineffable advantage over all the passers-by whom he elbows, of possessing a piece of the Princess Hermonthis, daughter of Pharaoh.

I looked upon all who did not possess, like myself, a paper-weight so authentically Egyptian as very ridiculous people, and it seemed to me that the proper occupation of every sensible man should consist in the mere fact of having a mummy's foot upon his desk.

Happily I met some friends, whose presence distracted me in my infatuation with this new acquisition. I went to dinner with them, for I could not very well have dined with myself.

When I came back that evening, with my brain slightly confused by a few glasses of wine, a vague whiff of Oriental perfume delicately titillated my olfactory nerves. The heat of the room had warmed the natron, bitumen, and myrrh in which the paraschistes, who cut open the bodies of the dead, had bathed the corpse of the princess. It was a perfume at once sweet and penetrating, a perfume that four thousand years had not been able to dissipate.

- 2 -

The Dream of Egypt was Eternity. Her odours have the solidity of granite and endure as long.

I soon drank deeply from the black cup of sleep. For a few hours all remained opaque to me. Oblivion and nothingness inundated me with their sombre waves.

Yet light gradually dawned upon the darkness of my mind. Dreams commenced to touch me softly in their silent flight.

The eyes of my soul were opened, and I beheld my chamber as it actually was. I might have believed myself awake but for a vague consciousness which assured me that I slept, and that something fantastic was about to take place.

The odour of the myrrh had augmented in intensity, and I felt a slight headache, which I very naturally attributed to several glasses of champagne that we had drunk to the unknown gods and our future fortunes.

I peered through my room with a feeling of expectation which I saw nothing to justify. Every article of furniture was in its proper place. The lamp, softly shaded by its globe of ground crystal, burned upon its bracket; the water-colour sketches shone under their Bohemian glass; the curtains hung down languidly; everything wore an aspect of tranquil slumber.

After a few moments, however, all this calm interior appeared to become disturbed. The woodwork cracked stealthily, the ash-covered log suddenly emitted a jet of blue flame, and the discs of the pateras seemed like great metallic eyes, watching, like myself, for the things which were about to happen.

My eyes accidentally fell upon the desk where I had placed the foot of the Princess Hermonthis.

Instead of remaining quiet, as behoved a foot which had been embalmed for four thousand years, it commenced to act in a nervous manner, contracted itself, and leaped over the papers like a startled frog. One would have imagined that it had suddenly been brought into contact with a galvanic battery. I could distinctly hear the dry sound made by its little heel, hard as the hoof of a gazelle.

I became rather discontented with my acquisition, inasmuch as I wished my paper-weights to be of a sedentary disposition, and thought it very unnatural that feet should walk about without legs, and I commenced to experience a feeling closely akin to fear.

Suddenly I saw the folds of my bed-curtain stir, and heard a bumping sound, like that caused by some person hopping on one foot across the floor. I must confess I became alternately hot and cold, that I felt a strange wind chill my back, and that my suddenly rising hair caused my night-cap to execute a leap of several yards.

The bed-curtains opened and I beheld the strangest figure imaginable before me.

It was a young girl of a very deep coffee-brown complexion, like the bayadère Amani, and possessing the purest Egyptian type of perfect beauty. Her eyes were almond shaped and oblique, with eyebrows so black that they seemed blue; her nose was exquisitely chiselled, almost Greek in its delicacy of outline; and she might indeed have been taken for a Corinthian statue of bronze but for the prominence of her cheek-bones and the slightly African fulness of her lips, which compelled one to recognise her as belonging beyond all doubt to the hieroglyphic race which dwelt upon the banks of the Nile.

Her arms, slender and spindle-shaped like those of very young girls, were encircled by a peculiar kind of metal bands and bracelets of glass beads; her hair was all twisted into little cords, and she wore upon her bosom a little idol-figure of green paste, bearing a whip with seven lashes, which proved it to be an image of Isis; her brow was adorned with a shining plate of gold, and a few traces of paint relieved the coppery tint of her cheeks.

As for her costume, it was very odd indeed.

Fancy a *pagne*, or skirt, all formed of little strips of material bedizened with red and black hieroglyphics, stiffened with bitumen, and apparently belonging to a freshly unbandaged mummy.

In one of those sudden flights of thought so common in dreams I heard the hoarse falsetto of the *bric-à-brac* dealer, repeating like a monotonous refrain the phrase he had uttered in his shop with so enigmatical an intonation:

"Old Pharaoh will not be well pleased He loved his daughter, the dear man!"

One strange circumstance, which was not at all calculated to restore my equanimity, was that the apparition had but one foot; the other was broken off at the ankle!

She approached the table where the foot was starting and fidgeting about more than ever, and there supported herself upon the edge of the desk. I saw her eyes fill with pearly gleaming tears.

Although she had not as yet spoken, I fully comprehended the thoughts which agitated her. She looked at her foot – for it was indeed her own – with an exquisitely graceful expression of coquettish sadness, but the foot leaped and ran hither and thither, as though impelled on steel springs.

Twice or thrice she extended her hand to seize it, but could not succeed.

Then commenced between the Princess Hermonthis and her foot – which appeared to be endowed with a special life of its own – a very fantastic dialogue in a most ancient Coptic tongue, such as might have been spoken thirty centuries ago in the syrinxes of the land of Ser. Luckily I understood Coptic perfectly well that night.

The Princess Hermonthis cried, in a voice sweet and vibrant as the tones of a crystal bell:

"Well, my dear little foot, you always flee from me, yet I always took good care of you. I bathed you with perfumed water in a bowl of alabaster; I smoothed your heel with pumice-stone mixed with palm-oil; your nails were cut with golden scissors and polished with a hippopotamus tooth; I was careful to select *tatbebs* for you, painted and embroidered and turned up at the toes, which were the envy of all the young girls in Egypt. You wore on your great toe rings bearing the device of the sacred Scarabseus, and you supported one of the lightest bodies that a lazy foot could sustain."

The foot replied in a pouting and chagrined tone:

"You know well that I do not belong to myself any longer. I have been bought and paid for. The old merchant knew what he was about. He bore you a grudge for having refused to espouse him. This is an ill turn which he has done you. The Arab who violated your royal coffin in the subterranean pits of the necropolis of Thebes was sent thither by him. He desired to prevent you from being present at the reunion of the shadowy nations in the cities below. Have you five pieces of gold for my ransom?"

"Alas, no! My jewels, my rings, my purses of gold and silver were all stolen from me," answered the Princess Hermonthis with a sob.

"Princess," I then exclaimed, "I never retained anybody's foot unjustly. Even though you have not got the five louis which it cost me, I present it to you gladly. I should feel unutterably wretched to think that I were the cause of so amiable a person as the Princess Hermonthis being lame."

I delivered this discourse in a royally gallant, troubadour tone which must have astonished the beautiful Egyptian girl.

She turned a look of deepest gratitude upon me, and her eyes shone with bluish gleams of light.

She took her foot, which surrendered itself willingly this time, like a woman about to put on her little shoe, and adjusted it to her leg with much skill.

This operation over, she took a few steps about the room, as though to assure herself that she was really no longer lame.

"Ah, how pleased my father will be! He who was so unhappy because of my mutilation, and who from the moment of my birth set a whole nation at work to hollow me out a tomb so deep that he might preserve me intact until that last day when souls must be weighed in the balance of Amenthi! Come with me to my father. He will receive you kindly, for you have given me back my foot."

I thought this proposition natural enough. I arrayed myself in a dressing-gown of large-flowered pattern, which lent me a very Pharaonic aspect, hurriedly put on a pair of Turkish slippers, and informed the Princess Hermonthis that I was ready to follow her.

Before starting, Hermonthis took from her neck the little idol of green paste, and laid it on the scattered sheets of paper which covered the table.

"It is only fair,' she observed, smilingly, 'that I should replace your paper-weight."

She gave me her hand, which felt soft and cold, like the skin of a serpent, and we departed.

We passed for some time with the velocity of an arrow through a fluid and grayish expanse, in which half-formed silhouettes flitted swiftly by us, to right and left.

For an instant we saw only sky and sea.

A few moments later obelisks commenced to tower in the distance; pylons and vast flights of steps guarded by sphinxes became clearly outlined against the horizon.

We had reached our destination.

The princess conducted me to a mountain of rose-coloured granite, in the face of which appeared an opening so narrow and low that it would have been difficult to distinguish it from the fissures in the rock, had not its location been marked by two stelae wrought with sculptures.

Hermonthis kindled a torch and led the way before me.

We traversed corridors hewn through the living rock. Their walls, covered with hieroglyphics and paintings of allegorical processions, might well have occupied thousands of arms for thousands of years in their formation. These corridors of interminable length opened into square chambers, in the midst of which pits had been contrived, through which we descended by cramp-irons or spiral stairways. These pits again conducted us into other chambers, opening into other corridors, likewise decorated with painted sparrow-hawks, serpents coiled in circles, the symbols of the *tau* and *pedum* – prodigious works of art which no living eye can ever examine – interminable legends of granite which only the dead have time to read through all eternity.

At last we found ourselves in a hall so vast, so enormous, so immeasurable, that the eye could not reach its limits. Files of monstrous columns stretched far out of sight on every side, between which twinkled livid stars of yellowish flame; points of light which revealed further depths incalculable in the darkness beyond.

The Princess Hermonthis still held my hand, and graciously saluted the mummies of her acquaintance.

My eyes became accustomed to the dim twilight, and objects became discernible.

I beheld the kings of the subterranean races seated upon thrones – grand old men, though dry, withered, wrinkled like parchment, and blackened with naphtha and bitumen – all wearing *pshents* of gold, and breastplates and gorgets glittering with precious stones, their eyes immovably fixed like the eyes of sphinxes, and their long beards whitened by the snow of centuries. Behind them stood their peoples, in the stiff and constrained posture enjoined by Egyptian art, all eternally preserving the attitude prescribed by the hieratic code. Behind these nations, the cats, ibixes, and crocodiles contemporary with them– rendered monstrous of aspect by their swathing bands – mewed, flapped their wings, or extended their jaws in a saurian giggle.

All the Pharaohs were there – Cheops, Chephrenes, Psammetichus, Sesostris, Amenotaph – all the dark rulers of the pyramids and syrinxes. On yet higher thrones sat Chronos and Xixouthros, who was contemporary with the deluge, and Tubal Cain, who reigned before it.

The beard of King Xixouthros had grown seven times around the granite table upon which he leaned, lost in deep reverie, and buried in dreams.

Further back, through a dusty cloud, I beheld dimly the seventy-two pre-adamite kings, with their seventy-two peoples, for ever passed away.

After permitting me to gaze upon this bewildering spectacle a few moments, the Princess Hermonthis presented me to her father Pharaoh, who favoured me with a most gracious nod.

"I have found my foot again! I have found my foot!" cried the princess, clapping her little hands together with every sign of frantic joy. "It was this gentleman who restored it to me."

The races of Kemi, the races of Nahasi – all the black, bronzed, and copper-coloured nations repeated in chorus:

"The Princess Hermonthis has found her foot again!"

Even Xixouthros himself was visibly affected.

He raised his heavy eyelids, stroked his moustache with his fingers, and turned upon me a glance weighty with centuries.

"By Oms, the dog of Hell, and Tmei, daughter of the Sun and of Truth, this is a brave and worthy lad!" exclaimed Pharaoh, pointing to me with his sceptre, which was terminated with a lotus-flower.

"What recompense do you desire?"

Filled with that daring inspired by dreams in which nothing seems impossible, I asked him for the hand of the Princess Hermonthis. The hand seemed to me a very proper antithetic recompense for the foot.

Pharaoh opened wide his great eyes of glass in astonishment at my witty request.

"What country do you come from, and what is your age?"

"I am a Frenchman, and I am twenty-seven years old venerable Pharaoh."

"Twenty-seven years old, and he wishes to espouse the Princess Hermonthis who is thirty centuries old!" cried out at once all the Thrones and all the Circles of Nations.

Only Hermonthis herself did not seem to think my request unreasonable.

"If you were even only two thousand years old," replied the ancient king, "I would willingly give you the princess, but the disproportion is too great; and, besides, we must give our daughters husbands who will last well. You do not know how to preserve yourselves any longer. Even those who died only fifteen centuries ago are already no more than a handful of dust. Behold, my flesh is solid as basalt, my bones are bars of steel!

"I will be present on the last day of the world with the same body and the same features which I had during my lifetime. My daughter Hermonthis will last longer than a statue of bronze.

"Then the last particles of your dust will have been scattered abroad by the winds, and even Isis herself, who was able to find the atoms of Osiris, would scarce be able to recompose your being.

"See how vigorous I yet remain, and how mighty is my grasp," he added, shaking my hand in the English fashion with a strength that buried my rings in the flesh of my fingers.

He squeezed me so hard that I awoke, and found my friend Alfred shaking me by the arm to make me get up.

"Oh, you everlasting sleeper! Must I have you carried out into the middle of the street, and fireworks exploded in your ears? It is afternoon. Don't you recollect your promise to take me with you to see M. Aguado's Spanish pictures?"

"God! I forgot all about it," I answered, dressing myself hurriedly. "We will go there at once. I have the permit lying there on my desk."

I started to find it, but fancy my astonishment when I beheld, instead of the mummy's foot I had purchased the evening before, the little green paste idol left in its place by the Princess Hermonthis!

SOME WORDS WITH A MUMMY

EDGAR ALLAN POE

The symposium of the preceding evening had been a little too much for my nerves. I had a wretched headache, and was desperately drowsy. Instead of going out therefore to spend the evening as I had proposed, it occurred to me that I could not do a wiser thing than just eat a mouthful of supper and go immediately to bed.

A light supper of course. I am exceedingly fond of Welsh rabbit. More than a pound at once, however, may not at all times be advisable. Still, there can be no material objection to two. And really between two and three, there is merely a single unit of difference. I ventured, perhaps, upon four. My wife will have it five; but, clearly, she has confounded two very distinct affairs. The abstract number, five, I am willing to admit; but, concretely, it has reference to bottles of Brown Stout, without which, in the way of condiment, Welsh rabbit is to be eschewed.

Having thus concluded a frugal meal, and donned my night-cap, with the serene hope of enjoying it till noon the next day, I placed my head upon the pillow, and, through the aid of a capital conscience, fell into a profound slumber forthwith.

But when were the hopes of humanity fulfilled? I could not have completed my third snore when there came a furious ringing at the street-door bell, and then an impatient thumping at the knocker, which awakened me at once. In a minute afterward, and while I was still rubbing my eyes, my wife thrust in my face a note, from my old friend, Doctor Ponnonner. It ran thus:

Come to me, by all means, my dear good friend, as soon as you receive this. Come and help us to rejoice. At last, by long persevering diplomacy, I have gained the assent of the Directors of the City Museum, to my examination of the Mummy – you know the one I mean. I have permission to unswathe it and open it, if desirable. A few friends only will be present – you, of course. The Mummy is now at my house, and we shall begin to unroll it at eleven tonight.
Yours, ever,
PONNONNER

By the time I had reached the "Ponnonner," it struck me that I was as wide awake as a man need be. I leaped out of bed in an ecstasy, overthrowing all in my way; dressed myself with a rapidity truly marvellous; and set off, at the top of my speed, for the doctor's.

There I found a very eager company assembled. They had been awaiting me with much impatience; the Mummy was extended upon the dining-table; and the moment I entered its examination was commenced.

It was one of a pair brought, several years previously, by Captain Arthur Sabretash, a cousin of Ponnonner's from a tomb near Eleithias, in the Lybian mountains, a considerable distance above Thebes on the Nile. The grottoes at this point, although less magnificent than the Theban sepulchres, are of higher interest, on account of affording more numerous illustrations of the private life of the Egyptians. The chamber from which our specimen was taken, was said to be very rich in such illustrations; the walls being completely covered with fresco paintings and bas-reliefs, while statues, vases, and Mosaic work of rich patterns, indicated the vast wealth of the deceased.

The treasure had been deposited in the Museum precisely in the same condition in which Captain Sabretash had found it; that is to say, the coffin had not been disturbed. For eight years it had thus stood, subject only externally to public inspection. We had now, therefore, the complete Mummy at our disposal; and to those who are aware how very rarely the unransacked antique reaches our shores, it will be evident, at once that we had great reason to congratulate ourselves upon our good fortune.

Approaching the table, I saw on it a large box, or case, nearly seven feet long, and perhaps three feet wide, by two feet and a half deep. It was oblong – not coffin-shaped. The material was at first supposed to be the wood of the sycamore (platanus), but, upon cutting into it, we found it to be pasteboard, or, more properly, papier mache, composed of papyrus. It was thickly ornamented with paintings, representing funeral scenes, and other mournful subjects – interspersed among which, in every variety of position, were certain series of hieroglyphical characters, intended, no doubt, for the name of the departed. By good luck, Mr. Gliddon formed one of our party; and he had no difficulty in translating the letters, which were simply phonetic, and represented the word Allamistakeo.

We had some difficulty in getting this case open without injury; but having at length accomplished the task, we came to a second, coffin-shaped, and very considerably less in size than the exterior one, but resembling it precisely in every other respect. The interval between the two was filled with resin, which had, in some degree, defaced the colors of the interior box.

Upon opening this latter (which we did quite easily), we arrived at a third case, also coffin-shaped, and varying from the second one in no particular, except in that of its material, which was cedar, and still emitted the peculiar and highly aromatic odor of that wood. Between the second and the third case there was no interval – the one fitting accurately within the other.

Removing the third case, we discovered and took out the body itself. We had expected to find it, as usual, enveloped in frequent rolls, or bandages, of linen; but, in place of these, we found a sort of sheath, made of papyrus, and coated with a layer of plaster, thickly gilt and painted. The paintings represented subjects connected with the various supposed duties of the soul, and its presentation to different divinities, with numerous identical human figures, intended, very probably, as portraits of the persons embalmed. Extending from head to foot was a columnar, or perpendicular, inscription, in phonetic hieroglyphics, giving again his name and titles, and the names and titles of his relations.

Around the neck thus ensheathed, was a collar of cylindrical glass beads, diverse in color, and so arranged as to form images of deities, of the scarabaeus, etc, with the winged globe. Around the small of the waist was a similar collar or belt.

Stripping off the papyrus, we found the flesh in excellent preservation, with no perceptible odor. The color was reddish. The skin was hard, smooth, and glossy. The teeth and hair were in good condition. The eyes (it seemed) had been removed, and glass ones substituted, which were very beautiful and wonderfully life-like, with the exception of somewhat too determined a stare. The fingers and the nails were brilliantly gilded.

Mr. Gliddon was of opinion, from the redness of the epidermis, that the embalmment had been effected altogether by asphaltum; but, on scraping the surface with a steel instrument, and throwing into the fire some of the powder thus obtained, the flavor of camphor and other sweet-scented gums became apparent.

We searched the corpse very carefully for the usual openings through which the entrails are extracted, but, to our surprise, we could discover none. No member of the party was at that period aware that entire or unopened mummies are not infrequently met. The brain it was customary to withdraw through the nose; the intestines through an incision in the side; the body was then shaved, washed, and salted; then laid aside for several weeks, when the operation of embalming, properly so called, began.

As no trace of an opening could be found, Doctor Ponnonner was preparing his instruments for dissection, when I observed that it was then past two o'clock. Hereupon it was agreed to postpone the internal examination until the next evening; and we were about to separate for the present, when some one suggested an experiment or two with the Voltaic pile.

The application of electricity to a mummy three or four thousand years old at the least, was an idea, if not very sage, still sufficiently original, and we all caught it at once. About one-tenth in earnest and nine-tenths in jest, we arranged a battery in the Doctor's study, and conveyed thither the Egyptian.

It was only after much trouble that we succeeded in laying bare some portions of the temporal muscle which appeared of less stony rigidity than other parts of the frame, but which, as we had anticipated, of course, gave no indication of galvanic susceptibility when brought in contact with the wire. This, the first trial, indeed, seemed decisive, and, with a hearty laugh at our own absurdity, we were bidding each other good night, when my eyes, happening to fall upon those of the Mummy, were there immediately riveted in amazement. My brief glance, in fact, had sufficed to assure me that the orbs which we had all supposed to be glass, and which were originally noticeable for a certain wild stare, were now so far covered by the lids, that only a small portion of the tunica albuginea remained visible.

With a shout I called attention to the fact, and it became immediately obvious to all.

I cannot say that I was alarmed at the phenomenon, because "alarmed" is, in my case, not exactly the word. It is possible, however, that, but for the Brown Stout, I might have been a little nervous. As for the rest of the company, they really made no attempt at concealing the downright fright which possessed them. Doctor Ponnonner was a man to be pitied. Mr. Gliddon, by some peculiar process, rendered himself invisible. Mr. Silk Buckingham, I fancy, will scarcely be so bold as to deny that he made his way, upon all fours, under the table.

After the first shock of astonishment, however, we resolved, as a matter of course, upon further experiment forthwith. Our operations were now directed against the great toe of the right foot. We made an incision over the outside of the exterior os sesamoideum pollicis pedis, and thus got at the root of the abductor muscle. Readjusting the battery, we now applied the fluid to the bisected nerves – when, with a movement of exceeding life-likeness, the Mummy first drew up its right knee so as to bring it nearly in contact with the abdomen, and then, straightening the limb with inconceivable force, bestowed a kick upon Doctor Ponnonner, which had the effect of discharging that gentleman, like an arrow from a catapult, through a window into the street below.

We rushed out en masse to bring in the mangled remains of the victim, but had the happiness to meet him upon the staircase, coming up in an unaccountable hurry, brimful of the most ardent philosophy, and more than ever impressed with the necessity of prosecuting our experiment with vigor and with zeal.

It was by his advice, accordingly, that we made, upon the spot, a profound incision into the tip of the subject's nose, while the Doctor himself, laying violent hands upon it, pulled it into vehement contact with the wire.

Morally and physically – figuratively and literally – was the effect electric. In the first place, the corpse opened its eyes and winked very rapidly for several minutes, as does Mr. Barnes in the pantomime, in the second place, it sneezed; in the third, it sat upon end; in the fourth, it shook its fist in Doctor Ponnonner's face; in the fifth, turning to Messieurs Gliddon and Buckingham, it addressed them, in very capital Egyptian, thus:

"I must say, gentlemen, that I am as much surprised as I am mortified at your behavior. Of Doctor Ponnonner nothing better was to be expected. He is a poor little fat fool who knows no better. I pity and forgive him. But you, Mr. Gliddon – and you, Silk – who have travelled and resided in Egypt until one might imagine you to the manner born – you, I say who have been so much among us that you speak Egyptian fully as well, I think, as you write your mother tongue – you, whom I have always been led to regard as the firm friend of the mummies – I really did anticipate more gentlemanly conduct from you. What am I to think of your standing quietly by and seeing me thus unhandsomely used? What am I to suppose by your permitting Tom, Dick, and Harry to strip me of my coffins, and my clothes, in this wretchedly cold climate? In what light (to come to the point) am I to regard your aiding and abetting that miserable little villain, Doctor Ponnonner, in pulling me by the nose?"

It will be taken for granted, no doubt, that upon hearing this speech under the circumstances, we all either made for the door, or fell into violent hysterics, or went off in a general swoon. One of these three things was, I say, to be expected. Indeed each and all of these lines of conduct might have been very plausibly pursued. And, upon my word, I am at a loss to know how or why it was that we pursued neither the one nor the other. But, perhaps, the true reason is to be sought in the spirit of the age, which proceeds by the rule of contraries altogether, and is now usually admitted as the solution of every thing in the way of paradox and impossibility. Or, perhaps, after all, it was only the Mummy's exceedingly natural and matter-of-course air that divested his words of the terrible. However this may be, the facts are clear, and no member of our party betrayed any very particular trepidation, or seemed to consider that any thing had gone very especially wrong.

For my part I was convinced it was all right, and merely stepped aside, out of the range of the Egyptian's fist. Doctor Ponnonner thrust his hands into his breeches' pockets, looked hard at the Mummy, and grew excessively red in the face. Mr. Glidden stroked his whiskers and drew up the collar of his shirt. Mr. Buckingham hung down his head, and put his right thumb into the left corner of his mouth.

The Egyptian regarded him with a severe countenance for some minutes and at length, with a sneer, said:

"Why don't you speak, Mr. Buckingham? Did you hear what I asked you, or not? Do take your thumb out of your mouth!"

Mr. Buckingham, hereupon, gave a slight start, took his right thumb out of the left corner of his mouth, and, by way of indemnification inserted his left thumb in the right corner of the aperture above-mentioned.

Not being able to get an answer from Mr. B., the figure turned peevishly to Mr. Glidden, and, in a peremptory tone, demanded in general terms what we all meant.

Mr. Glidden replied at great length, in phonetics; and but for the deficiency of American printing-offices in hieroglyphical type, it would afford me much pleasure to record here, in the original, the whole of his very excellent speech.

I may as well take this occasion to remark, that all the subsequent conversation in which the Mummy took a part, was carried on in primitive

Egyptian, through the medium (so far as concerned myself and other untravelled members of the company) – through the medium, I say, of Messieurs Gliddon and Buckingham, as interpreters. These gentlemen spoke the mother tongue of the Mummy with inimitable fluency and grace; but I could not help observing that (owing, no doubt, to the introduction of images entirely modern, and, of course, entirely novel to the stranger) the two travellers were reduced, occasionally, to the employment of sensible forms for the purpose of conveying a particular meaning. Mr. Gliddon, at one period, for example, could not make the Egyptian comprehend the term "politics," until he sketched upon the wall, with a bit of charcoal a little carbuncle-nosed gentleman, out at elbows, standing upon a stump, with his left leg drawn back, right arm thrown forward, with his fist shut, the eyes rolled up toward Heaven, and the mouth open at an angle of ninety degrees. Just in the same way Mr. Buckingham failed to convey the absolutely modern idea "wig," until (at Doctor Ponnonner's suggestion) he grew very pale in the face, and consented to take off his own.

It will be readily understood that Mr. Gliddon's discourse turned chiefly upon the vast benefits accruing to science from the unrolling and disembowelling of mummies; apologizing, upon this score, for any disturbance that might have been occasioned him, in particular, the individual Mummy called Allamistakeo; and concluding with a mere hint (for it could scarcely be considered more) that, as these little matters were now explained, it might be as well to proceed with the investigation intended. Here Doctor Ponnonner made ready his instruments.

In regard to the latter suggestions of the orator, it appears that Allamistakeo had certain scruples of conscience, the nature of which I did not distinctly learn; but he expressed himself satisfied with the apologies tendered, and, getting down from the table, shook hands with the company all round.

When this ceremony was at an end, we immediately busied ourselves in repairing the damages which our subject had sustained from the scalpel. We sewed up the wound in his temple, bandaged his foot, and applied a square inch of black plaster to the tip of his nose.

It was now observed that the Count (this was the title, it seems, of Allamistakeo) had a slight fit of shivering – no doubt from the cold. The Doctor immediately repaired to his wardrobe, and soon returned with a black dress coat, made in Jennings' best manner, a pair of sky-blue plaid pantaloons with straps, a pink gingham chemise, a flapped vest of brocade, a white sack overcoat, a walking cane with a hook, a hat with no brim, patent-leather boots, straw-colored kid gloves, an eye-glass, a pair of whiskers, and a waterfall cravat. Owing to the disparity of size between the Count and the doctor (the proportion being as two to one), there was some little difficulty in adjusting these habiliments upon the person of the Egyptian; but when all was arranged, he might have been said to be dressed. Mr. Gliddon, therefore, gave him his arm, and led him to a comfortable chair by the fire, while the Doctor rang the bell upon the spot and ordered a supply of cigars and wine.

The conversation soon grew animated. Much curiosity was, of course, expressed in regard to the somewhat remarkable fact of Allamistakeo's still remaining alive.

"I should have thought," observed Mr. Buckingham, "that it is high time you were dead."

"Why," replied the Count, very much astonished, "I am little more than seven hundred years old! My father lived a thousand, and was by no means in his dotage when he died."

Here ensued a brisk series of questions and computations, by means of which it became evident that the antiquity of the Mummy had been grossly misjudged. It had been five thousand and fifty years and some months since he had been consigned to the catacombs at Eleithias.

"But my remark," resumed Mr. Buckingham, "had no reference to your age at the period of interment (I am willing to grant, in fact, that you are still a young man), and my illusion was to the immensity of time during which, by your own showing, you must have been done up in asphaltum."

"In what?" said the Count.

"In asphaltum," persisted Mr. B.

"Ah, yes; I have some faint notion of what you mean; it might be made to answer, no doubt – but in my time we employed scarcely any thing else than the Bichloride of Mercury."

"But what we are especially at a loss to understand," said Doctor Ponnonner, "is how it happens that, having been dead and buried in Egypt five thousand years ago, you are here to-day all alive and looking so delightfully well."

"Had I been, as you say, dead," replied the Count, "it is more than probable that dead, I should still be; for I perceive you are yet in the infancy of Calvanism, and cannot accomplish with it what was a common thing among us in the old days. But the fact is, I fell into catalepsy, and it was considered by my best friends that I was either dead or should be; they accordingly embalmed me at once – I presume you are aware of the chief principle of the embalming process?"

"Why not altogether."

"Why, I perceive – a deplorable condition of ignorance! Well I cannot enter into details just now: but it is necessary to explain that to embalm (properly speaking), in Egypt, was to arrest indefinitely all the animal functions subjected to the process. I use the word 'animal' in its widest sense, as including the physical not more than the moral and vital being. I repeat that the leading principle of embalmment consisted, with us, in the immediately arresting, and holding in perpetual abeyance, all the animal functions subjected to the process. To be brief, in whatever condition the individual was, at the period of embalmment, in that condition he remained. Now, as it is my good fortune to be of the blood of the Scarabaeus, I was embalmed alive, as you see me at present."

"The blood of the Scarabaeus!" exclaimed Doctor Ponnonner.

"Yes. The Scarabaeus was the insignium or the 'arms,' of a very distinguished and very rare patrician family. To be 'of the blood of the Scarabaeus,' is merely to be one of that family of which the Scarabaeus is the insignium. I speak figuratively."

"But what has this to do with you being alive?"

"Why, it is the general custom in Egypt to deprive a corpse, before embalmment, of its bowels and brains; the race of the Scarabaei alone did not coincide with the custom. Had I not been a Scarabeus, therefore,

I should have been without bowels and brains; and without either it is inconvenient to live."

"I perceive that," said Mr. Buckingham, "and I presume that all the entire mummies that come to hand are of the race of Scarabaei."

"Beyond doubt."

"I thought," said Mr. Gliddon, very meekly, "that the Scarabaeus was one of the Egyptian gods."

"One of the Egyptian *what*?" exclaimed the Mummy, starting to its feet.

"Gods!" repeated the traveller.

"Mr. Gliddon, I really am astonished to hear you talk in this style," said the Count, resuming his chair. "No nation upon the face of the earth has ever acknowledged more than one god. The Scarabaeus, the Ibis, etc., were with us (as similar creatures have been with others) the symbols, or media, through which we offered worship to the Creator too august to be more directly approached."

There was here a pause. At length the colloquy was renewed by Doctor Ponnonner.

"It is not improbable, then, from what you have explained," said he, "that among the catacombs near the Nile there may exist other mummies of the Scarabaeus tribe, in a condition of vitality?"

"There can be no question of it," replied the Count; "all the Scarabaei embalmed accidentally while alive, are alive now. Even some of those purposely so embalmed, may have been overlooked by their executors, and still remain in the tomb."

"Will you be kind enough to explain," I said, "what you mean by 'purposely so embalmed'?"

"With great pleasure!" answered the Mummy, after surveying me leisurely through his eye-glass – for it was the first time I had ventured to address him a direct question.

"With great pleasure," he said. "The usual duration of man's life, in my time, was about eight hundred years. Few men died, unless by most extraordinary accident, before the age of six hundred; few lived longer than a decade of centuries; but eight were considered the natural term. After the discovery of the embalming principle, as I have already described it to you, it occurred to our philosophers that a laudable curiosity might be gratified, and, at the same time, the interests of science much advanced, by living this natural term in installments. In the case of history, indeed, experience demonstrated that something of this kind was indispensable. An historian, for example, having attained the age of five hundred, would write a book with great labor and then get himself carefully embalmed; leaving instructions to his executors pro tem., that they should cause him to be revivified after the lapse of a certain period – say five or six hundred years. Resuming existence at the expiration of this time, he would invariably find his great work converted into a species of hap-hazard note-book – that is to say, into a kind of literary arena for the conflicting guesses, riddles, and personal squabbles of whole herds of exasperated commentators. These guesses, etc., which passed under the name of annotations, or emendations, were found so completely to have enveloped, distorted, and overwhelmed the text, that the author had to go about with a lantern to discover his own book. When discovered, it was never worth the trouble of the search. After re-writing it throughout, it was regarded as the bounden duty of the historian to set himself to work immediately in correcting, from his own private knowledge and experience, the traditions of the day concerning the epoch at which he had originally lived. Now this process of re-scription and personal rectification, pursued by various individual sages from time to time, had the effect of preventing our history from degenerating into absolute fable."

"I beg your pardon," said Doctor Ponnonner at this point, laying his hand gently upon the arm of the Egyptian – "I beg your pardon, sir, but may I presume to interrupt you for one moment?"

"By all means, sir," replied the Count, drawing up.

"I merely wished to ask you a question," said the Doctor. "You mentioned the historian's personal correction of traditions respecting his own epoch. Pray, sir, upon an average what proportion of these Kabbala were usually found to be right?"

"The Kabbala, as you properly term them, sir, were generally discovered to be precisely on a par with the facts recorded in the un-re-written histories themselves; – that is to say, not one individual iota of either was ever known, under any circumstances, to be not totally and radically wrong."

"But since it is quite clear," resumed the Doctor, "that at least five thousand years have elapsed since your entombment, I take it for granted that your histories at that period, if not your traditions were sufficiently explicit on that one topic of universal interest, the Creation, which took place, as I presume you are aware, only about ten centuries before."

"Sir!" said the Count Allamistakeo.

The Doctor repeated his remarks, but it was only after much additional explanation that the foreigner could be made to comprehend them. The latter at length said, hesitatingly:

"The ideas you have suggested are to me, I confess, utterly novel. During my time I never knew any one to entertain so singular a fancy as that the universe (or this world if you will have it so) ever had a beginning at all. I remember once, and once only, hearing something remotely hinted, by a man of many speculations, concerning the origin of the human race; and by this individual, the very word Adam (or Red Earth), which you make use of, was employed. He employed it, however, in a generical sense, with reference to the spontaneous germination from rank soil (just as a thousand of the lower genera of creatures are germinated) – the spontaneous germination, I say, of five vast hordes of men, simultaneously upspringing in five distinct and nearly equal divisions of the globe."

Here, in general, the company shrugged their shoulders, and one or two of us touched our foreheads with a very significant air. Mr. Silk Buckingham, first glancing slightly at the occiput and then at the sinciput of Allamistakeo, spoke as follows:

"The long duration of human life in your time, together with the occasional practice of passing it, as you have explained, in installments, must have had, indeed, a strong tendency to the general development and conglomeration of knowledge. I presume, therefore, that we are to attribute the marked inferiority of the old Egyptians in all particulars of science, when compared with the moderns, and more especially with the Yankees, altogether to the superior solidity of the Egyptian skull."

"I confess again," replied the Count, with much suavity, "that I am somewhat at a loss to comprehend you; pray, to what particulars of science do you allude?"

Here our whole party, joining voices, detailed, at great length, the assumptions of phrenology and the marvels of animal magnetism.

Having heard us to an end, the Count proceeded to relate a few anecdotes, which rendered it evident that prototypes of Gall and Spurzheim had flourished and faded in Egypt so long ago as to have been nearly forgotten, and that the manoeuvres of Mesmer were really very contemptible tricks when put in collation with the positive miracles of the Theban savans, who created lice and a great many other similar things.

I here asked the Count if his people were able to calculate eclipses. He smiled rather contemptuously, and said they were.

This put me a little out, but I began to make other inquiries in regard to his astronomical knowledge, when a member of the company, who had never as yet opened his mouth, whispered in my ear, that for information on this head, I had better consult Ptolemy (whoever Ptolemy is), as well as one Plutarch de facie lunae.

I then questioned the Mummy about burning-glasses and lenses, and, in general, about the manufacture of glass; but I had not made an end of my queries before the silent member again touched me quietly on the elbow, and begged me for God's sake to take a peep at Diodorus Siculus. As for the Count, he merely asked me, in the way of reply, if we moderns possessed any such microscopes as would enable us to cut cameos in the style of the Egyptians. While I was thinking how I should answer this question, little Doctor Ponnonner committed himself in a very extraordinary way.

"Look at our architecture!" he exclaimed, greatly to the indignation of both the travellers, who pinched him black and blue to no purpose.

"Look," he cried with enthusiasm, "at the Bowling-Green Fountain in New York! Or if this be too vast a contemplation, regard for a moment the Capitol at Washington, D. C.!" – and the good little medical man went on to detail very minutely, the proportions of the fabric to which he referred. He explained that the portico alone was adorned with no less than four and twenty columns, five feet in diameter, and ten feet apart.

The Count said that he regretted not being able to remember, just at that moment, the precise dimensions of any one of the principal buildings of the city of Aznac, whose foundations were laid in the night of Time, but the ruins of which were still standing, at the epoch of his entombment, in a vast plain of sand to the westward of Thebes. He recollected, however, (talking of the porticoes,) that one affixed to an inferior palace in a kind of suburb called Carnac, consisted of a hundred and forty-four columns, thirty-seven feet in circumference, and twenty-five feet apart. The approach to this portico, from the Nile, was through an avenue two miles long, composed of sphynxes, statues, and obelisks, twenty, sixty, and a hundred feet in height. The palace itself (as well as he could remember) was, in one direction, two miles long, and might have been altogether about seven in circuit. Its walls were richly painted all over, within and without, with hieroglyphics. He would not pretend to assert that even fifty or sixty of the Doctor's Capitols might have been built within these walls, but he was by no means sure that two or three hundred of them might not have been squeezed in with some trouble. That palace at Carnac was an insignificant little building after all. He (the Count), however, could not conscientiously refuse to admit the ingenuity, magnificence, and superiority of the Fountain at the Bowling Green, as described by the Doctor. Nothing like it, he was forced to allow, had ever been seen in Egypt or elsewhere.

I here asked the Count what he had to say to our railroads.

"Nothing," he replied, "in particular." They were rather slight, rather ill-conceived, and clumsily put together. They could not be compared, of course, with the vast, level, direct, iron-grooved causeways upon which the Egyptians conveyed entire temples and solid obelisks of a hundred and fifty feet in altitude.

I spoke of our gigantic mechanical forces.

He agreed that we knew something in that way, but inquired how I should have gone to work in getting up the imposts on the lintels of even the little palace at Carnac.

This question I concluded not to hear, and demanded if he had any idea of Artesian wells; but he simply raised his eyebrows; while Mr. Gliddon winked at me very hard and said, in a low tone, that one had been recently discovered by the engineers employed to bore for water in the Great Oasis.

I then mentioned our steel; but the foreigner elevated his nose, and asked me if our steel could have executed the sharp carved work seen on the obelisks, and which was wrought altogether by edge-tools of copper.

This disconcerted us so greatly that we thought it advisable to vary the attack to Metaphysics. We sent for a copy of a book called the "Dial," and read out of it a chapter or two about something that is not very clear, but which the Bostonians call the Great Movement of Progress.

The Count merely said that Great Movements were awfully common things in his day, and as for Progress, it was at one time quite a nuisance, but it never progressed.

We then spoke of the great beauty and importance of Democracy, and were at much trouble in impressing the Count with a due sense of the advantages we enjoyed in living where there was suffrage ad libitum, and no king.

He listened with marked interest, and in fact seemed not a little amused. When we had done, he said that, a great while ago, there had occurred something of a very similar sort. Thirteen Egyptian provinces determined all at once to be free, and to set a magnificent example to the rest of mankind. They assembled their wise men, and concocted the most ingenious constitution it is possible to conceive. For a while they managed remarkably well; only their habit of bragging was prodigious. The thing ended, however, in the consolidation of the thirteen states, with some fifteen or twenty others, in the most odious and insupportable despotism that was ever heard of upon the face of the Earth.

I asked what was the name of the usurping tyrant.

As well as the Count could recollect, it was Mob.

Not knowing what to say to this, I raised my voice, and deplored the Egyptian ignorance of steam.

The Count looked at me with much astonishment, but made no answer. The silent gentleman, however, gave me a violent nudge in the ribs with his elbows – told me I had sufficiently exposed myself for once – and demanded if I was really such a fool as not to know that the modern steam-engine is derived from the invention of Hero, through Solomon de Caus.

We were now in imminent danger of being discomfited; but, as good luck would have it, Doctor Ponnonner, having rallied, returned to our rescue, and inquired if the people of Egypt would seriously pretend to rival the moderns in the all – important particular of dress.

The Count, at this, glanced downward to the straps of his pantaloons, and then taking hold of the end of one of his coat-tails, held it up close to his eyes for some minutes. Letting it fall, at last, his mouth extended itself very gradually from ear to ear; but I do not remember that he said any thing in the way of reply.

Hereupon we recovered our spirits, and the Doctor, approaching the Mummy with great dignity, desired it to say candidly, upon its honor as a gentleman, if the Egyptians had comprehended, at any period, the manufacture of either Ponnonner's lozenges or Brandreth's pills.

We looked, with profound anxiety, for an answer – but in vain. It was not forthcoming. The Egyptian blushed and hung down his head. Never was triumph more consummate; never was defeat borne with so ill a grace. Indeed, I could not endure the spectacle of the poor Mummy's mortification. I reached my hat, bowed to him stiffly, and took leave.

Upon getting home I found it past four o'clock, and went immediately to bed. It is now ten A.M. I have been up since seven, penning these memoranda for the benefit of my family and of mankind. The former I shall behold no more.

My wife is a shrew. The truth is, I am heartily sick of this life and of the nineteenth century in general. I am convinced that every thing is going wrong. Besides, I am anxious to know who will be President in 2045. As soon, therefore, as I shave and swallow a cup of coffee, I shall just step over to Ponnonner's and get embalmed for a couple of hundred years.

LOST IN A PYRAMID

LOUISA MAY ALCOTT

"And what are these, Paul?" asked Evelyn, opening a tarnished gold box and examining its contents curiously.

"Seeds of some unknown Egyptian plant," replied Forsyth, with a sudden shadow on his dark face, as he looked down at the three scarlet grains lying in the white hand lifted to him.

"Where did you get them?" asked the girl.

"That is a weird story, which will only haunt you if I tell it," said Forsyth, with an absent expression that strongly excited the girl's curiosity.

"Please tell it, I like weird tales, and they never trouble me. Ah, do tell it; your stories are always so interesting," she cried, looking up with such a pretty blending of entreaty and command in her charming face, that refusal was impossible.

"You'll be sorry for it, and so shall I, perhaps; I warn you beforehand, that harm is foretold to the possessor of those mysterious seeds," said Forsyth, smiling, even while he knit his black brows, and regarded the blooming creature before him with a fond yet foreboding glance.

"Tell on, I'm not afraid of these pretty atoms," she answered, with an imperious nod.

"To hear is to obey. Let me read the facts, and then I will begin," returned Forsyth, pacing to and fro with the far-off look of one who turns the pages of the past.

Evelyn watched him a moment, and then returned to her work, or play, rather, for the task seemed well suited to the vivacious little creature, half-child, half-woman.

"While in Egypt," commenced Forsyth, slowly, "I went one day with my guide and Professor Niles, to explore the Cheops. Niles had a mania for antiquities of all sorts, and forgot time, danger and fatigue in the ardor of his pursuit. We rummaged up and down the narrow passages, half choked with dust and close air; reading inscriptions on the walls, stumbling over shattered mummy-cases, or coming face to face with some shriveled specimen perched like a hobgoblin on the little shelves where the dead used to be stowed away for ages. I was desperately tired after a few hours of it, and begged the professor to return. But he was bent on exploring certain places, and would not desist. We had but one guide, so I was forced to stay; but Jumal, my man, seeing how weary I was, proposed to us to rest in one of the larger passages, while he went to procure another guide for Niles. We consented, and assuring us that we were perfectly safe, if we did not quit the spot, Jumal left us, promising to return speedily. The professor sat down to take notes of his researches, and stretching my self on the soft sand, I fell asleep.

"I was roused by that indescribable thrill which instinctively warns us of danger, and springing up, I found myself alone. One torch burned faintly where Jumal had struck it, but Niles and the other light were gone. A dreadful sense of loneliness oppressed me for a moment; then I collected myself and looked well about me. A bit of paper was pinned to my hat, which lay near me, and on it, in the professor's writing were these words:

I've gone back a little to refresh my memory on certain points. Don't follow me till Jumal comes. I can find my way back to you, for I have a clue. Sleep well, and dream gloriously of the Pharaohs. N N.

"I laughed at first over the old enthusiast, then felt anxious then restless, and finally resolved to follow him, for I discovered a strong cord fastened to a fallen stone, and knew that this was the clue he spoke of. Leaving a line for Jumal, I took my torch and retraced my steps, following the cord along the winding ways. I often shouted, but received no reply, and pressed on, hoping at each turn to see the old man poring over some musty relic of antiquity. Suddenly the cord ended, and lowering my torch, I saw that the footsteps had gone on.

"'Rash fellow, he'll lose himself, to a certainty,' I thought, really alarmed now.

"As I paused, a faint call reached me, and I answered it, waited, shouted again, and a still fainter echo replied.

"Niles was evidently going on, misled by the reverberations of the low passages. No time was to be lost, and, forgetting myself, I stuck my torch in the deep sand to guide me back to the clue, and ran down the straight path before me, whooping like a madman as I went. I did not mean to lose sight of the light, but in my eagerness to find Niles I turned from the main passage, and, guided by his voice, hastened on. His torch soon gladdened my eyes, and the clutch of his trembling hands told me what agony he had suffered.

"'Let us get out of this horrible place at once,' he said, wiping the great drops off his forehead.

"'Come, we're not far from the clue. I can soon reach it, and then we are safe'; but as I spoke, a chill passed over me, for a perfect labyrinth of narrow paths lay before us.

"Trying to guide myself by such land-marks as I had observed in my hasty passage, I followed the tracks in the sand till I fancied we must be near my light. No glimmer appeared, however, and kneeling down to examine the footprints nearer, I discovered, to my dismay, that I had been following the wrong ones, for among those marked by a deep boot-heel, were prints of bare feet; we had had no guide there, and Jumal wore sandals.

"Rising, I confronted Niles, with the one despairing word, 'Lost!' as I pointed from the treacherous sand to the fast-waning light.

"I thought the old man would be overwhelmed but, to my surprise, he grew quite calm and steady, thought a moment, and then went on, saying, quietly:

"'Other men have passed here before us; let us follow their steps, for, if I do not greatly err, they lead toward great passages, where one's way is easily found.'

"On we went, bravely, till a misstep threw the professor violently to the ground with a broken leg, and nearly extinguished the torch. It was a horrible predicament, and I gave up all hope as I sat beside the poor fellow, who lay exhausted with fatigue, remorse and pain, for I would not leave him.

"'Paul,' he said suddenly, 'if you will not go on, there is one more effort we can make. I remember hearing that a party lost as we are, saved themselves by building a fire. The smoke penetrated further than sound or light, and the guide's quick wit understood the unusual mist; he followed it, and rescued the party. Make a fire and trust to Jumal.'

"'A fire without wood?' I began; but he pointed to a shelf behind me, which had escaped me in the gloom; and on it I saw a slender mummy-case. I understood him, for these dry cases, which lie about in hundreds, are freely used as firewood. Reaching up, I pulled it down, believing it to be empty, but as it fell, it burst open, and out rolled a mummy. Accustomed as I was to such sights, it startled me a little, for danger had unstrung my nerves. Laying the little brown chrysalis aside, I smashed the case, lit the pile with my torch, and soon a light cloud of smoke drifted down the three passages which diverged from the cell-like place where we had paused.

"While busied with the fire, Niles, forgetful of pain and peril, had dragged the mummy nearer, and was examining it with the interest of a man whose ruling passion was strong even in death.

"'Come and help me unroll this. I have always longed to be the first to see and secure the curious treasures put away among the folds of these uncanny winding-sheets. This is a woman, and we may find something rare and precious here,' he said, beginning to unfold the outer coverings, from which a strange aromatic odor came.

"Reluctantly I obeyed, for to me there was something sacred in the bones of this unknown woman. But to beguile the time and amuse the poor fellow, I lent a hand, wondering as I worked, if this dark, ugly thing had ever been a lovely, soft-eyed Egyptian girl.

"From the fibrous folds of the wrappings dropped precious gums and spices, which half intoxicated us with their potent breath, antique coins, and a curious jewel or two, which Niles eagerly examined.

"All the bandages but one were cut off at last, and a small head laid bare, round which still hung great plaits of what had once been luxuriant hair. The shriveled hands were folded on the breast, and clasped in them lay that gold box."

"Ah!" cried Evelyn, dropping it from her rosy palm with a shudder.

"Nay; don't reject the poor little mummy's treasure. I never have quite forgiven myself for stealing it, or for burning her," said Forsyth, painting rapidly, as if the recollection of that experience lent energy to his hand.

"Burning her! Oh, Paul, what do you mean?" asked the girl, sitting up with a face full of excitement.

"I'll tell you. While busied with Madame la Momie, our fire had burned low, for the dry case went like tinder. A faint, far-off sound made our hearts leap, and Niles cried out: 'Pile on the wood; Jumal is tracking us; don't let the smoke fail now or we are lost!'

"'There is no more wood; the case was very small, and is all gone,' I answered, tearing off such of my garments as would burn readily, and piling them upon the embers.

"Niles did the same, but the light fabrics were quickly consumed, and made no smoke.

"'Burn that!' commanded the professor, pointing to the mummy.

"I hesitated a moment. Again came the faint echo of a horn. Life was dear to me. A few dry bones might save us, and I obeyed him in silence.

"A dull blaze sprung up, and a heavy smoke rose from the burning mummy, rolling in volumes through the low passages, and threatening to suffocate us with its fragrant mist. My brain grew dizzy, the light danced before my eyes, strange phantoms seemed to people the air, and, in the act of asking Niles why he gasped and looked so pale, I lost consciousness."

Evelyn drew a long breath, and put away the scented toys from her lap as if their odor oppressed her.

Forsyth's swarthy face was all aglow with the excitement of his story, and his black eyes glittered as he added, with a quick laugh:

"That's all; Jumal found and got us out, and we both forswore pyramids for the rest of our days."

"But the box: how came you to keep it?" asked Evelyn, eyeing it askance as it lay gleaming in a streak of sunshine.

"Oh, I brought it away as a souvenir, and Niles kept the other trinkets."

"But you said harm was foretold to the possessor of those scarlet seeds," persisted the girl, whose fancy was excited by the tale, and who fancied all was not told.

"Among his spoils, Niles found a bit of parchment, which he deciphered, and this inscription said that the mummy we had so ungallantly burned was that of a famous sorceress who bequeathed her curse to whoever should disturb her rest. Of course I don't believe that curse has anything to do with it, but it's a fact that Niles never prospered from that day. He says it's because he has never recovered from the fall and fright and I dare say it is so; but I sometimes wonder if I am to share the curse, for I've a vein of superstition in me, and that poor little mummy haunts my dreams still."

A long silence followed these words. Paul painted mechanically and Evelyn lay regarding him with a thoughtful face. But gloomy fancies were as foreign to her nature as shadows are to noonday, and presently she laughed a cheery laugh, saying as she took up the box again:

"Why don't you plant them, and see what wondrous flower they will bear?"

"I doubt if they would bear anything after lying in a mummy's hand for centuries," replied Forsyth, gravely.

"Let me plant them and try. You know wheat has sprouted and grown that was taken from a mummy's coffin; why should not these pretty seeds? I should so like to watch them grow; may I, Paul?"

"No, I'd rather leave that experiment untried. I have a queer feeling about the matter, and don't want to meddle myself or let anyone I love meddle with these seeds. They may be some horrible poison, or possess some evil power, for the sorceress evidently valued them, since she clutched them fast even in her tomb."

"Now, you are foolishly superstitious, and I laugh at you. Be generous; give me one seed, just to learn if it will grow. See I'll pay for it," and Evelyn, who now stood beside him, dropped a kiss on his forehead as she made her request, with the most engaging air.

But Forsyth would not yield. He smiled and returned the embrace with lover-like warmth, then flung the seeds into the fire, and gave her back the golden box, saying, tenderly:

"My darling, I'll fill it with diamonds or bonbons, if you please, but I will not let you play with that witch's spells. You've enough of your own, so forget the 'pretty seeds' and see what a Light of the Harem I've made of you."

Evelyn frowned, and smiled, and presently the lovers were out in the spring sunshine reveling in their own happy hopes, untroubled by one foreboding fear.

- 2 -

"I have a little surprise for you, love," said Forsyth, as he greeted his cousin three months later on the morning of his wedding day.

"And I have one for you," she answered, smiling faintly.

"How pale you are, and how thin you grow! All this bridal bustle is too much for you, Evelyn." he said, with fond anxiety, as he watched the strange pallor of her face, and pressed the wasted little hand in his.

"I am so tired," she said, and leaned her head wearily on her lover's breast. "Neither sleep, food, nor air gives me strength, and a curious mist seems to cloud my mind at times. Mamma says it is the heat, but I shiver even in the sun, while at night I burn with fever. Paul, dear, I'm glad you are going to take me away to lead a quiet, happy life with you, but I'm afraid it will be a very short one."

"My fanciful little wife! You are tired and nervous with all this worry, but a few weeks of rest in the country will give us back our blooming Eve again. Have you no curiosity to learn my surprise?" he asked, to change her thoughts.

The vacant look stealing over the girl's face gave place to one of interest, but as she listened it seemed to require an effort to fix her mind on her lover's words.

"You remember the day we rummaged in the old cabinet?"

"Yes," and a smile touched her lips for a moment.

"And how you wanted to plant those queer red seeds I stole from the mummy?"

"I remember," and her eyes kindled with sudden fire.

"Well, I tossed them into the fire, as I thought, and gave you the box. But when I went back to cover up my picture, and found one of those seeds on the rug, a sudden fancy to gratify your whim led me to send it to Niles and ask him to plant and report on its progress. Today I hear from him for the first time, and he reports that the seed has grown marvelously, has budded, and that he intends to take the first flower, if it blooms in time, to a meeting of famous scientific men, after which he will send me its true name and the plant itself. From his description, it must be very curious, and I'm impatient to see it."

"You need not wait; I can show you the flower in its bloom," and Evelyn beckoned with the *mechante* smile so long a stranger to her lips.

Much amazed, Forsyth followed her to her own little boudoir, and there, standing in the sunshine, was the unknown plant. Almost rank in their luxuriance were the vivid green leaves on the slender purple stems, and rising from the midst, one ghostly-white flower, shaped like the head of a hooded snake, with scarlet stamens like forked tongues, and on the petals glittered spots like dew.

"A strange, uncanny flower! Has it any odor?" asked Forsyth, bending to examine it, and forgetting, in his interest, to ask how it came there.

"None, and that disappoints me, I am so fond of perfumes," answered the girl, caressing the green leaves which trembled at her touch, while the purple stems deepened their tint.

"Now tell me about it," said Forsyth, after standing silent for several minutes.

"I had been before you, and secured one of the seeds, for two fell on the rug. I planted it under a glass in the richest soil I could find, watered it faithfully, and was amazed at the rapidity with which it grew when once it appeared above the earth. I told no-one, for I meant to surprise you with it; but this bud has been so long in blooming, I have had to wait. It is a good omen that it blossoms today, and as it is nearly white, I mean to wear it, for I've learned to love it, having been my pet for so long."

"I would not wear it, for, in spite of its innocent color, it is an evil-looking plant, with its adder's tongue and unnatural dew. Wait till Niles tells us what it is, then pet it if it is harmless."

"Perhaps my sorceress cherished it for some symbolic beauty--those old Egyptians were full of fancies. It was very sly of you to turn the tables on me in this way. But I forgive you, since in a few hours, I shall chain this mysterious hand forever. How cold it is! Come out into the garden and get some warmth and color for tonight, my love."

But when night came, no one could reproach the girl with her pallor, for she glowed like a pomegranate-flower, her eyes were full of fire, her lips scarlet, and all her old vivacity seemed to have returned. A more brilliant bride never blushed under a misty veil, and when her lover saw her, he was absolutely startled by the almost unearthly beauty which transformed the pale, languid creature of the morning into this radiant woman.

They were married, and if love, many blessings, and all good gifts lavishly showered upon them could make them happy, then this young pair were truly blest. But even in the rapture of the moment that made her his, Forsyth observed how icy cold was the little hand he held, how feverish the deep color on the soft cheek he kissed, and what a strange fire burned in the tender eyes that looked so wistfully at him.

Blithe and beautiful as a spirit, the smiling bride played her part in all the festivities of that long evening, and when at last light, life and color began to fade, the loving eyes that watched her thought it but the natural weariness of the hour. As the last guest departed, Forsyth was met by a servant, who gave him a letter marked "Haste." Tearing it open, he read these lines, from a friend of the professor's:

DEAR SIR – Poor Niles died suddenly two days ago, while at the Scientific Club, and his last words were: 'Tell Paul Forsyth to beware of the Mummy's Curse, for this fatal flower has killed me.' The circumstances of his death were so peculiar, that I add them as a sequel to this message. For several months, as he told us, he had been watching an unknown plant, and that evening he brought us the flower to examine. Other matters of interest absorbed us till a late hour, and the plant was forgotten. The professor wore it in his buttonhole – a strange white, serpent-headed blossom, with pale glittering spots, which slowly changed to a glittering scarlet, till the leaves looked as if sprinkled with blood. It was observed that instead of the pallor and feebleness which had recently come over him, that the professor was unusually animated, and seemed in an almost unnatural state of high spirits. Near the close of the meeting, in the midst of a lively discussion, he suddenly dropped, as if smitten with apoplexy. He was conveyed home insensible, and after one lucid interval, in which he gave me the message I have recorded above, he died in great agony, raving of mummies, pyramids, serpents, and some fatal curse which had fallen upon him.

After his death, livid scarlet spots, like those on the flower, appeared upon his skin, and he shriveled like a withered leaf. At my desire, the mysterious plant was examined, and pronounced by the best authority one of the most deadly poisons known to the Egyptian sorceresses. The plant slowly absorbs the vitality of whoever cultivates it, and the blossom, worn for two or three hours, produces either madness or death.

Down dropped the paper from Forsyth's hand; he read no further, but hurried back into the room where he had left his young wife. As if worn out with fatigue, she had thrown herself upon a couch, and lay there motionless, her face half-hidden by the light folds of the veil, which had blown over it.

"Evelyn, my dearest! Wake up and answer me. Did you wear that strange flower today?" whispered Forsyth, putting the misty screen away.

There was no need for her to answer, for there, gleaming spectrally on her bosom, was the evil blossom, its white petals spotted now with flecks of scarlet, vivid as drops of newly spilt blood.

But the unhappy bridegroom scarcely saw it, for the face above it appalled him by its utter vacancy. Drawn and pallid, as if with some wasting malady, the young face, so lovely an hour ago, lay before him aged and blighted by the baleful influence of the plant which had drunk up her life. No recognition in the eyes, no word upon the lips, no motion of the hand--only the faint breath, the fluttering pulse, and wide-opened eyes, betrayed that she was alive.

Alas for the young wife! The superstitious fear at which she had smiled had proved true: the curse that had bided its time for ages was fulfilled at last, and her own hand wrecked her happiness for ever. Death in life was her doom, and for years Forsyth secluded himself to tend with pathetic devotion the pale ghost, who never, by word or look, could thank him for the love that outlived even such a fate as this.

THE RING OF THOTH

ARTHUR CONAN DOYLE

Mr. John Vansittart Smith, F.R.S., of 147-A Gower Street, was a man whose energy of purpose and clearness of thought might have placed him in the very first rank of scientific observers. He was the victim, however, of a universal ambition which prompted him to aim at distinction in many subjects rather than pre-eminence in one. In his early days he had shown an aptitude for zoology and for botany which caused his friends to look upon him as a second Darwin, but when a professorship was almost within his reach he had suddenly discontinued his studies and turned his whole attention to chemistry. Here his researches upon the spectra of the metals had won him his fellowship in the Royal Society; but again he played the coquette with his subject, and after a year's absence from the laboratory he joined the Oriental Society, and delivered a paper on the Hieroglyphic and Demotic inscriptions of El Kab, thus giving a crowning example both of the versatility and of the inconstancy of his talents.

The most fickle of wooers, however, is apt to be caught at last, and so it was with John Vansittart Smith. The more he burrowed his way into Egyptology the more impressed he became by the vast field which it opened to the inquirer, and by the extreme importance of a subject which promised to throw a light upon the first germs of human civilisation and the origin of the greater part of our arts and sciences. So struck was Mr. Smith that he straightway married an Egyptological young lady who had written upon the sixth dynasty, and having thus secured a sound base of operations he set himself to collect materials for a work which should unite the research of Lepsius and the ingenuity of Champollion. The preparation of this *magnum opus* entailed many hurried visits to the magnificent Egyptian collections of the Louvre, upon the last of which, no longer ago than the middle of last October, he became involved in a most strange and noteworthy adventure.

The trains had been slow and the Channel had been rough, so that the student arrived in Paris in a somewhat befogged and feverish condition. On reaching the Hotel de France, in the Rue Laffitte, he had thrown himself upon a sofa for a couple of hours, but finding that he was unable to sleep, he determined, in spite of his fatigue, to make his way to the Louvre, settle the point which he had come to decide, and take the evening train back to Dieppe. Having come to this conclusion, he donned his greatcoat, for it was a raw rainy day, and made his way across the Boulevard des Italiens and down the Avenue de l'Opera. Once in the Louvre he was on familiar ground, and he speedily made his way to the collection of papyri which it was his intention to consult.

The warmest admirers of John Vansittart Smith could hardly claim for him that he was a handsome man. His high-beaked nose and prominent chin had something of the same acute and incisive character which distinguished his intellect. He held his head in a birdlike fashion, and birdlike, too, was the pecking motion with which, in conversation, he threw out his objections and retorts. As he stood, with the high collar of his greatcoat raised to his ears, he might have seen from the reflection in the glass-case before him that his appearance was a singular one. Yet it came upon him as a sudden jar when an English voice behind him exclaimed in very audible tones, "What a queer-looking mortal!"

The student had a large amount of petty vanity in his composition which manifested itself by an ostentatious and overdone disregard of all personal considerations. He straightened his lips and looked rigidly at the roll of papyrus, while his heart filled with bitterness against the whole race of travelling Britons.

"Yes," said another voice, "he really is an extraordinary fellow."

"Do you know," said the first speaker, "one could almost believe that by the continual contemplation of mummies the chap has become half a mummy himself?"

"He has certainly an Egyptian cast of countenance," said the other.

John Vansittart Smith spun round upon his heel with the intention of shaming his countrymen by a corrosive remark or two. To his surprise and relief, the two young fellows who had been conversing had their shoulders turned towards him, and were gazing at one of the Louvre attendants who was polishing some brass-work at the other side of the room.

"Carter will be waiting for us at the Palais Royal," said one tourist to the other, glancing at his watch, and they clattered away, leaving the student to his labours.

"I wonder what these chatterers call an Egyptian cast of countenance," thought John Vansittart Smith, and he moved his position slightly in order to catch a glimpse of the man's face. He started as his eyes fell upon it. It was indeed the very face with which his studies had made him familiar. The regular statuesque features, broad brow, well-rounded chin, and dusky complexion were the exact counterpart of the innumerable statues, mummy-cases, and pictures which adorned the walls of the apartment. The thing was beyond all coincidence. The man must be an Egyptian. The national angularity of the shoulders and narrowness of the hips were alone sufficient to identify him.

John Vansittart Smith shuffled towards the attendant with some intention of addressing him. He was not light of touch in conversation, and found it difficult to strike the happy mean between the brusqueness of the superior and the geniality of the equal. As he came nearer, the man presented his side face to him, but kept his gaze still bent upon his work. Vansittart Smith, fixing his eyes upon the fellow's skin, was conscious of a sudden impression that there was something inhuman and preternatural about its appearance. Over the temple and cheek-bone it was as glazed and as shiny as varnished parchment. There was no suggestion of pores. One could not fancy a drop of moisture upon that arid surface. From brow to chin, however, it was cross-hatched by a million delicate wrinkles, which shot and interlaced as though Nature in some Maori mood had tried how wild and intricate a pattern she could devise.

"*Ou est la collection de Memphis?*" asked the student with the awkward air of a man who is devising a question merely for the purpose of opening a conversation.

"*C'est la,*" replied the man brusquely, nodding his head at the other side of the room.

"*Vous etes un Egyptien, n'est-ce pas?*" asked the Englishman.

The attendant looked up and turned his strange dark eyes upon his questioner. They were vitreous, with a misty dry shininess, such as Smith had never seen in a human head before. As he gazed into them he saw some strong emotion gather in their depths, which rose and deepened until it broke into a look of something akin both to horror and to hatred.

"*Non, monsieur; je suis francais.*" The man turned abruptly and bent low over his polishing. The student gazed at him for a moment in astonishment, and then turning to a chair in a retired corner behind one of the doors he proceeded to make notes of his researches among the papyri. His thoughts, however, refused to return into their natural groove. They would run upon the enigmatical attendant with the sphinx-like face and the parchment skin.

"Where have I seen such eyes?" said Vansittart Smith to himself. "There is something saurian about them, something reptilian. There's the *membrana nictitans* of the snakes," he mused, bethinking himself of his zoological studies.

83

"It gives a shiny effect. But there was something more here. There was a sense of power, of wisdom – so I read them – and of weariness, utter weariness, and ineffable despair. It may be all imagination, but I never had so strong an impression. By Jove, I must have another look at them!" He rose and paced round the Egyptian rooms, but the man who had excited his curiosity had disappeared.

The student sat down again in his quiet corner, and continued to work at his notes. He had gained the information which he required from the papyri, and it only remained to write it down while it was still fresh in his memory. For a time his pencil travelled rapidly over the paper, but soon the lines became less level, the words more blurred, and finally the pencil tinkled down upon the floor, and the head of the student dropped heavily forward upon his chest. Tired out by his journey, he slept so soundly in his lonely post behind the door that neither the clanking civil guard, nor the footsteps of sightseers, nor even the loud hoarse bell which gives the signal for closing, were sufficient to arouse him.

Twilight deepened into darkness, the bustle from the Rue de Rivoli waxed and then waned, distant Notre Dame clanged out the hour of midnight, and still the dark and lonely figure sat silently in the shadow. It was not until close upon one in the morning that, with a sudden gasp and an intaking of the breath, Vansittart Smith returned to consciousness. For a moment it flashed upon him that he had dropped asleep in his study-chair at home. The moon was shining fitfully through the unshuttered window, however, and as his eye ran along the lines of mummies and the endless array of polished cases, he remembered clearly where he was and how he came there. The student was not a nervous man. He possessed that love of a novel situation which is peculiar to his race. Stretching out his cramped limbs, he looked at his watch, and burst into a chuckle as he observed the hour. The episode would make an admirable anecdote to be introduced into his next paper as a relief to the graver and heavier speculations. He was a little cold, but wide awake and much refreshed. It was no wonder that the guardians had overlooked him, for the door threw its heavy black shadow right across him.

The complete silence was impressive. Neither outside nor inside was there a creak or a murmur. He was alone with the dead men of a dead civilisation. What though the outer city reeked of the garish nineteenth century! In all this chamber there was scarce an article, from the shrivelled ear of wheat to the pigment-box of the painter, which had not held its own against four thousand years. Here was the flotsam and jetsam washed up by the great ocean of time from that far-off empire. From stately Thebes, from lordly Luxor, from the great temples of Heliopolis, from a hundred rifled tombs, these relics had been brought. The student glanced round at the long silent figures who flickered vaguely up through the gloom, at the busy toilers who were now so restful, and he fell into a reverent and thoughtful mood. An unwonted sense of his own youth and insignificance came over him. Leaning back in his chair, he gazed dreamily down the long vista of rooms, all silvery with the moonshine, which extend through the whole wing of the widespread building. His eyes fell upon the yellow glare of a distant lamp.

John Vansittart Smith sat up on his chair with his nerves all on edge. The light was advancing slowly towards him, pausing from time to time, and then coming jerkily onwards. The bearer moved noiselessly. In the utter silence there was no suspicion of the pat of a footfall. An idea of robbers entered the Englishman's head. He snuggled up further into the corner. The light was two rooms off. Now it was in the next chamber, and still there was no sound. With something approaching to a thrill of fear the student observed a face, floating in the air as it were, behind the flare of the lamp. The figure was wrapped in shadow, but the light fell full upon the strange eager face. There was no mistaking the metallic glistening eyes and the cadaverous skin. It was the attendant with whom he had conversed.

Vansittart Smith's first impulse was to come forward and address him. A few words of explanation would set the matter clear, and lead doubtless to his being conducted to some side door from which he might make his way to his hotel. As the man entered the chamber, however, there was something so stealthy in his movements, and so furtive in his expression, that the Englishman altered his intention. This was clearly no ordinary official walking the rounds. The fellow wore felt-soled slippers, stepped with a rising chest, and glanced quickly from left to right, while his hurried gasping breathing thrilled the flame of his lamp. Vansittart Smith crouched silently back into the corner and watched him keenly, convinced that his errand was one of secret and probably sinister import.

There was no hesitation in the other's movements. He stepped lightly and swiftly across to one of the great cases, and, drawing a key from his pocket, he unlocked it. From the upper shelf he pulled down a mummy, which he bore away with him, and laid it with much care and solicitude upon the ground. By it he placed his lamp, and then squatting down beside it in Eastern fashion he began with long quivering fingers to undo the cerecloths and bandages which girt it round. As the crackling rolls of linen peeled off one after the other, a strong aromatic odour filled the chamber, and fragments of scented wood and of spices pattered down upon the marble floor.

It was clear to John Vansittart Smith that this mummy had never been unswathed before. The operation interested him keenly. He thrilled all over with curiosity, and his birdlike head protruded further and further from behind the door. When, however, the last roll had been removed from the four-thousand-year-old head, it was all that he could do to stifle an outcry of amazement. First, a cascade of long, black, glossy tresses poured over the workman's hands and arms. A second turn of the bandage revealed a low, white forehead, with a pair of delicately arched eyebrows. A third uncovered a pair of bright, deeply fringed eyes, and a straight, well-cut nose, while a fourth and last showed a sweet, full, sensitive mouth, and a beautifully curved chin. The whole face was one of extraordinary loveliness, save for the one blemish that in the centre of the forehead there was a single irregular, coffee-coloured splotch. It was a triumph of the embalmer's art. Vansittart Smith's eyes grew larger and larger as he gazed upon it, and he chirruped in his throat with satisfaction.

Its effect upon the Egyptologist was as nothing, however, compared with that which it produced upon the strange attendant. He threw his hands up into the air, burst into a harsh clatter of words, and then, hurling himself down upon the ground beside the mummy, he threw his arms round her, and kissed her repeatedly upon the lips and brow. *"Ma petite!"* he groaned in French. *"Ma pauvre petite!"* His voice broke with emotion, and his innumerable wrinkles quivered and writhed, but the student observed in the lamplight that his shining eyes were still dry and tearless as two beads of steel. For some minutes he lay, with a twitching face, crooning and moaning over the beautiful head. Then he broke into a sudden smile, said some words in an unknown tongue, and sprang to his feet with the vigorous air of one who has braced himself for an effort.

In the centre of the room there was a large circular case which contained, as the student had frequently remarked, a magnificent collection of early Egyptian rings and precious stones. To this the attendant strode, and, unlocking it, threw it open. On the edge at the side he placed his lamp, and beside it a small earthenware jar which he had drawn from his pocket. He then took a handful of rings from the case, and with the most serious and anxious face he proceeded to smear each in turn with some liquid substance from the earthen pot, holding them to the light as he did so. He was clearly disappointed with the first lot, for he threw them petulantly back into the case and drew out some more. One of these, a massive ring with a large crystal set in it, he seized and eagerly tested with the contents of the jar. Instantly he uttered a cry of joy, and threw out his arms in a wild gesture which upset the pot and sent the liquid streaming across the floor to the very feet of the Englishman. The attendant drew a red handkerchief from his bosom, and, mopping up the mess, he followed it into the corner, where in a moment he found himself face to face with his observer.

"Excuse me," said John Vansittart Smith, with all imaginable politeness; "I have been unfortunate enough to fall asleep behind this door."

"And you have been watching me?" the other asked in English, with a most venomous look on his corpse-like face.

The student was a man of veracity. "I confess," said he, "that I have noticed your movements, and that they have aroused my curiosity and interest in the highest degree."

The man drew a long flamboyant-bladed knife from his bosom. "You have had a very narrow escape," he said; "had I seen you ten minutes ago, I should have driven this through your heart. As it is, if you touch me or interfere with me in any way you are a dead man."

"I have no wish to interfere with you," the student answered. "My presence here is entirely accidental. All I ask is that you will have the extreme kindness to show me out through some side door." He spoke with great suavity, for the man was still pressing the tip of his dagger against the palm of his left hand, as though to assure himself of its sharpness, while his face preserved its malignant expression.

"If I thought – " said he. "But no, perhaps it is as well. What is your name?"

The Englishman gave it.

"Vansittart Smith," the other repeated. "Are you the same Vansittart Smith who gave a paper in London upon El Kab? I saw a report of it. Your knowledge of the subject is contemptible."

"Sir!" cried the Egyptologist.

"Yet it is superior to that of many who make even greater pretensions. The whole keystone of our old life in Egypt was not the inscriptions or monuments of which you make so much, but was our hermetic philosophy and mystic knowledge of which you say little or nothing."

"Our old life!" repeated the scholar, wide-eyed; and then suddenly, "Good God, look at the mummy's face!"

The strange man turned and flashed his light upon the dead woman, uttering a long doleful cry as he did so. The action of the air had already undone all the art of the embalmer. The skin had fallen away, the eyes had sunk inwards, the discoloured lips had writhed away from the yellow teeth, and the brown mark upon the forehead alone showed that it was indeed the same face which had shown such youth and beauty a few short minutes before.

The man flapped his hands together in grief and horror. Then mastering himself by a strong effort he turned his hard eyes once more upon the Englishman.

"It does not matter," he said, in a shaking voice. "It does not really matter. I came here tonight with the fixed determination to do something. It is now done. All else is as nothing. I have found my quest. The old curse is broken. I can rejoin her. What matter about her inanimate shell so long as her spirit is awaiting me at the other side of the veil!"

"These are wild words," said Vansittart Smith. He was becoming more and more convinced that he had to do with a madman.

"Time presses, and I must go," continued the other. "The moment is at hand for which I have waited this weary time. But I must show you out first. Come with me."

Taking up the lamp, he turned from the disordered chamber, and led the student swiftly through the long series of the Egyptian, Assyrian, and Persian apartments. At the end of the latter he pushed open a small door let into the wall and descended a winding stone stair. The Englishman felt the cold fresh air of the night upon his brow. There was a door opposite him which appeared to communicate with the street. To the right of this another door stood ajar, throwing a spurt of yellow light across the passage. "Come in here!" said the attendant shortly.

Vansittart Smith hesitated. He had hoped that he had come to the end of his adventure. Yet his curiosity was strong within him. He could not leave the matter unsolved, so he followed his strange companion into the lighted chamber.

It was a small room, such as is devoted to a *concierge*. A wood fire sparkled in the grate. At one side stood a truckle bed, and at the other a coarse wooden chair, with a round table in the centre, which bore the remains of a meal. As the visitor's eye glanced round he could not but remark with an ever-recurring thrill that all the small details of the room were of the most quaint design and antique workmanship. The candlesticks, the vases upon the chimneypiece, the fire-irons, the ornaments upon the walls, were all such as he had been wont to associate with the remote past. The gnarled heavy-eyed man sat himself down upon the edge of the bed, and motioned his guest into the chair.

"There may be design in this," he said, still speaking excellent English. "It may be decreed that I should leave some account behind as a warning to all rash mortals who would set their wits up against workings of Nature. I leave it with you. Make such use as you will of it. I speak to you now with my feet upon the threshold of the other world.

"I am, as you surmised, an Egyptian – not one of the down-trodden race of slaves who now inhabit the Delta of the Nile, but a survivor of that fiercer and harder people who tamed the Hebrew, drove the Ethiopian back into the southern deserts, and built those mighty works which have been the envy and the wonder of all after generations. It was in the reign of Tuthmosis, sixteen hundred years before the birth of Christ, that I first saw the light. You shrink away from me. Wait, and you will see that I am more to be pitied than to be feared.

"My name was Sosra. My father had been the chief priest of Osiris in the great temple of Abaris, which stood in those days upon the Bubastic branch of the Nile. I was brought up in the temple and was trained in all those mystic arts which are spoken of in your own Bible. I was an apt pupil. Before I was sixteen I had learned all which the wisest priest could teach me. From that time on I studied Nature's secrets for myself, and shared my knowledge with no man.

"Of all the questions which attracted me there were none over which I laboured so long as over those which concern themselves with the nature of life. I probed deeply into the vital principle. The aim of medicine had been to drive away disease when it appeared. It seemed to me that a method might be devised which should so fortify the body as to prevent weakness or death from ever taking hold of it. It is useless that I should recount my researches. You would scarce comprehend them if I did. They were carried out partly upon animals, partly upon slaves, and partly on myself. Suffice it that their result was to furnish me with a substance which, when injected into the blood, would endow the body with strength to resist the effects of time, of violence, or of disease. It would not indeed confer immortality, but its potency would endure for many thousands of years. I used it upon a cat, and afterwards drugged the creature with the most deadly poisons. That cat is alive in Lower Egypt at the present moment. There was nothing of mystery or magic in the matter. It was simply a chemical discovery, which may well be made again.

"Love of life runs high in the young. It seemed to me that I had broken away from all human care now that I had abolished pain and driven death to such a distance. With a light heart I poured the accursed stuff into my veins. Then I looked round for some one whom I could benefit. There was a young priest of Thoth, Parmes by name, who had won my goodwill by his earnest nature and his devotion to his studies. To him I whispered my secret, and at his request I injected him with my elixir. I should now, I reflected, never be without a companion of the same age as myself.

"After this grand discovery I relaxed my studies to some extent, but Parmes continued his with redoubled energy. Every day I could see him working with his flasks and his distiller in the Temple of Thoth, but he said little to me as to the result of his labours. For my own part, I used to walk through the city and look around me with exultation as I reflected that all this was destined to pass away, and that only I should remain. The people would bow to me as they passed me, for the fame of my knowledge had gone abroad.

"There was war at this time, and the Great King had sent down his soldiers to the eastern boundary to drive away the Hyksos. A Governor, too, was sent to Abaris, that he might hold it for the King. I had heard much of the beauty of the daughter of this Governor, but one day as I walked out with Parmes we met her, borne upon the shoulders of her slaves. I was struck with love as with lightning.

My heart went out from me. I could have thrown myself beneath the feet of her bearers. This was my woman. Life without her was impossible. I swore by the head of Horus that she should be mine. I swore it to the Priest of Thoth. He turned away from me with a brow which was as black as midnight.

"There is no need to tell you of our wooing. She came to love me even as I loved her. I learned that Parmes had seen her before I did, and had shown her that he too loved her, but I could smile at his passion, for I knew that her heart was mine. The white plague had come upon the city and many were stricken, but I laid my hands upon the sick and nursed them without fear or scathe. She marvelled at my daring. Then I told her my secret, and begged her that she would let me use my art upon her.

"'Your flower shall then be unwithered, Atma,' I said. 'Other things may pass away, but you and I, and our great love for each other, shall outlive the tomb of King Chefru.'

"But she was full of timid, maidenly objections. 'Was it right?' she asked, 'was it not a thwarting of the will of the gods? If the great Osiris had wished that our years should be so long, would he not himself have brought it about?'

"With fond and loving words I overcame her doubts, and yet she hesitated. It was a great question, she said. She would think it over for this one night. In the morning I should know of her resolution. Surely one night was not too much to ask. She wished to pray to Isis for help in her decision.

"With a sinking heart and a sad foreboding of evil I left her with her tirewomen. In the morning, when the early sacrifice was over, I hurried to her house. A frightened slave met me upon the steps. Her mistress was ill, she said, very ill. In a frenzy I broke my way through the attendants, and rushed through hall and corridor to my Atma's chamber. She lay upon her couch, her head high upon the pillow, with a pallid face and a glazed eye. On her forehead there blazed a single angry purple patch. I knew that hell-mark of old. It was the scar of the white plague, the sign-manual of death.

"Why should I speak of that terrible time? For months I was mad, fevered, delirious, and yet I could not die. Never did an Arab thirst after the sweet wells as I longed after death. Could poison or steel have shortened the thread of my existence, I should soon have rejoined my love in the land with the narrow portal. I tried, but it was of no avail. The accursed influence was too strong upon me. One night as I lay upon my couch, weak and weary, Parmes, the priest of Thoth, came to my chamber. He stood in the circle of the lamplight, and he looked down upon me with eyes which were bright with a mad joy.

"'Why did you let the maiden die?' he asked; 'why did you not strengthen her as you strengthened me?'

"'I was too late,' I answered. 'But I had forgot. You also loved her.

You are my fellow in misfortune. Is it not terrible to think of the centuries which must pass ere we look upon her again? Fools, fools, that we were to take death to be our enemy!'

"'You may say that,' he cried with a wild laugh; 'the words come well from your lips. For me they have no meaning.'

"'What mean you?' I cried, raising myself upon my elbow. 'Surely, friend, this grief has turned your brain.' His face was aflame with joy, and he writhed and shook like one who hath a devil.

"'Do you know whither I go?' he asked.

"'Nay,' I answered, 'I cannot tell.'

"'I go to her,' said he. 'She lies embalmed in the further tomb by the double palm-tree beyond the city wall.'

"'Why do you go there?' I asked.

"'To die!' he shrieked, 'to die! I am not bound by earthen fetters.'

"'But the elixir is in your blood,' I cried.

"'I can defy it,' said he; 'I have found a stronger principle which will destroy it. It is working in my veins at this moment, and in an hour I shall be a dead man. I shall join her, and you shall remain behind.'

"As I looked upon him I could see that he spoke words of truth. The light in his eye told me that he was indeed beyond the power of the elixir.

"'You will teach me!' I cried.

"'Never!' he answered.

"'I implore you, by the wisdom of Thoth, by the majesty of Anubis!'

"'It is useless,' he said coldly.

"'Then I will find it out,' I cried.

"'You cannot,' he answered; 'it came to me by chance. There is one ingredient which you can never get. Save that which is in the ring of Thoth, none will ever more be made.'

"'In the ring of Thoth!' I repeated, 'where then is the ring of Thoth?'

"'That also you shall never know,' he answered. 'You won her love. Who has won in the end? I leave you to your sordid earth life. My chains are broken. I must go!' He turned upon his heel and fled from the chamber. In the morning came the news that the Priest of Thoth was dead.

"My days after that were spent in study. I must find this subtle poison which was strong enough to undo the elixir. From early dawn to midnight I bent over the test-tube and the furnace. Above all, I collected the papyri and the chemical flasks of the Priest of Thoth. Alas! they taught me little. Here and there some hint or stray expression would raise hope in my bosom, but no good ever came of it. Still, month after month, I struggled on. When my heart grew faint I would make my way to the tomb

by the palm-trees. There, standing by the dead casket from which the jewel had been rifled, I would feel her sweet presence, and would whisper to her that I would rejoin her if mortal wit could solve the riddle.

"Parmes had said that his discovery was connected with the ring of Thoth. I had some remembrance of the trinket. It was a large and weighty circlet, made, not of gold, but of a rarer and heavier metal brought from the mines of Mount Harbal. Platinum, you call it. The ring had, I remembered, a hollow crystal set in it, in which some few drops of liquid might be stored. Now, the secret of Parmes could not have to do with the metal alone, for there were many rings of that metal in the Temple. Was it not more likely that he had stored his precious poison within the cavity of the crystal? I had scarce come to this conclusion before, in hunting through his papers, I came upon one which told me that it was indeed so, and that there was still some of the liquid unused.

"But how to find the ring? It was not upon him when he was stripped for the embalmer. Of that I made sure. Neither was it among his private effects. In vain I searched every room that he had entered, every box and vase and chattel that he had owned. I sifted the very sand of the desert in the place where he had been wont to walk; but, do what I would, I could come upon no traces of the ring of Thoth. Yet it may be that my labours would have overcome all obstacles had it not been for a new and unlooked-for misfortune.

"A great war had been waged against the Hyksos, and the Captains of the Great King had been cut off in the desert, with all their bowmen and horsemen. The shepherd tribes were upon us like the locusts in a dry year. From the wilderness of Shur to the great bitter lake there was blood by day and fire by night. Abaris was the bulwark of Egypt, but we could not keep the savages back. The city fell. The Governor and the soldiers were put to the sword, and I, with many more, was led away into captivity.

"For years and years I tended cattle in the great plains by the Euphrates. My master died, and his son grew old, but I was still as far from death as ever. At last I escaped upon a swift camel, and made my way back to Egypt. The Hyksos had settled in the land which they had conquered, and their own King ruled over the country. Abaris had been torn down, the city had been burned, and of the great Temple there was nothing left save an unsightly mound. Everywhere the tombs had been rifled and the monuments destroyed. Of my Atma's grave no sign was left. It was buried in the sands of the desert, and the palm-trees which marked the spot had long disappeared. The papers of Parmes and the remains of the Temple of Thoth were either destroyed or scattered far and wide over the deserts of Syria. All search after them was vain.

"From that time I gave up all hope of ever finding the ring or discovering the subtle drug. I set myself to live as patiently as might be until the effect of the elixir should wear away. How can you understand how terrible a thing time is, you who have experience only of the narrow course which lies between the cradle and the grave! I know it to my cost, I who have floated down the whole stream of history. I was old when Ilium fell. I was very old when Herodotus came to Memphis. I was bowed down with years when the new gospel came upon earth. Yet you see me much as other men are, with the cursed elixir still sweetening my blood, and guarding me against that which I would court. Now at last, at last I have come to the end of it!

"I have travelled in all lands and I have dwelt with all nations. Every tongue is the same to me. I learned them all to help pass the weary time. I need not tell you how slowly they drifted by, the long dawn of modern civilisation, the dreary middle years, the dark times of barbarism. They are all behind me now. I have never looked with the eyes of love upon another woman. Atma knows that I have been constant to her.

"It was my custom to read all that the scholars had to say upon Ancient Egypt. I have been in many positions, sometimes affluent, sometimes poor, but I have always found enough to enable me to buy the journals which deal with such matters. Some nine months ago I was in San Francisco, when I read an account of some discoveries made in the neighbourhood of Abaris. My heart leapt into my mouth as I read it. It said that the excavator had busied himself in exploring some tombs recently unearthed. In one there had been found an unopened mummy with an inscription upon the outer case setting forth that it contained the body of the daughter of the Governor of the city in the days of Tuthmosis. It added that on removing the outer case there had been exposed a large platinum ring set with a crystal, which had been laid upon the breast of the embalmed woman. This, then, was where Parmes had hid the ring of Thoth. He might well say that it was safe, for no Egyptian would ever stain his soul by moving even the outer case of a buried friend.

"That very night I set off from San Francisco, and in a few weeks I found myself once more at Abaris, if a few sand-heaps and crumbling walls may retain the name of the great city. I hurried to the Frenchmen who were digging there and asked them for the ring. They replied that both the ring and the mummy had been sent to the Boulak Museum at Cairo. To Boulak I went, but only to be told that Mariette Bey had claimed them and had shipped them to the Louvre. I followed them, and there at last, in the Egyptian chamber, I came, after close upon four thousand years, upon the remains of my Atma, and upon the ring for which I had sought so long.

"But how was I to lay hands upon them? How was I to have them for my very own? It chanced that the office of attendant was vacant. I went to the Director. I convinced him that I knew much about Egypt. In my eagerness I said too much. He remarked that a Professor's chair would suit me better than a seat in the conciergerie. I knew more, he said, than he did. It was only by blundering, and letting him think that he had over-estimated my knowledge, that I prevailed upon him to let me move the few effects which I have retained into this chamber. It is my first and my last night here.

"Such is my story, Mr. Vansittart Smith. I need not say more to a man of your perception. By a strange chance you have this night looked upon the face of the woman whom I loved in those far-off days. There were many rings with crystals in the case, and I had to test for the platinum to be sure of the one which I wanted. A glance at the crystal has shown me that the liquid is indeed within it, and that I shall at last be able to shake off that accursed health which has been worse to me than the foulest disease. I have nothing more to say to you. I have unburdened myself. You may tell my story or you may withhold it at your pleasure. The choice rests with you. I owe you some amends, for you have had a narrow escape of your life this night. I was a desperate man, and not to be baulked in my purpose. Had I seen you before the thing was done, I might have put it beyond your power to oppose me or to raise an alarm. This is the door. It leads into the Rue de Rivoli. Good night."

The Englishman glanced back. For a moment the lean figure of Sosra the Egyptian stood framed in the narrow doorway. The next the door had slammed, and the heavy rasping of a bolt broke on the silent night.

It was on the second day after his return to London that Mr. John Vansittart Smith saw the following concise narrative in the Paris correspondence of the *Times*:

CURIOUS OCCURRENCE IN THE LOUVRE

Yesterday morning a strange discovery was made in the principal Eastern chamber. The *ouvriers* who are employed to clean out the rooms in the morning found one of the attendants lying dead upon the floor with his arms round one of the mummies. So close was his embrace that it was only with the utmost difficulty that they were separated. One of the cases containing valuable rings had been opened and rifled. The authorities are of opinion that the man was bearing away the mummy with some idea of selling it to a private collector, but that he was struck down in the very act by long-standing disease of the heart. It is said that he was a man of uncertain age and eccentric habits, without any living relations to mourn over his dramatic and untimely end.

LOT NO. 249

ARTHUR CONAN DOYLE

- I -

Of the dealings of Edward Bellingham with William Monkhouse Lee, and of the cause of the great terror of Abercrombie Smith, it may be that no absolute and final judgment will ever be delivered. It is true that we have the full and clear narrative of Smith himself, and such corroboration as he could look for from Thomas Styles the servant, from the Reverend Plumptree Peterson, Fellow of Old's, and from such other people as chanced to gain some passing glance at this or that incident in a singular chain of events. Yet, in the main, the story must rest upon Smith alone, and the most will think that it is more likely that one brain, however outwardly sane, has some subtle warp in its texture, some strange flaw in its workings, than that the path of Nature has been overstepped in open day in so famed a centre of learning and light as the University of Oxford. Yet when we think how narrow and how devious this path of Nature is, how dimly we can trace it, for all our lamps of science, and how from the darkness which girds it round great and terrible possibilities loom ever shadowly upwards, it is a bold and confident man who will put a limit to the strange by-paths into which the human spirit may wander.

In a certain wing of what we will call Old College in Oxford there is a corner turret of an exceeding great age. The heavy arch which spans the open door has bent downwards in the centre under the weight of its years, and the grey, lichen-blotched blocks of stone are bound and knitted together with withes and strand of ivy, as though the old mother had set herself to brace them up against wind and weather. From a door a stone stair curves upwards spirally, passing two landings, and terminating in a third one, its steps all shapeless and hollowed by the tread of so many generations of the seekers after knowledge. Life has flowed like water down this winding stair, and, waterlike, has left these smooth-worn grooves behind it. From the long-gowned, pedantic scholars of Plantagenet days down to the young bloods of a later age, how full and strong had been that tide of young English life. And what was left now of all those hopes, those strivings, those fiery energies, save here and there in some old-world churchyard a few scratches upon a stone, and perchance a handful of dust in a mouldering coffin? Yet here were the silent stair and the grey old wall, with bend and saltire and many another heraldic device still to be read upon its surface, like grotesque shadows thrown back from the days that had passed.

In the month of May, in the year 1884, three young men occupied the sets of rooms which opened on to the separate landings of the old stair. Each set consisted simply of a sitting-room and a bedroom, while the two corresponding rooms upon the ground-floor were used, the one as a coal-cellar, and the other as the living-room of the servant, or scout, Thomas Styles, whose duty it was to wait upon the three men above him. To right and to left was a line of lecture-rooms and of offices, so that the dwellers in the old turret enjoyed a certain seclusion, which made the chambers popular among the more studious undergraduates. Such were the three who occupied them now – Abercrombie Smith above, Edward Bellingham beneath him, and William Monkhouse Lee upon the lowest story.

It was ten o'clock on a bright spring night, and Abercrombie Smith lay back in his armchair, his feet upon the fender, and his briar-root pipe between his lips. In a similar chair, and equally at his ease, there lounged on the other side of the fireplace his old school friend Jephro Hastie. Both men were in flannels, for they had spent their evening upon the river, but apart from their dress no one could look at their hard-cut, alert faces without seeing that they were open-air men – men whose minds and tastes turned naturally to all that was manly and robust. Hastie, indeed, was stroke of his college boat, and Smith was an even better oar, but a coming examination had already cast its shadow over him and held him to his work, save for the few hours a week which health demanded. A litter of medical books upon the table, with scattered bones, models, and anatomical plates, pointed to the extent as well as the nature of his studies, while a couple of single-sticks and a set of boxing-gloves above the mantelpiece hinted at the means by which, with Hastie's help, he might take his exercise in its most compressed and least distant form. They knew each other very well – so well that they could sit now in that soothing silence which is the very highest development of companionship.

"Have some whisky," said Abercrombie Smith at last between two cloudbursts. "Scotch in the jug and Irish in the bottle."

"No, thanks. I'm in for the sculls. I don't liquor when I'm training. How about you?"

"I'm reading hard. I think it best to leave it alone."

Hastie nodded, and they relapsed into a contented silence.

"By the way, Smith," asked Hastie, presently, "have you made the acquaintance of either of the fellows on your stair yet?"

"Just a nod when we pass. Nothing more."

"Hum! I should be inclined to let it stand at that. I know something of them both. Not much, but as much as I want. I don't think I should take them to my bosom if I were you. Not that there's much amiss with Monkhouse Lee."

"Meaning the thin one?"

"Precisely. He is a gentlemanly little fellow. I don't think there is any vice in him. But then you can't know him without knowing Bellingham."

"Meaning the fat one?"

"Yes, the fat one. And he's a man whom I, for one, would rather not know."

Abercrombie Smith raised his eyebrows and glanced across at his companion.

"What's up, then?" he asked. "Drink? Cards? Cad? You used not to be censorious."

"Ah! You evidently don't know the man, or you wouldn't ask. There's something damnable about him – something reptilian. My gorge always rises at him. I should put him down as a man with secret vices – an evil liver. He's no fool, though. They say that he is one of the best men in his line that they have ever had in the college."

"Medicine or classics?"

"Eastern languages. He's a demon at them. Chillingworth met him somewhere above the second cataract last long, and he told me that he just prattled to the Arabs as if he had been born and nursed and weaned among them. He talked Coptic to the Copts, and Hebrew to the Jews, and Arabic to the Bedouins, and they were all ready to kiss the hem of his frock-coat. There are some old hermit Johnnies up in those parts who sit on rocks and scowl and spit at the casual stranger. Well, when they saw this chap Bellingham, before he had said five words they just lay down on their bellies and wriggled. Chillingworth said that he never saw anything like it. Bellingham seemed to take it as his right, too, and strutted about among them and talked down to them like a Dutch uncle. Pretty good for an undergrad of Old's, wasn't it?"

"Why do you say you can't know Lee without knowing Bellingham?"

"Because Bellingham is engaged to his sister Eveline. Such a bright little girl, Smith! I know the whole family well. It's disgusting to see that brute with her. A toad and a dove, that's what they always remind me of."

Abercrombie Smith grinned and knocked his ashes out against the side of the grate.

"You show every card in your hand, old chap," said he. "What a prejudiced, green-eyed, evil-thinking old man it is! You have really nothing against the fellow except that."

"Well, I've known her ever since she was as long as that cherry-wood pipe, and I don't like to see her taking risks. And it is a risk. He looks beastly. And he has a beastly temper, a venomous temper. You remember his row with Long Norton?"

"No; you always forget that I am a freshman."

"Ah, it was last winter. Of course. Well, you know the towpath along by the river. There were several fellows going along it, Bellingham in front, when they came on an old market-woman coming the other way. It had been raining – you know what those fields are like when it has rained – and the path ran between the river and a great puddle that was nearly as broad. Well, what does this swine do but keep the path, and push the old girl into the mud, where she and her marketings came to terrible grief. It was a blackguard thing to do, and Long Norton, who is as gentle a fellow as ever stepped, told him what he thought of it. One word led to another, and it ended in Norton laying his stick across the fellow's shoulders. There was the deuce of a fuss about it, and it's a treat to see the way in which Bellingham looks at Norton when they meet now. By Jove, Smith, it's nearly eleven o'clock!"

"No hurry. Light your pipe again."

"Not I. I'm supposed to be in training. Here I've been sitting gossiping when I ought to have been safely tucked up. I'll borrow your skull, if you can share it. Williams has had mine for a month. I'll take the little bones of your ear, too, if you are sure you won't need them. Thanks very much. Never mind a bag, I can carry them very well under my arm. Good-night, my son, and take my tip as to your neighbour."

When Hastie, bearing his anatomical plunder, had clattered off down the winding stair, Abercrombie Smith hurled his pipe into the wastepaper basket, and drawing his chair nearer to the lamp, plunged into a formidable

102

green-covered volume, adorned with great coloured maps of that strange internal kingdom of which we are the hapless and helpless monarchs. Though a freshman at Oxford, the student was not so in medicine, for he had worked for four years at Glasgow and at Berlin, and this coming examination would place him finally as a member of his profession. With his firm mouth, broad forehead, and clear-cut, somewhat hard-featured face, he was a man who, if he had no brilliant talent, was yet so dogged, so patient, and so strong that he might in the end overtop a more showy genius. A man who can hold his own among Scotchmen and North Germans is not a man to be easily set back. Smith had left a name at Glasgow and at Berlin, and he was bent now upon doing as much at Oxford, if hard work and devotion could accomplish it.

He had sat reading for about an hour, and the hands of the noisy carriage clock upon the side table were rapidly closing together upon the twelve, when a sudden sound fell upon the student's ear – a sharp, rather shrill sound, like the hissing intake of a man's breath who gasps under some strong emotion. Smith laid down his book and slanted his ear to listen. There was no one on either side or above him, so that the interruption came certainly from the neighbour beneath – the same neighbour of whom Hastie had given so unsavory an account. Smith knew him only as a flabby, pale-faced man of silent and studious habits, a man whose lamp threw a golden bar from the old turret even after he had extinguished his own. This community in lateness had formed a certain silent bond between them. It was soothing to Smith when the hours stole on towards dawning to feel that there was another so close who set as small a value upon his sleep as he did. Even now, as his thoughts turned towards him, Smith's feelings were kindly. Hastie was a good fellow, but he was rough, strong-fibred, with no imagination or sympathy. He could not tolerate departures from what he looked upon as the model type of manliness. If a man could not be measured by a public-school standard, then he was beyond the pale with Hastie. Like so many who are themselves robust, he was apt to confuse the constitution with the character, to ascribe to want of principle what was really a want of circulation. Smith, with his stronger mind, knew his friend's habit, and made allowance for it now as his thoughts turned towards the man beneath him.

There was no return of the singular sound, and Smith was about to turn to his work once more, when suddenly there broke out in the silence of the night a hoarse cry, a positive scream – the call of a man who is moved and shaken beyond all control. Smith sprang out of his chair and dropped his book. He was a man of fairly firm fibre, but there was something in this sudden, uncontrollable shriek of horror which chilled his blood and pringled in his skin. Coming in such a place and at such an hour, it brought a thousand fantastic possibilities into his head. Should he rush down, or was it better to wait? He had all the national hatred of making a scene, and he knew so little of his neighbour that he would not lightly intrude upon his affairs. For a moment he stood in doubt and even as he balanced the matter there was a quick rattle of footsteps upon the stairs, and young Monkhouse Lee, half dressed and as white as ashes, burst into his room.

"Come down!" he gasped. "Bellingham's ill."

Abercrombie Smith followed him closely downstairs into the sitting-room which was beneath his own, and intent as he was upon the matter in hand, he could not but take an amazed glance around him as he crossed the threshold. It was such a chamber as he had never seen before – a museum rather than a study. Walls and ceiling were thickly covered with a thousand strange relics from Egypt and the East. Tall, angular figures bearing burdens or weapons stalked in an uncouth frieze round the apartments. Above were bull-headed, stork-headed, cat-headed, owl-headed statues, with viper-crowned, almond-eyed monarchs, and strange, beetle-like deities cut out of the blue Egyptian lapis lazuli. Horus and Isis and Osiris peeped down from every niche and shelf, while across the ceiling a true son of Old Nile, a great, hanging-jawed crocodile, was slung in a double noose.

In the centre of this singular chamber was a large, square table, littered with papers, bottles, and the dried leaves of some graceful, palm-like plant. These varied objects had all been heaped together in order to make room for a mummy case, which had been conveyed from the wall, as was evident from the gap there, and laid across the front of the table. The mummy itself, a horrid, black, withered thing, like a charred head on a gnarled bush, was lying half out of the case, with its clawlike hand and bony forearm resting upon the table. Propped up against the sarcophagus was an old yellow scroll of papyrus, and in front of it, in a wooden armchair, sat the owner of the room, his head thrown back, his widely-opened eyes directed in a horrified stare to the crocodile above him, and his blue, thick lips puffing loudly with every expiration.

"My God! He's dying!" cried Monkhouse Lee distractedly.

He was a slim, handsome young fellow, olive-skinned and dark-eyed, of a Spanish rather than of an English type, with a Celtic intensity of manner which contrasted with the Saxon phlegm of Abercrombie Smith.

"Only a faint, I think," said the medical student. "Just give me a hand with him. You take his feet. Now on to the sofa. Can you kick all those little wooden devils off? What a litter it is! Now he will be all right if we undo his collar and give him some water. What has he been up to at all?"

"I don't know. I heard him cry out. I ran up. I know him pretty well, you know. It is very good of you to come down."

"His heart is going like a pair of castanets," said Smith, laying his hand on the breast of the unconscious man. "He seems to me to be frightened all to pieces. Chuck the water over him! What a face he has got on him!"

It was indeed a strange and most repellent face, for colour and outline were equally unnatural. It was white, not with the ordinary pallor of fear, but with an absolutely bloodless white, like the under side of a sole. He was very fat, but gave the impression of having at some time been considerably fatter, for his skin hung loosely in creases and folds, and was shot with a meshwork of wrinkles. Short, stubbly brown hair bristled up from his scalp, with a pair of thick, wrinkled ears protruding at the sides. His light grey eyes were still open, the pupils dilated and the balls projecting in a fixed and horrid stare. It seemed to Smith as he looked down upon him that he had never seen Nature's danger signals flying so plainly upon a man's countenance, and his thoughts turned more seriously to the warning which Hastie had given him an hour before.

"What the deuce can have frightened him so?" he asked.

"It's the mummy."

"The mummy? How, then?"

"I don't know. It's beastly and morbid. I wish he would drop it. It's the second fright he has given me. It was the same last winter. I found him just like this, with that horrid thing in front of him."

"What does he want with the mummy, then?"

"Oh, he's a crank, you know. It's his hobby. He knows more about these things than any man in England. But I wish he wouldn't! Ah, he's beginning to come to."

A faint tinge of colour had begun to steal back into Bellingham's ghastly cheeks, and his eyelids shivered like a sail after a calm. He clasped and unclasped his hands, drew a long, thin breath between his teeth, and suddenly jerking up his head, threw a glance of recognition around him. As his eyes fell upon the mummy, he sprang off the sofa, seized the roll of papyrus, thrust it into a drawer, turned the key, and then staggered back on to the sofa.

"What's up?" he asked. "What do you chaps want?"

"You've been shrieking out and making no end of a fuss," said Monkhouse Lee. "If our neighbour here from above hadn't come down, I'm sure I don't know what I should have done with you."

"Ah, it's Abercrombie Smith," said Bellingham, glancing up at him. "How very good of you to come in! What a fool I am! Oh, my God, what a fool I am!"

He sunk his head on to his hands, and burst into peal after peal of hysterical laughter.

"Look here! Drop it!" cried Smith, shaking him roughly by the shoulder.

"Your nerves are all in a jangle. You must drop these little midnight games with mummies, or you'll be going off your chump. You're all on wires now."

"I wonder," said Bellingham, "whether you would be as cool as I am if you had seen –"

"What then?"

"Oh, nothing. I meant that I wonder if you could sit up at night with a mummy without trying your nerves. I have no doubt that you are quite right. I dare say that I have been taking it out of myself too much lately. But I am all right now. Please don't go, though. Just wait for a few minutes until I am quite myself."

"The room is very close," remarked Lee, throwing open the window and letting in the cool night air.

"It's balsamic resin," said Bellingham. He lifted up one of the dried palmate leaves from the table and frizzled it over the chimney of the lamp. It broke away into heavy smoke wreaths, and a pungent, biting odour filled the chamber. "It's the sacred plant – the plant of the priests," he remarked. "Do you know anything of Eastern languages, Smith?"

"Nothing at all. Not a word."

The answer seemed to lift a weight from the Egyptologist's mind.

"By the way," he continued, "how long was it from the time that you ran down, until I came to my senses?"

"Not long. Some four or five minutes."

"I thought it could not be very long," said he, drawing a long breath. "But what a strange thing unconsciousness is! There is no measurement to it. I could not tell from my own sensations if it were seconds or weeks. Now that gentleman on the table was packed up in the days of the eleventh dynasty, some forty centuries ago, and yet if he could find his tongue, he would tell us that this lapse of time has been but a closing of the eyes and a reopening of them. He is a singularly fine mummy, Smith."

Smith stepped over to the table and looked down with a professional eye at the black and twisted form in front of him. The features, though horribly discoloured, were perfect, and two little nut-like eyes still lurked in the depths of the black, hollow sockets. The blotched skin was drawn tightly from bone to bone, and a tangled wrap of black coarse hair fell over the ears. Two thin teeth, like those of a rat, overlay the shrivelled lower lip. In its crouching position, with bent joints and craned head, there was a suggestion of energy about the horrid thing which made Smith's gorge rise. The gaunt ribs, with their parchment-like covering, were exposed, and the sunken, leaden-hued abdomen, with the long slit where the embalmer had left his mark; but the lower limbs were wrapped round with coarse yellow bandages. A number of little clove-like pieces of myrrh and of cassia were sprinkled over the body, and lay scattered on the inside of the case.

"I don't know his name," said Bellingham, passing his hand over the shrivelled head. "You see the outer sarcophagus with the inscriptions is missing. Lot 249 is all the title he has now. You see it printed on his case. That was his number in the auction at which I picked him up."

"He has been a very pretty sort of fellow in his day," remarked Abercrombie Smith.

"He has been a giant. His mummy is six feet seven in length, and that would be a giant over there, for they were never a very robust race. Feel these great knotted bones, too. He would be a nasty fellow to tackle."

"Perhaps these very hands helped to build the stones into the pyramids," suggested Monkhouse Lee, looking down with disgust in his eyes at the crooked, unclean talons.

"No fear. This fellow has been pickled in natron, and looked after in the most approved style. They did not serve hodsmen in that fashion. Salt or bitumen was enough for them. It has been calculated that this sort of thing cost about seven hundred and thirty pounds in our money. Our friend was a noble at the least. What do you make of that small inscription near his feet, Smith?"

"I told you that I know no Eastern tongue."

"Ah, so you did. It is the name of the embalmer, I take it. A very conscientious worker he must have been. I wonder how many modern works will survive four thousand years?"

He kept on speaking lightly and rapidly, but it was evident to Abercrombie Smith that he was still palpitating with fear. His hands shook, his lower lip trembled, and look where he would, his eye always came sliding round to his gruesome companion. Through all his fear, however, there was a suspicion of triumph in his tone and manner. His eyes shone, and his footstep, as he paced the room, was brisk and jaunty. He gave the impression of a man who has gone through an ordeal, the marks of which he still bears upon him, but which has helped him to his end.

"You're not going yet?" he cried, as Smith rose from the sofa.

At the prospect of solitude, his fears seemed to crowd back upon him, and he stretched out a hand to detain him.

"Yes, I must go. I have my work to do. You are all right now. I think that with your nervous system you should take up some less morbid study."

"Oh, I am not nervous as a rule; and I have unwrapped mummies before."

"You fainted last time," observed Monkhouse Lee.

"Ah, yes, so I did. Well, I must have a nerve tonic or a course of electricity. You are not going, Lee?"

"I'll do whatever you wish, Ned."

"Then I'll come down with you and have a shakedown on your sofa. Good-night, Smith. I am so sorry to have disturbed you with my foolishness."

They shook hands, and as the medical student stumbled up the spiral and irregular stair he heard a key turn in a door, and the steps of his two new acquaintances as they descended to the lower floor.

- 2 -

In this strange way began the acquaintance between Edward Bellingham and Abercrombie Smith, an acquaintance which the latter, at least, had no desire to push forward. Bellingham, however, appeared to have taken a fancy to his rough-spoken neighbour, and made his advances in such a way that he could hardly be repulsed without absolute brutality. Twice he called to thank Smith for his assistance, and many times afterwards he looked in with books, papers and such other civilities as two bachelor neighbours can offer each other. He was, as Smith soon found, a man of wide reading, with catholic tastes and an extraordinary memory. His manner, too, was so pleasing and suave that one came, after a time, to overlook his repellent appearance. For a jaded and wearied man he was no unpleasant companion, and Smith found himself, after a time, looking forward to his visits, and even returning them.

Clever as he undoubtedly was, however, the medical student seemed to detect a dash of insanity in the man. He broke out at times into a high, inflated style of talk which was in contrast with the simplicity of his life.

"It is a wonderful thing," he cried, "to feel that one can command powers of good and of evil – a ministering angel or a demon of vengeance." And again, of Monkhouse Lee, he said, – "Lee is a good fellow, an honest fellow, but he is without strength or ambition. He would not make a fit partner for a man with a great enterprise. He would not make a fit partner for me."

At such hints and innuendoes stolid Smith, puffing solemnly at his pipe, would simply raise his eyebrows and shake his head, with little interjections of medical wisdom as to earlier hours and fresher air.

One habit Bellingham had developed of late which Smith knew to be a frequent herald of a weakening mind. He appeared to be forever talking to himself. At late hours of the night, when there could be no visitor with him, Smith could still hear his voice beneath him in a low, muffled monologue, sunk almost to a whisper, and yet very audible in the silence. This solitary babbling annoyed and distracted the student, so that he spoke more than once to his neighbour about it. Bellingham, however, flushed up at the charge, and denied curtly that he had uttered a sound; indeed, he showed more annoyance over the matter than the occasion seemed to demand.

Had Abercrombie Smith had any doubt as to his own ears he had not to go far to find corroboration. Tom Styles, the little wrinkled man-servant who had attended to the wants of the lodgers in the turret for a longer time than any man's memory could carry him, was sorely put to it over the same matter.

"If you please, sir," said he, as he tidied down the top chamber one morning, "do you think Mr. Bellingham is all right, sir?"

"All right, Styles?"

"Yes, sir. Right in his head, sir."

"Why should he not be, then?"

"Well, I don't know, sir. His habits has changed of late. He's not the same man he used to be, though I make free to say that he was never quite one of my gentlemen, like Mr. Hastie or yourself, sir. He's took to talkin' to himself something awful. I wonder it don't disturb you. I don't know what to make of him, sir."

"I don't know what business it is of yours, Styles."

"Well, I takes an interest, Mr. Smith. It may be forward of me, but I can't help it. I feel sometimes as if I was mother and father to my young gentlemen. It all falls on me when things go wrong and the relations come. But Mr. Bellingham, sir. I want to know what it is that walks about his room sometimes when he's out and when the door's locked on the outside."

"Eh? You're talking nonsense, Styles."

"Maybe so, sir; but I heard it more'n once with my own ears."

"Rubbish, Styles."

"Very good, sir. You'll ring the bell if you want me."

Abercrombie Smith gave little heed to the gossip of the old man-servant, but a small incident occurred a few days later which left an unpleasant effect upon his mind, and brought the words of Styles forcibly to his memory.

Bellingham had come up to see him late one night, and was entertaining him with an interesting account of the rock tombs of Beni Hassan in Upper Egypt, when Smith, whose hearing was remarkably acute, distinctly heard the sound of a door opening on the landing below.

"There's some fellow gone in or out of your room," he remarked.

Bellingham sprang up and stood helpless for a moment, with the expression of a man who is half incredulous and half afraid.

"I surely locked it. I am almost positive that I locked it," he stammered. "No one could have opened it."

"Why, I hear some one coming up the steps now," said Smith.

Bellingham rushed out through the door, slammed it loudly behind him, and hurried down the stairs. About half-way down Smith heard him stop, and thought he caught the sound of whispering. A moment later the door beneath him shut, a key creaked in a lock, and Bellingham, with beads of moisture upon his pale face, ascended the stairs once more, and re-entered the room.

"It's all right," he said, throwing himself down in a chair. "It was that fool of a dog. He had pushed the door open. I don't know how I came to forget to lock it."

"I didn't know you kept a dog," said Smith, looking very thoughtfully at the disturbed face of his companion.

"Yes, I haven't had him long. I must get rid of him. He's a great nuisance."

"He must be, if you find it so hard to shut him up. I should have thought that shutting the door would have been enough, without locking it."

"I want to prevent old Styles from letting him out. He's of some value, you know, and it would be awkward to lose him."

"I am a bit of a dog-fancier myself," said Smith, still gazing hard at his companion from the corner of his eyes. "Perhaps you'll let me have a look at it."

"Certainly. But I am afraid it cannot be tonight; I have an appointment. Is that clock right? Then I am a quarter of an hour late already. You'll excuse me, I am sure."

He picked up his cap and hurried from the room. In spite of his appointment, Smith heard him re-enter his own chamber and lock his door upon the inside.

This interview left a disagreeable impression upon the medical student's mind. Bellingham had lied to him, and lied so clumsily that it looked as if he had desperate reasons for concealing the truth. Smith knew that his neighbour had no dog. He knew, also, that the step which he had heard upon the stairs was not the step of an animal. But if it were not, then what could it be? There was old Styles's statement about the something which used to pace the room at times when the owner was absent. Could it be a woman? Smith rather inclined to the view. If so, it would mean disgrace and expulsion to Bellingham if it were discovered by the authorities, so that his anxiety and falsehoods might be accounted for. And yet it was inconceivable that an undergraduate could keep a woman in his rooms without being instantly detected. Be the explanation what it might, there was something ugly about it, and Smith determined, as he turned to his books, to discourage all further attempts at intimacy on the part of his soft-spoken and ill-favoured neighbour.

But his work was destined to interruption that night. He had hardly caught up the broken threads when a firm, heavy footfall came three steps at a time from below, and Hastie, in blazer and flannels, burst into the room.

"Still at it!" said he, plumping down into his wonted arm-chair. "What a chap you are to stew! I believe an earthquake might come and knock Oxford into a cocked hat, and you would sit perfectly placid with your books among the ruins. However, I won't bore you long. Three whiffs of baccy, and I am off."

"What's the news, then?" asked Smith, cramming a plug of bird's-eye into his briar with his forefinger.

"Nothing very much. Wilson made 70 for the freshmen against the eleven. They say that they will play him instead of Buddicomb, for Buddicomb is clean off colour. He used to be able to bowl a little, but it's nothing but half-volleys and long hops now."

"Medium right," suggested Smith, with the intense gravity which comes upon a 'varsity man when he speaks of athletics.

"Inclining to fast, with a work from leg. Comes with the arm about three inches or so. He used to be nasty on a wet wicket. Oh, by-the-way, have you heard about Long Norton?"

"What's that?"

"He's been attacked."

"Attacked?"

"Yes, just as he was turning out of the High Street, and within a hundred yards of the gate of Old's."

"But who –"

"Ah, that's the rub! If you said 'what,' you would be more grammatical. Norton swears that it was not human, and, indeed, from the scratches on his throat, I should be inclined to agree with him."

"What, then? Have we come down to spooks?"

Abercrombie Smith puffed his scientific contempt.

"Well, no; I don't think that is quite the idea, either. I am inclined to think that if any showman has lost a great ape lately, and the brute is in these parts, a jury would find a true bill against it. Norton passes that way every night, you know, about the same hour. There's a tree that hangs low over the path – the big elm from Rainy's garden. Norton thinks the thing dropped on him out of the tree. Anyhow, he was nearly strangled by two arms, which, he says, were as strong and as thin as steel bands. He saw nothing; only those beastly arms that tightened and tightened on him. He yelled his head nearly off, and a couple of chaps came running, and the thing went over the wall like a cat. He never got a fair sight of it the whole time. It gave Norton a shake up, I can tell you. I tell him it has been as good as a change at the seaside for him."

"A garrotter, most likely," said Smith.

"Very possible. Norton says not; but we don't mind what he says. The garrotter had long nails, and was pretty smart at swinging himself over walls. By-the-way, your beautiful neighbour would be pleased if he heard about it. He had a grudge against Norton, and he's not a man, from what I know of him, to forget his little debts. But hallo, old chap, what have you got in your noddle?"

"Nothing," Smith answered curtly.

He had started in his chair, and the look had flashed over his face which comes upon a man who is struck suddenly by some unpleasant idea.

"You looked as if something I had said had taken you on the raw. By-the-way, you have made the acquaintance of Master B. since I looked in last, have you not? Young Monkhouse Lee told me something to that effect."

"Yes; I know him slightly. He has been up here once or twice."

"Well, you're big enough and ugly enough to take care of yourself. He's not what I should call exactly a healthy sort of Johnny, though, no doubt, he's very clever, and all that. But you'll soon find out for yourself. Lee is all right; he's a very decent little fellow. Well, so long, old chap! I row Mullins for the Vice-Chancellor's pot on Wednesday week, so mind you come down, in case I don't see you before."

Bovine Smith laid down his pipe and turned stolidly to his books once more. But with all the will in the world, he found it very hard to keep his mind upon his work. It would slip away to brood upon the man beneath him, and upon the little mystery which hung round his chambers. Then his thoughts turned to this singular attack of which Hastie had spoken, and to the grudge which Bellingham was said to owe the object of it. The two ideas would persist in rising together in his mind, as though there were some close and intimate connection between them. And yet the suspicion was so dim and vague that it could not be put down in words.

"Confound the chap!" cried Smith, as he shied his book on pathology across the room. "He has spoiled my night's reading, and that's reason enough, if there were no other, why I should steer clear of him in the future."

For ten days the medical student confined himself so closely to his studies that he neither saw nor heard anything of either of the men beneath him. At the hours when Bellingham had been accustomed to visit him, he took care to sport his oak, and though he more than once heard a knocking at his outer door, he resolutely refused to answer it. One afternoon, however, he was descending the stairs when, just as he was passing it, Bellingham's door flew open, and young Monkhouse Lee came out with his eyes sparkling and a dark flush of anger upon his olive cheeks. Close at his heels followed Bellingham, his fat, unhealthy face all quivering with malignant passion.

"You fool!" he hissed. "You'll be sorry."

"Very likely," cried the other. "Mind what I say. It's off! I won't hear of it!"

"You've promised, anyhow."

"Oh, I'll keep that! I won't speak. But I'd rather little Eva was in her grave. Once for all, it's off. She'll do what I say. We don't want to see you again."

So much Smith could not avoid hearing, but he hurried on, for he had no wish to be involved in their dispute. There had been a serious breach between them, that was clear enough, and Lee was going to cause the engagement with his sister to be broken off. Smith thought of Hastie's comparison of the toad and the dove, and was glad to think that the matter was at an end. Bellingham's face when he was in a passion was not pleasant to look upon. He was not a man to whom an innocent girl could be trusted for life. As he walked, Smith wondered languidly what could have caused the quarrel, and what the promise might be which Bellingham had been so anxious that Monkhouse Lee should keep.

It was the day of the sculling match between Hastie and Mullins, and a stream of men were making their way down to the banks of the Isis. A May sun was shining brightly, and the yellow path was barred with the black shadows of the tall elm-trees. On either side the grey colleges lay back from the road, the hoary old mothers of minds looking out from their high, mullioned windows at the tide of young life which swept so merrily past them. Black-clad tutors, prim officials, pale reading men, brown-faced, straw-hatted young athletes in white sweaters or many-coloured blazers, all were hurrying towards the blue winding river which curves through the Oxford meadows.

Abercrombie Smith, with the intuition of an old oarsman, chose his position at the point where he knew that the struggle, if there were a struggle, would come. Far off he heard the hum which announced the start, the gathering roar of the approach, the thunder of running feet, and the shouts of the men in the boats beneath him. A spray of half-clad, deep-breathing runners shot past him, and craning over their shoulders, he saw Hastie pulling a steady thirty-six, while his opponent, with a jerky forty, was a good boat's length behind him. Smith gave a cheer for his friend, and pulling out his watch, was starting off again for his chambers, when he felt a touch upon his shoulder, and found that young Monkhouse Lee was beside him.

"I saw you there," he said, in a timid, deprecating way. "I wanted to speak to you, if you could spare me a half-hour. This cottage is mine. I share it with Harrington of King's. Come in and have a cup of tea."

"I must be back presently," said Smith. "I am hard on the grind at present. But I'll come in for a few minutes with pleasure. I wouldn't have come out only Hastie is a friend of mine."

"So he is of mine. Hasn't he a beautiful style? Mullins wasn't in it. But come into the cottage. It's a little den of a place, but it is pleasant to work in during the summer months."

It was a small, square, white building, with green doors and shutters, and a rustic trellis-work porch, standing back some fifty yards from the river's bank. Inside, the main room was roughly fitted up as a study – deal table, unpainted shelves with books, and a few cheap oleographs upon the wall. A kettle sang upon a spirit-stove, and there were tea things upon a tray on the table.

"Try that chair and have a cigarette," said Lee. "Let me pour you out a cup of tea. It's so good of you to come in, for I know that your time is a good deal taken up. I wanted to say to you that, if I were you, I should change my rooms at once."

"Eh?"

Smith sat staring with a lighted match in one hand and his unlit cigarette in the other.

"Yes; it must seem very extraordinary, and the worst of it is that I cannot give my reasons, for I am under a solemn promise – a very solemn promise. But

I may go so far as to say that I don't think Bellingham is a very safe man to live near. I intend to camp out here as much as I can for a time."

"Not safe! What do you mean?"

"Ah, that's what I mustn't say. But do take my advice, and move your rooms. We had a grand row today. You must have heard us, for you came down the stairs."

"I saw that you had fallen out."

"He's a horrible chap, Smith. That is the only word for him. I have had doubts about him ever since that night when he fainted – you remember, when you came down. I taxed him today, and he told me things that made my hair rise, and wanted me to stand in with him. I'm not strait-laced, but I am a clergyman's son, you know, and I think there are some things which are quite beyond the pale. I only thank God that I found him out before it was too late, for he was to have married into my family."

"This is all very fine, Lee," said Abercrombie Smith curtly. "But either you are saying a great deal too much or a great deal too little."

"I give you a warning."

"If there is real reason for warning, no promise can bind you. If I see a rascal about to blow a place up with dynamite no pledge will stand in my way of preventing him."

"Ah, but I cannot prevent him, and I can do nothing but warn you."

"Without saying what you warn me against."

"Against Bellingham."

"But that is childish. Why should I fear him, or any man?"

"I can't tell you. I can only entreat you to change your rooms. You are in danger where you are. I don't even say that Bellingham would wish to injure you. But it might happen, for he is a dangerous neighbour just now."

"Perhaps I know more than you think," said Smith, looking keenly at the young man's boyish, earnest face. "Suppose I tell you that some one else shares Bellingham's rooms."

Monkhouse Lee sprang from his chair in uncontrollable excitement.

"You know, then?" he gasped.

"A woman."

Lee dropped back again with a groan.

"My lips are sealed," he said. "I must not speak."

"Well, anyhow," said Smith, rising, "it is not likely that I should allow myself to be frightened out of rooms which suit me very nicely. It would be a little too feeble for me to move out all my goods and chattels because you say that Bellingham might in some unexplained way do me an injury. I think that I'll just take my chance, and stay where I am, and as I see that it's nearly five o'clock, I must ask you to excuse me."

He bade the young student adieu in a few curt words, and made his way homeward through the sweet spring evening, feeling half-ruffled, half-amused, as any other strong, unimaginative man might who has been menaced by a vague and shadowy danger.

There was one little indulgence which Abercrombie Smith always allowed himself, however closely his work might press upon him. Twice a week, on the Tuesday and the Friday, it was his invariable custom to walk over to Farlingford, the residence of Doctor Plumptree Peterson, situated about a mile and a half out of Oxford. Peterson had been a close friend of Smith's elder brother Francis, and as he was a bachelor, fairly well-to-do, with a good cellar and a better library, his house was a pleasant goal for a man who was in need of a brisk walk. Twice a week, then, the medical student would swing out there along the dark country roads, and spend a pleasant hour in Peterson's comfortable study, discussing, over a glass of old port, the gossip of the 'varsity or the latest developments of medicine or of surgery.

On the day which followed his interview with Monkhouse Lee, Smith shut up his books at a quarter past eight, the hour when he usually started for his friend's house. As he was leaving his room, however, his eyes chanced to fall upon one of the books which Bellingham had lent him, and his conscience pricked him for not having returned it. However repellent the man might be, he should not be treated with discourtesy. Taking the book, he walked downstairs and knocked at his neighbour's door. There was no answer; but on turning the handle he found that it was unlocked. Pleased at the thought of avoiding an interview, he stepped inside, and placed the book with his card upon the table.

The lamp was turned half down, but Smith could see the details of the room plainly enough. It was all much as he had seen it before – the frieze, the animal-headed gods, the hanging crocodile, and the table littered over with papers and dried leaves. The mummy case stood upright against the wall, but the mummy itself was missing. There was no sign of any second occupant of the room, and he felt as he withdrew that he had probably done Bellingham an injustice. Had he a guilty secret to preserve, he would hardly leave his door open so that all the world might enter.

The spiral stair was as black as pitch, and Smith was slowly making his way down its irregular steps, when he was suddenly conscious that something had passed him in the darkness. There was a faint sound, a whiff of air, a light brushing past his elbow, but so slight that he could scarcely be certain of it. He stopped and listened, but the wind was rustling among the ivy outside, and he could hear nothing else.

"Is that you, Styles?" he shouted.

There was no answer, and all was still behind him. It must have been a sudden gust of air, for there were crannies and cracks in the old turret. And yet he could almost have sworn that he heard a footfall by his very side. He had emerged into the quadrangle, still turning the matter over in his head, when a man came running swiftly across the smooth-cropped lawn.

"Is that you, Smith?"

"Hullo, Hastie!"

"For God's sake come at once! Young Lee is drowned! Here's Harrington of King's with the news. The doctor is out. You'll do, but come along at once. There may be life in him."

"Have you brandy?"

"No."

"I'll bring some. There's a flask on my table."

Smith bounded up the stairs, taking three at a time, seized the flask, and was rushing down with it, when, as he passed Bellingham's room, his eyes fell upon something which left him gasping and staring upon the landing.

The door, which he had closed behind him, was now open, and right in front of him, with the lamp-light shining upon it, was the mummy case. Three minutes ago it had been empty. He could swear to that. Now it framed the lank body of its horrible occupant, who stood, grim and stark, with his black shrivelled face towards the door. The form was lifeless and inert, but it seemed to Smith as he gazed that there still lingered a lurid spark of vitality, some faint sign of consciousness in the little eyes which lurked in the depths of the hollow sockets. So astounded and shaken was he that he had forgotten his errand, and was still staring at the lean, sunken figure when the voice of his friend below recalled him to himself.

"Come on, Smith!" he shouted. "It's life and death, you know. Hurry up! Now, then," he added, as the medical student reappeared, "let us do a sprint. It is well under a mile, and we should do it in five minutes. A human life is better worth running for than a pot."

Neck and neck they dashed through the darkness, and did not pull up until panting and spent, they had reached the little cottage by the river. Young Lee, limp and dripping like a broken water-plant, was stretched upon the sofa, the green scum of the river upon his black hair, and a fringe of white foam upon his leaden-hued lips. Beside him knelt his fellow student, Harrington, endeavouring to chafe some warmth back into his rigid limbs.

"I think there's life in him," said Smith, with his hand to the lad's side. "Put your watch glass to his lips. Yes, there's dimming on it. You take one arm, Hastie. Now work it as I do, and we'll soon pull him round."

For ten minutes they worked in silence, inflating and depressing the chest of the unconscious man. At the end of that time a shiver ran through his body, his lips trembled, and he opened his eyes. The three students burst out into an irrepressible cheer.

"Wake up, old chap. You've frightened us quite enough."

"Have some brandy. Take a sip from the flask."

"He's all right now," said his companion Harrington. "Heavens, what a fright I got! I was reading here, and had gone out for a stroll as far as the river, when I heard a scream and a splash. Out I ran, and by the time I could find him and fish him out, all life seemed to have gone. Then Simpson couldn't get a doctor, for he has a game-leg, and I had to run, and I don't know what I'd have done without you fellows. That's right, old chap. Sit up."

Monkhouse Lee had raised himself on his hands, and looked wildly about him.

"What's up?" he asked. "I've been in the water. Ah, yes; I remember."

A look of fear came into his eyes, and he sank his face into his hands.

"How did you fall in?"

"I didn't fall in."

"How then?"

"I was thrown in. I was standing by the bank, and something from behind picked me up like a feather and hurled me in. I heard nothing, and I saw nothing. But I know what it was, for all that."

"And so do I," whispered Smith.

Lee looked up with a quick glance of surprise.

"You've learned, then?" he said. "You remember the advice I gave you?"

"Yes, and I begin to think that I shall take it."

"I don't know what the deuce you fellows are talking about," said Hastie, "but I think, if I were you, Harrington, I should get Lee to bed at once. It will be time enough to discuss the why and the wherefore when he is a little stronger. I think, Smith, you and I can leave him alone now. I am walking back to college; if you are coming in that direction, we can have a chat."

But it was little chat that they had upon their homeward path. Smith's mind was too full of the incidents of the evening, the absence of the mummy from his neighbour's rooms, the step that passed him on the stair, the reappearance – the extraordinary, inexplicable reappearance of the grisly thing – and then this attack upon Lee, corresponding so closely to the previous outrage upon another man against whom Bellingham bore a grudge. All this settled in his thoughts, together with the many little incidents which had previously turned him against his neighbour, and the singular circumstances under which he was first called in to him. What had been a dim suspicion, a vague, fantastic conjecture, had suddenly taken form, and stood out in his mind as a grim fact, a thing not to be denied. And yet, how monstrous it was! How unheard of! How entirely beyond all bounds of human experience. An impartial judge, or even the friend who walked by his side, would simply tell him that his eyes had deceived him, that the mummy had been there all the time, that young Lee had tumbled into the river as any other man tumbles into a river, and that blue pill was the best thing for a disordered liver. He felt that he would have said as much if the positions had been reversed. And yet he could swear that Bellingham was a murderer at heart, and that he wielded a weapon such as no man had ever used in all the grim history of crime.

Hastie had branched off to his rooms with a few crisp and emphatic comments upon his friend's unsociability, and Abercrombie Smith crossed the quadrangle to his corner turret with a strong feeling of repulsion for his chambers and their associations. He would take Lee's advice, and move his quarters as soon as possible, for how could a man study when his ear was ever straining for every murmur or footstep in the room below? He observed, as he crossed over the lawn, that the light was still shining in Bellingham's window, and as he passed up the staircase the door opened, and the man himself looked out at him. With his fat, evil face he was like some bloated spider fresh from the weaving of his poisonous web.

"Good-evening," said he. "Won't you come in?"

"No," cried Smith fiercely.

"No? You are busy as ever? I wanted to ask you about Lee. I was sorry to hear that there was a rumour that something was amiss with him."

His features were grave, but there was the gleam of a hidden laugh in his eyes as he spoke. Smith saw it, and he could have knocked him down for it.

"You'll be sorrier still to hear that Monkhouse Lee is doing very well, and is out of all danger," he answered. "Your hellish tricks have not come off this time. Oh, you needn't try to brazen it out. I know all about it."

Bellingham took a step back from the angry student, and half-closed the door as if to protect himself.

"You are mad," he said. "What do you mean? Do you assert that I had anything to do with Lee's accident?"

"Yes," thundered Smith. "You and that bag of bones behind you; you worked it between you. I tell you what it is, Master B., they have given up burning folk like you, but we still keep a hangman, and, by George, if any man in this college meets his death while you are here, I'll have you up, and if you don't swing for it, it won't be my fault. You'll find that your filthy Egyptian tricks won't answer in England."

"You're a raving lunatic," said Bellingham.

"All right. You just remember what I say, for you'll find that I'll be better than my word."

The door slammed, and Smith went fuming up to his chamber, where he locked the door upon the inside, and spent half the night in smoking his old briar and brooding over the strange events of the evening.

Next morning Abercrombie Smith heard nothing of his neighbour, but Harrington called upon him in the afternoon to say that Lee was almost himself again. All day Smith stuck fast to his work, but in the evening he determined to pay the visit to his friend Doctor Peterson upon which he had started the night before. A good walk and a friendly chat would be welcome to his jangled nerves.

Bellingham's door was shut as he passed, but glancing back when he was some distance from the turret, he saw his neighbour's head at the window outlined against the lamp-light, his face pressed apparently against the glass as he gazed out into the darkness. It was a blessing to be away from all contact with him, if but for a few hours, and Smith stepped out briskly, and breathed the soft spring air into his lungs. The half-moon lay in the west between two Gothic pinnacles, and threw upon the silvered street a dark tracery from the stone-work above. There was a brisk breeze, and light, fleecy clouds drifted swiftly across the sky. Old's was on the very border of the town, and in five minutes Smith found himself beyond the houses and between the hedges of a May-scented Oxfordshire lane.

It was a lonely and little frequented road which led to his friend's house. Early as it was, Smith did not meet a single soul upon his way. He walked briskly along until he came to the avenue gate, which opened into the long gravel drive leading up to Farlingford. In front of him he could see the cosy red light of the windows glimmering through the foliage. He stood with his hand upon the iron latch of the swinging gate, and he glanced back at the road along which he had come. Something was coming swiftly down it.

It moved in the shadow of the hedge, silently and furtively, a dark, crouching figure, dimly visible against the black background. Even as he gazed back at it, it had lessened its distance by twenty paces, and was fast closing upon him. Out of the darkness he had a glimpse of a scraggy neck, and of two eyes that will ever haunt him in his dreams. He turned, and with a cry of terror he ran for his life up the avenue. There were the red lights, the signals of safety, almost within a stone's-throw of him. He was a famous runner, but never had he run as he ran that night.

The heavy gate had swung into place behind him, but he heard it dash open again before his pursuer. As he rushed madly and wildly through the night, he could hear a swift, dry patter behind him, and could see, as he threw back a glance, that this horror was bounding like a tiger at his heels, with blazing eyes and one stringy arm out-thrown. Thank God, the door was ajar. He could see the thin bar of light which shot from the lamp in the hall. Nearer yet sounded the clatter from behind. He heard a hoarse gurgling at his very shoulder. With a shriek he flung himself against the door, slammed and bolted it behind him, and sank half-fainting on to the hall chair.

"My goodness, Smith, what's the matter?" asked Peterson, appearing at the door of his study.

"Give me some brandy."

Peterson disappeared, and came rushing out again with a glass and a decanter.

"You need it," he said, as his visitor drank off what he poured out for him. "Why, man, you are as white as a cheese."

Smith laid down his glass, rose up, and took a deep breath.

"I am my own man again now," said he. "I was never so unmanned before. But, with your leave, Peterson, I will sleep here tonight, for I don't think I could face that road again except by daylight. It's weak, I know, but I can't help it."

Peterson looked at his visitor with a very questioning eye.

"Of course you shall sleep here if you wish. I'll tell Mrs. Burney to make up the spare bed. Where are you off to now?"

"Come up with me to the window that overlooks the door. I want you to see what I have seen."

They went up to the window of the upper hall whence they could look down upon the approach to the house. The drive and the fields on either side lay quiet and still, bathed in the peaceful moonlight.

"Well, really, Smith," remarked Peterson, "it is well that I know you to be an abstemious man. What in the world can have frightened you?"

"I'll tell you presently. But where can it have gone? Ah, now, look, look! See the curve of the road just beyond your gate."

"Yes, I see; you needn't pinch my arm off. I saw some one pass. I should say a man, rather thin, apparently, and tall, very tall. But what of him? And what of yourself? You are still shaking like an aspen leaf."

"I have been within hand-grip of the devil, that's all. But come down to your study, and I shall tell you the whole story."

He did so. Under the cheery lamp-light, with a glass of wine on the table beside him, and the portly form and florid face of his friend in front, he narrated, in their order, all the events, great and small, which had formed so singular a chain, from the night on which he had found Bellingham fainting in front of the mummy case until this horrid experience of an hour ago.

"There now," he said as he concluded, "that's the whole black business. It is monstrous and incredible, but it is true."

Doctor Plumptree Peterson sat for some time in silence with a very puzzled expression upon his face.

"I never heard of such a thing in my life, never!" he said at last. "You have told me the facts. Now tell me your inferences."

"You can draw your own."

"But I should like to hear yours. You have thought over the matter, and I have not."

"Well, it must be a little vague in detail, but the main points seem to me to be clear enough. This fellow Bellingham, in his Eastern studies, has got hold of some infernal secret by which a mummy – or possibly only this particular mummy – can be temporarily brought to life. He was trying this disgusting business on the night when he fainted. No doubt the sight of the creature moving had shaken his nerve, even though he had expected it. You remember that almost the first words he said were to call out upon himself as a fool. Well, he got more hardened afterwards, and carried the matter through without fainting. The vitality which he could put into it was evidently only a passing thing, for I have seen it continually in its case as dead as this table. He has some elaborate process, I fancy, by which he brings the thing to pass. Having done it, he naturally bethought him that he might use the creature as an agent. It has intelligence and it has strength. For some purpose he took Lee into his confidence; but Lee, like a decent Christian, would have nothing to do with such a business. Then they had a row, and Lee vowed that he would tell his sister of Bellingham's true character. Bellingham's game was to prevent him, and he nearly managed it, by setting this creature of his on his track. He had already tried its powers upon another man – Norton – towards whom he had a grudge. It is the merest chance that he has not two murders upon his soul. Then, when I taxed him with the matter, he had the strongest reasons for wishing me out of the way, before I could convey my knowledge to any one else. He got his chance when I went out, for he knew my habits and where I was bound for. I have had a narrow shave, Peterson, and it is mere luck you didn't find me on your doorstep in the morning. I'm not a nervous man as a rule, and I never thought to have the fear of death put upon me as it was tonight."

"My dear boy, you take the matter too seriously," said his companion. "Your nerves are out of order with your work, and you make too much of it. How could such a thing as this stride about the streets of Oxford, even at night, without being seen?"

"It has been seen. There is quite a scare in the town about an escaped ape, as they imagine the creature to be. It is the talk of the place."

"Well, it's a striking chain of events. And yet, my dear fellow, you must allow that each incident in itself is capable of a more natural explanation."

"What! Even my adventure of tonight?"

"Certainly. You come out with your nerves all unstrung, and your head full of this theory of yours. Some gaunt, half-famished tramp steals after you, and seeing you run, is emboldened to pursue you. Your fears and imagination do the rest."

"It won't do, Peterson; it won't do."

"And again, in the instance of your finding the mummy case empty, and then a few moments later with an occupant, you know that it was lamp-light, that the lamp was half turned down, and that you had no special reason to look hard at the case. It is quite possible that you may have overlooked the creature in the first instance."

"No, no; it is out of the question."

"And then Lee may have fallen into the river, and Norton been garrotted. It is certainly a formidable indictment that you have against Bellingham; but if you were to place it before a police magistrate, he would simply laugh in your face."

"I know he would. That is why I mean to take the matter into my own hands."

"Eh?"

"Yes; I feel that a public duty rests upon me, and, besides, I must do it for my own safety, unless I choose to allow myself to be hunted by this beast out of the college, and that would be a little too feeble. I have quite made up my mind what I shall do. And first of all, may I use your paper and pens for an hour?"

"Most certainly. You will find all that you want upon that side-table."

Abercrombie Smith sat down before a sheet of foolscap, and for an hour, and then for a second hour his pen travelled swiftly over it. Page after page was finished and tossed aside while his friend leaned back in his arm-chair, looking across at him with patient curiosity. At last, with an exclamation of satisfaction, Smith sprang to his feet, gathered his papers up into order, and laid the last one upon Peterson's desk.

"Kindly sign this as a witness," he said.

"A witness? Of what?"

"Of my signature, and of the date. The date is the most important. Why, Peterson, my life might hang upon it."

"My dear Smith, you are talking wildly. Let me beg you to go to bed."

"On the contrary, I never spoke so deliberately in my life. And I will promise to go to bed the moment you have signed it."

"But what is it?"

"It is a statement of all that I have been telling you tonight. I wish you to witness it."

"Certainly," said Peterson, signing his name under that of his companion. "There you are! But what is the idea?"

"You will kindly retain it, and produce it in case I am arrested."

"Arrested? For what?"

"For murder. It is quite on the cards. I wish to be ready for every event. There is only one course open to me, and I am determined to take it."

"For Heaven's sake, don't do anything rash!"

"Believe me, it would be far more rash to adopt any other course. I hope that we won't need to bother you, but it will ease my mind to know that you have this statement of my motives. And now I am ready to take your advice and to go to roost, for I want to be at my best in the morning."

- 3 -

Abercrombie Smith was not an entirely pleasant man to have as an enemy. Slow and easy-tempered, he was formidable when driven to action. He brought to every purpose in life the same deliberate resoluteness which had distinguished him as a scientific student. He had laid his studies aside for a day, but he intended that the day should not be wasted. Not a word did he say to his host as to his plans, but by nine o'clock he was well on his way to Oxford.

In the High Street he stopped at Clifford's the gunmaker's, and bought a heavy revolver, with a box of central-fire cartridges. Six of them he slipped into the chambers, and half-cocking the weapon, placed it in the pocket of his coat. He then made his way to Hastie's rooms, where the big oarsman was lounging over his breakfast, with the Sporting Times propped up against the coffee-pot.

"Hullo! What's up?" he asked. "Have some coffee?"

"No, thank you. I want you to come with me, Hastie, and do what I ask you."

"Certainly, my boy."

"And bring a heavy stick with you."

"Hullo!" Hastie stared. "Here's a hunting crop that would fell an ox."

"One other thing. You have a box of amputating knives. Give me the longest of them."

"There you are. You seem to be fairly on the war trail. Anything else?"

"No; that will do." Smith placed the knife inside his coat, and led the way to the quadrangle. "We are neither of us chickens, Hastie," said he.

"I think I can do this job alone, but I take you as a precaution. I am going to have a little talk with Bellingham. If I have only him to deal with, I won't, of course, need you. If I shout, however, up you come, and lam out with your whip as hard as you can lick. Do you understand?"

"All right. I'll come if I hear you bellow."

"Stay here, then. I may be a little time, but don't budge until I come down."

"I'm a fixture."

Smith ascended the stairs, opened Bellingham's door and stepped in. Bellingham was seated behind his table, writing. Beside him, among his litter of strange possessions, towered the mummy case, with its sale number 249 still stuck upon its front, and its hideous occupant stiff and stark within it. Smith looked very deliberately round him, closed the door, and then stepping across to the fireplace, struck a match and set the fire alight. Bellingham sat staring, with amazement and rage upon his bloated face.

"Well, really now, you make yourself at home," he gasped.

Smith sat himself deliberately down, placing his watch upon the table, drew out his pistol, cocked it, and laid it in his lap. Then he took the long amputating knife from his bosom, and threw it down in front of Bellingham.

"Now, then," said he, "just get to work and cut up that mummy."

"Oh, is that it?" said Bellingham with a sneer.

"Yes, that is it. They tell me that the law can't touch you. But I have a law that will set matters straight. If in five minutes you have not set to work, I swear by the God who made me that I will put a bullet through your brain!"

"You would murder me?"

Bellingham had half risen, and his face was the colour of putty.

"Yes."

"And for what?"

"To stop your mischief. One minute has gone."

"But what have I done?"

"I know and you know."

"This is mere bullying."

"Two minutes are gone."

"But you must give reasons. You are a madman – a dangerous madman. Why should I destroy my own property? It is a valuable mummy."

"You must cut it up, and you must burn it."

"I will do no such thing."

"Four minutes are gone."

Smith took up the pistol and he looked towards Bellingham with an inexorable face. As the second hand stole round, he raised his hand, and the finger twitched upon the trigger.

"There! There! I'll do it!" screamed Bellingham.

In frantic haste he caught up the knife and hacked at the figure of the mummy, ever glancing round to see the eye and the weapon of his terrible visitor bent upon him. The creature crackled and snapped under every stab of the keen blade. A thick yellow dust rose up from it. Spices and dried essences rained down upon the floor. Suddenly, with a rending crack, its backbone snapped asunder, and it fell, a brown heap of sprawling limbs, upon the floor.

"Now into the fire!" said Smith.

The flames leaped and roared as the dried and tinder-like debris was piled upon it. The little room was like the stoke-hole of a steamer and the sweat ran down the faces of the two men; but still the one stooped and worked, while the other sat watching him with a set face. A thick, fat smoke oozed out from the fire, and a heavy smell of burned rosin and singed hair filled the air. In a quarter of an hour a few charred and brittle sticks were all that was left of Lot No. 249.

"Perhaps that will satisfy you," snarled Bellingham, with hate and fear in his little grey eyes as he glanced back at his tormentor.

"No; I must make a clean sweep of all your materials. We must have no more devil's tricks. In with all these leaves! They may have something to do with it."

"And what now?" asked Bellingham, when the leaves also had been added to the blaze.

"Now the roll of papyrus which you had on the table that night. It is in that drawer, I think."

"No, no," shouted Bellingham. "Don't burn that! Why, man, you don't know what you do. It is unique; it contains wisdom which is nowhere else to be found."

"Out with it!"

"But look here, Smith, you can't really mean it. I'll share the knowledge with you. I'll teach you all that is in it. Or, stay, let me only copy it before you burn it!"

Smith stepped forward and turned the key in the drawer. Taking out the yellow, curled roll of paper, he threw it into the fire, and pressed it down with his heel. Bellingham screamed, and grabbed at it; but Smith pushed him back and stood over it until it was reduced to a formless grey ash.

"Now, Master B.," said he, "I think I have pretty well drawn your teeth. You'll hear from me again, if you return to your old tricks. And now good-morning, for I must go back to my studies."

And such is the narrative of Abercrombie Smith as to the singular events which occurred in Old College, Oxford, in the spring of '84. As Bellingham left the university immediately afterwards, and was last heard of in the Soudan, there is no one who can contradict his statement. But the wisdom of men is small, and the ways of Nature are strange, and who shall put a bound to the dark things which may be found by those who seek for them?

THE UNSEEN MAN'S STORY

JULIAN HAWTHORNE

The captain picked up his cigar and relighted it; the rest of us sat silent for a minute at least. Then Sam, without making any comment, addressed the individual on his left hand, who, owing to his position, was the only person at table whom I had not been able to see.

"If I'm not mistaken," said Sam, "you've been abroad, too. Would you mind telling us about something entertaining over there?"

Whereupon, the person in question opened his mouth and discoursed to the following effect:

The friends whom I expected to meet in Athens had been gone two days when I arrived. This was the first of October. I spent three weeks exploring the Grecian capital and its environs, and then I ran across my old college mate, Haymaker, one of the most useful men living, for he knows everyone and everything, has been everywhere, and is as full of enthusiasm and energy as on the day he entered the freshman class.

He asked me whether I had been to Egypt. I said that I had not. "Then now is your time!" was his reply; and taking out a notebook, he proceeded to jot down for me an itinerary, containing such useful details as the names of the best hotels, merchants and dragomen, the things to be seen and the order in which to see them, the number of days or weeks to be spent in various places, the fees to be paid to government officers and others, and the approximate total expenses of a six months trip.

"There you are, my dear boy," said he, handing me the paper, "and when you get home, if you don't confess that your winter on the Nile was the pleasantest experience of your travels, I'll stand a dinner for a dozen at Delmonico's, and you shall make a speech!" As we shook hands at parting, he added, "Mind and don't forget to look up old Carigliano. Charming old maniac – worth all the rest of the trip put together!"

I embarked for Alexandria a few days later, and on the fifth of November we sighted the Pharos, in a temperature of seventy-eight degrees, and in the midst of a color, a movement, a picturesqueness, and a strangeness, such as are to be met with only in the East. The wharves crowded with shipping, the ports, the villas and the palaces, glowed in the calm clear light of the oriental afternoon. Handed at the custom house in a perfect Babel and jostled by a crowd of dark-hued faces, bare legs, and scanty but gorgeously fine clothing. In a whirl of gesticulation, broken English, and rapacious, good-humored excitement, I had my trunks examined and was driven (following Haymaker's advice) to the Hotel Europe. There I secured the services of Ahmed Hassan as dragoman, and my Egyptian campaign began.

Everybody has made the same campaign, or has read accounts of it, so that I will not enlarge upon my individual experiences. I stayed in Alexandria a week, and then took the train through the green antiquity of immemorial Egypt, as far as Cairo. There I remained a month – long enough to begin to feel in harmony with the oriental idea. In other words, I began to get used to turbans, to nakedness, to the union of inconceivable squalor and splendor; to streets a yard wide crammed with donkeys, camels, merchandise, and the population of a score of barbarous countries; to the awful repose of the living desert, and to the immortal simplicity of the mysterious pyramids and of the

Sphinx. I became accustomed to a sky from which no rain ever fell, and to a valley whose verdure was derived from a spring which no man had ever discovered. I grew familiar with the cry of the muezzin from the minarets, and with the calm and shadowy interior of the domed and splendid mosques. Egypt is the stimulus and the despair of adjectives! I welcomed the unveiled sunshine to the marrow of my bones, and thought of Cleopatra and the Pharaohs. There is no other land so strange as this, nor any in which the stranger so soon comes to feel himself prehistorically at home. At last I hired a *dahabeah*, and, on the fifteenth of December, I began the ascent of the Nile, not sorry to exchange the jolt and wriggle of the donkey-back for the smooth glide and musical ripple of the Egyptian sail boat.

Now ensued three weeks of enforced but delicious inactivity, during which I had leisure to digest what I had seen, and to prepare myself for what might be to come. Though the Nile flows out of the dead past, it is itself anything but lifeless. The current runs rapidly; boats flit in all directions, impelled by oar or sail; voices are continually heard, in song, shout, and laughter; wild geese sit on the long sand strip or fly honking overhead.

Cairo, with its silvery domes and minarets, sinks slowly beneath the northern horizon; on our left, beyond the desert, are the notched hills of Mokattam; on our right, the wide valley, green with abundant grain, beautiful with rows of palms, noisy with the shrill voices of dark-robed women clustered on the banks, populous with mud villages and squatting, staring Arabs. Here and there a *shadoof* laboriously irrigates the plain, or, higher up the river, the creaking *sakia* not less primitively fulfils its office. The days are a long glory of sunshine; the nights, a soft splendor of stars. We are sailing into the earliest twilight of human history; but earth and sky were never clearer or more bright. We lose all sense of time; the mere luxury of existence obliterates it; what is a lifetime compared with the immeasurable ages which gaze down upon us from the margins of this mighty stream?

It was at the close of the first week in January of the new year, that, coming on deck one morning early, I saw opening before me the great valley of Thebes. It was a splendid morning – it seemed to me even more splendid than usual. A couple of vultures, sitting on the high western bank, rose in the air and sailed away towards the Lybian hills, whose clear gray outline cut the purple sky. Were they going to seek for food in the tombs there? The plain, of vast extent, and green as the emerald, is unequally divided by the broad, swift running of the Nile; of the ancient city nothing is yet visible; though, with a good telescope, one might perhaps discern in the southern distance the forms of the twin colossi of the Pharaoh Amunoph, and the matchless obelisk of Hatasoo Thothmes.

Nevertheless, a glow of memory and anticipation came upon me; for here was the scene of a civilization more sumptuous and earlier than any in recorded history. For each stalk of grain that waves now in the northern breeze, there was once a living man, with ancestors before him and a posterity to follow; and the energy, power, and magnificence of their existence has dwarfed and made pallid all that came after them. As we continued to move slowly up the stream, the world-famous ruins loomed larger and more distinct; and mud villages of the present inhabitants, clustered near or upon these gigantic fragments, were like the nests of swallows under the eaves of a cathedral. It seemed as if no being of less stature and ability than Memnon himself could have hewn out and piled together such immeasurable miracles of stone.

I had made my arrangements for a prolonged stay in Thebes; and as inns are not plentiful in that region, I made a hotel, and a very comfortable one, of my *dahabeah*. We made fast near the bank, close to the temple of Luxor, and while I ate my dinner Ahmed Hassan engaged in personal conflict with fifty or a hundred Arabs, who wanted to sell the *howadji* all the spoils of Egypt, from the time of Menes, the eternal, down to the latest Ptolemy. Presently I came on deck, and getting into our boat, Ahmed and I were rowed across to the western shore, where donkeys and more Arabs were awaiting us, and prepared to take a preliminary gallop in the direction of Karnak, a mile or two down the river.

Among the Arabs I noticed one man, who, though with them, was evidently not of them. He was tall, and of dignified bearing, and his full beard, which was nearly white, fell down over his breast. His eyes were blue, and very bright; their glance was penetrating, but restless. His complexion, though tanned by the sun, had been originally fair; his broad forehead was partly concealed by a white turban, and he wore full Turkish trousers gathered at the knee, while over his close-fitting undergarment was thrown a flowing cloak, which he gathered about him as he stood. In spite of his oriental costume, however, I was quite sure this man was not of Eastern birth; and the manner in which he had scrutinized my face and appearance seemed to indicate that his interest in me, if he had any, was of another kind than would be felt by a real son of the desert.

"Who is that?" I inquired of Ahmed, as we jogged along.

"He? Oh, he ver strange man, come here long time, tink from Europe. Five year – ten year – allays see he; he ver wise – say he crazy."

"What is his name?"

"Oh, not know right name; call he Kehr-el-Lans Effendi. He go much tomba; mebbe hunt antika; but not know."

"Does he live here?"

"Tink he live Temple Medinet Abou. We go by – mebbe find he. Plenty time talk he."

There was an impression on my mind that I had heard something about this mysterious personage; but it was too vague at the moment, to enable me to analyze it; and the overpowering spectacle of Karnak effectually put the matter out of my head for the time being. But, a few days afterward, we visited Medinet Abou; and while I was endeavoring to determine, with the aid of Ahmed and a guide book, which portion of the ruins was the later work, and which that of the sister of Thothmes, the same dignified figure that I had seen on the river bank suddenly appeared from behind a neighboring column; and after saluting me gravely, proceeded, with much courtesy, and in the French tongue, to enlighten me on the question. It was soon evident that he was profoundly versed in the lore of ancient Egypt; and I was particularly struck with his manner when mentioning Hatasoo Thothmes; or, as he called her, Queen Amunuhet. His voice, when pronouncing her name, was lowered to a reverential murmur; and he passed the palm of his hand down his face from his forehead to his chin – an oriental gesture signifying homage.

"She was a remarkable woman," I ventured to observe.

"There was none like her," he replied. "She had many subjects, many worshipers; and one at least," he added, with a sigh, and clasping his hands on his heart, "still survives, and walks the earth in the likeness of a man!"

At this moment I was visited by an inspiration of memory; the recollection of my friend Haymaker's injunction flashed over me. "Pardon me if the question is indiscreet," I said, "but have I not the honor of addressing Monsieur Carigliano?"

He bowed slightly. "I once bore that name," he replied. "But, for twenty years, since I have lived here, it has been as a mask which I have cast aside. My true name might, perhaps, be found on one of these stones; but it has never been uttered by living lips."

"So this," I thought to myself, "is Haymaker's 'charming old maniac!' His acquaintance certainly seems to be worth cultivating. To hear him talk, one would suppose he had enjoyed personal relations with a princess who died thirty-five hundred years ago! That is a form of mania that ought to be enquired into." Aloud I said, "I wish I might hope to enjoy the benefit of further intercourse with you. I am deeply interested in all that appertains to the history of the Pharaohs; and especially," I added, meeting his eyes, "in the age of the great Thothmes."

The change of expression that lightened his face showed me that I had touched a favorable chord. "It is a long time," he said, "since I have held converse with a member of what are called the civilized races; but I feel moved to speak to you; and, since you express interest in a matter nearly affecting me, it will give me pleasure to oblige you. If you will come to this spot to-morrow evening alone, I will take you to my abode, and do my best to give you satisfaction." I thanked him heartily and promised to be on hand; he bowed, again saluted me gravely, and, retiring, was soon lost to sight behind the huge, thickly planted columns of the wondrous temple.

When I explained to Ahmed the purport of our conversation, he strongly advised me to have nothing to do with the adventure. He declared that "Kehr-el-Lans Effendi" was a powerful magician, and was quite capable of putting me under a spell and shutting me up for a thousand years in some forgotten tomb of the hills. He was often heard conversing in an unknown tongue with spectres; and was suspected of kidnapping the babies of the neighboring poor people, and offering them up as sacrifices to the heathen deities, whom he was supposed to worship. At the very least, Ahmed added, this redoubtable wizard would in some way compel me to pay for my escape from his clutches with an immense sum of money. In spite of these warnings, however, I held to my purpose; and about sunset the next day, I presented myself, alone, at the appointed spot. In a few minutes Carigliano made his appearance; and I followed him through the ruins for a distance of perhaps fifty yards. I then saw him stoop, and push against a slab of granite, set in an apparently solid portion of the temple wall. It moved, as if upon a hidden pivot, and disclosed a flight of steps leading downward. The darkness was intense; and for a moment I hesitated. Having come so far, however, I was determined to see the end of the adventure, and I accordingly descended. I heard his footsteps preceding me; and then a light flashed up, and I found myself in a subterranean chamber which bore evidence of being used as an abode. It was of fair height, and about twenty feet in length by fifteen in width. The walls were of polished stone, engraved with pictures and hieroglyphics. It contained a mattress, and various simple but sufficient appliances of life. Everything was neat and clean, and the air was pure, though the method of ventilation was not apparent. The light proceeded from a large lamp of antique design which depended from the ceiling.

Some cushions at the head of the room served as a divan, and upon this Carigliano motioned me to be seated, while he brought forward two long-stemmed pipes, which we lighted and smoked. For some time our conversation was laconic, and on indifferent topics. But at length my entertainer took the pipe from his lips, fixed his eyes upon me, and spoke as follows:

"I have admitted you to this chamber, whither no other guest has ever penetrated, not merely for the sake of gratifying your curiosity, but because the time has come when – if ever – the history of my life must be unfolded. Tomorrow it will be twenty years since the event occurred which revealed to me my destiny; and yours are the last mortal eyes that will behold me. Before I vanish forever, I desire to leave some testimony behind me as to my past and my future.

"I came to Egypt at twenty-eight years of age, as an attaché of a scientific expedition sent hereby the French government. My technical duties were to decipher and to take copies of the more important hieroglyphic writings and inscriptions in the tombs and temples. But I had, for a number of years previous, given my whole attention to the study of ancient Egyptian subjects, and was, even at that time, more profoundly versed than any other scholar in its problems and mysteries. I had always felt an especial and peculiar inclination toward these researches; it seemed to me far more like recalling what I had once known, than as breaking absolutely new ground in knowledge. The scenes and persons of the days of the Pharaohs were as vivid in my imagination as the memories of yesterday; I spoke their language and I comprehended their wisdom. And when, for the first time, I breathed the air of the Nile valley, and felt the sand of the desert beneath my feet, and beheld the mighty monuments of a vanished past, a voice in my heart seemed to tell me that this was no foreign country, but my home.

"It was here in Thebes that my duties chief lay, and it was here, also, that the mysterious home-feeling was most strong. From the first, I needed no guide; each step I took was on familiar ground; and as I gazed over the valley of ruins, some secret faculty of my mind reconstructed the scenes of four thousand years ago, and I saw once more the splendid city throbbing with life and sparkling with wealth, and witnessed the triumph of the kings, the processions and sacrifices of the priests, the glittering array of the soldiers, and the throng and tumult of the people. It was awaking dream, but it made the reality of the present seem unsubstantial. And ever and anon – especially when sauntering about the ruins of this temple – I was sensible of another feeling: a strange tremor and yearning of the heart, which I could not under- stand, yet which, could I have fathomed it, would, I thought, have proved the key whereby all else that was perplexing might be unlocked.

"One morning I arose early, and took my sketching materials, intending to spend the day in one or another of the great tombs that honeycomb the western hills. A foot-path leads over the ridge beyond Medinet Abou – a track of powdered limestone – and so, by a steep descent, brings one to the naked and desolate gorges beyond, where the Pharaohs were entombed. On reaching the summit of this ridge, I turned, and for a few moments gazed back on the wide valley of the Egyptian capital. The sun had just risen; its light flashed across the long curve of the Nile, and touched the lips of Memnon, as he sat eternal on his throne, his shadow falling far behind him over the green expanse of waving grain at his base. Involuntarily I bent forward, as if to catch the music of the response which, as tradition says, the colossal deity was wont to make to the salutation of the sun-god. And, in truth, a deep, melodious sound seemed to resound in the air – though whether proceeding from Memnon's lips, or from the heavens above, or from the depths of my own breast, I could not tell; a sound that resolved itself into words, saying, 'Pass on, thou favored one, and fear not! Thy queen awaits thee!' And down I rode into the shadow and silence of the abyss of tombs.

"Threading my way among loose boulders, and down a narrow and devious track, I reached the bottom of the descent, and wound along the length of the ravine. It had been my first intention to enter one of the tombs of the kings; but I was impelled to press onward, and at length I entered another gorge, lying further toward the heart of the hills, which, as I knew, had been set apart for the interment of the queens of Egypt. Here, a sense of solitude more profound than any I had before experienced came over me; but accompanying it, and even arising out of it, was a feeling of being conducted and inspired by some intelligence or personality not my own. I fell into an abstracted mood, in which I scarcely noted the way I was going; until at length I came involuntarily to a pause, and, as it were, awoke, and gazed around me.

"I was in a region so wild and savage, so naked, and desolate, that it seemed as if no human being before me, could ever have penetrated there. Rocky walls, wholly devoid of vegetation, arose on each side, and climbed heavenward, as if they would meet in the depths of the purple sky. Loose fragments of limestone hung on the ledges of the precipices, or lay in confused masses on the narrow floor of the tortuous valley. The sun, now some hours high, flung its white luster on the western walls, yet only the upper portion of them was illuminated. No sign of life, not even an insect or a bird, disturbed the stillness; no sound was audible but the hoof-tramps of the ass that I rode, which were echoed in exaggerated volume from the imprisoning cliffs. On my left hand was a vertical face of rock, the base seeming to rest upon a mounded slope, composed of detached and shattered blocks. I dismounted and clambered up this ascent, and then beheld, to my surprise, the distinct outlines of a picture graven into the limestone. It covered a space about four feet in length and breadth; and from its unusual situation, as well as from its remarkable intrinsic character, it strongly fixed my attention. It represented the body of a woman, apparently of high rank, lying on a pallet; and as I judged from certain accessories, about to be prepared for embalming. But beside her stood the figure of a man in soldier's garb, who, with outstretched hand, seemed about to take the woman's heart from her bosom. Some of the details of the picture indicated that it dated back as far as the time of

Thothmes – the period of the Hebrew Exodus; and yet the cutting of the lines was as sharp and undefaced as if the artist had but just given the finishing stroke of the chisel.

"I lost no time in setting up my easel, and, preparing to make a careful copy of this picture, I sat on a detached fragment of stone, with my right hand toward the face of the cliff; and in drawing I rested my hand on the mahl-stick, the end of which, for convenience, I rested against the design I was copying. As, from time to time, I had occasion to alter the position of my hand and of the mahl-stick, it happened that its point at length rested upon that part of the picture where was represented the heart of the woman upon the pallet. At the same moment I was conscious of a slight jar, causing me to make a false stroke; and the mahl-stick slipped from its place. I looked up and saw – what I had not noticed before – that the entire surface of the stone upon which the picture was engraven was sunk some distance below the surrounding surface of the rock. The depression was slight, not more than half an inch; but as I looked, it became gradually deeper and yet more deep; it was now two inches and still increasing.

"In the course of a few minutes, the pictured stone had receded as much as a foot, with a steady but slowly accelerating movement. Overcome with wonder, I continued to gaze at this singular phenomenon, until the stone was nearly out of sight. The direction it took was slightly inclined upward; and I perceived that the polished surfaces upon which it traveled were finely grooved, the grooves corresponding with ridges in the moving stone, which fitted into the former.

"By this time I had in some degree recovered my self-possession, and resolved to pursue the investigation of this marvel. I had brought a small lamp with me, for use in the tombs, and this I now lighted, and holding it in my hand, I crawled into the cavity left by the receding stone. This cavity was now about ten feet in depth, the sides as smooth as glass, and ascending at an angle of about twenty degrees. But after following it a little further, there was a sudden enlargement to double the former dimensions. I was now able to stand upright, and to walk on a passage beside the moving stone, instead of following in its track, as heretofore. It continued to travel upward beside me; and I now discovered that the immediate cause of its ascent was a fine but strong cable of bronze, which was fastened to its inner side, and was being drawn inward by some force beyond.

"The push which I had accidentally given with the mahl-stick to that particular spot in the picture which represented the woman's heart, had probably given the impetus which set the machinery in motion.

"After proceeding up the slippery incline for perhaps a hundred feet, I came to a level space, reaching to an unknown extent beyond, above, and on each hand. And here, by the dusky light of my lamp, I saw the semblance of a human figure, slowly and steadily turning the handle of a machine resembling a windlass, to the body of which the bronze cable was attached, and around which it was being wound. The figure wore the Egyptian head-dress and garb, and his face and limbs were of a brown hue; but so regular and rigid were his movements, and so imperfect was the light that I could not decide whether he was indeed a human being, or only himself a cunningly wrought part of the machine. I spoke to him but he returned no answer; and my own voice died away in a hollow whisper. As I stood there, the stone which had closed the entrance to the passage reached the summit of the ascent; and the figure, after putting a check in the cog of his wheel, sank down beside it, with his face upon his knees, and his hands clasped around his ankles, and became motionless in the attitude which, perhaps, had been undisturbed till now for more than thirty centuries.

"Shading my lamp with my hand, I moved along the walls of the chamber, which lay transversely across the ascending passage by which I had come. It was lined with white stucco on which were painted in brilliant colors such scenes of the daily life and habits of the Egyptians, as are customarily found on the walls of tombs. At length I came to an opening nearly opposite that by which I had entered; a corridor extending further into the mountain. After following it for awhile, I was brought to another corridor at right angles to it, going in both directions. I chose the turn to the left, and soon came to another turn, which descended for a long distance, and, just as it seemed to come to an end, admitted me into a hall much larger than the first, and more richly decorated. Here were represented the various ceremonies of the dead, the liturgies relating to their travels in the realm of shades, together with astronomical designs, and figures of monsters and of deities. In the center of the room, moreover, stood a large sarcophagus, richly engraved and ornamented, but empty. Here my explorations had apparently come to an end, for there was no visible outlet from the chamber. Accustomed as I was, however, to the concealments of these gigantic excavations, I felt assured that the end was not yet; and when I applied my shoulder to the upper end of the sarcophagus, it yielded to the pressure, and sliding forward, disclosed an oblong aperture in the floor beneath it, into which I unhesitatingly descended; and after wandering blindly for some minutes, first in one direction and then in another, I discerned a gleam of light in front of me, and, the next moment, entered an apartment the solemn grandeur of which seemed a fitting culmination of all that had preceded it.

"In the center of the lofty ceiling was a representation of the winged sun; and from it, or through it, proceeded a soft but powerful light, like that of phosphorescence in its nature, though bright enough to fill every corner of the vast hall with a clear radiance. The walls glowed with color, and here were the sacred figures of Isis and Osiris, of Horus, of Athor, Anubis, Ptah, and Nofre Atmos. But these things scarcely impressed themselves on my senses, for I was arrested by a far greater marvel. The figures on the walls were but shadows; but the floor of this mighty chamber was populous with forms of concrete substance; with men and women who breathed and moved and lived. They lived, and yet it scarcely seemed like life, so slow, so almost imperceptible were their movements. It was as if the space of an ordinary lifetime had been drawn out, for them, to the measure of myriad years; that days were to them as moments, and years as hours, and centuries as years; that while the breath came and went through their nostrils, a moon might wax and wane; and that the lifting of their faces was as the turning of the earth upon its axis. It was, perhaps, the dry, unchanging atmosphere of this region, hidden deep beneath the heart of the mountain, and separated from the world without for so many hundred years, that had wrought this torpor in them; I myself had become already sensible of an alteration in the beating of my pulse and a subtle lethargy in my movements. At first, as I looked upon this strange assemblage, they seemed each one to have paused, in the accomplishment of some characteristic act. One swarthy figure was shaping a necklet of gold brought from the deadly mines of Ethiopia; another, with mallet uplifted, was chiseling a statue; still another, held in his hand a scarabaeus, which he was about to polish. In another place, a man was in the act of blowing glass; near him was one with colors and a brush, making as if to add another touch to his picture; others were in the attitude of turning the potters wheel, of breaking flax, or of playing draughts. In one corner of the room were a group of women seated on the ground, with a ball which they seemed about to toss from one to another. But, as I contemplated them, their apparent insensibility resolved itself into motion, and I saw that they were not carven images, but that the hearts which had begun to beat when Moses was an infant, still sent the blood through their veins, though in pulses as measured as the tides of ocean.

"Meanwhile, my presence was seemingly unnoticed; no eye had met mine, and I was as apparently invisible to them as if the abyss of ages that lay between us had been as wide in space as it was in time. But, as I paused near the entrance of the hall, uncertain what to do, my ears caught a faint sound of solemn music; a portal of stone at the opposite extremity of the vista was slowly unfolded and from it issued, with lingering but majestic step, a stately procession. First came boys, bearing censers in the form of a golden arm, in the hollowed hand of which burned fragrant balls of *kyphi*, diffusing a heavy perfume. Then followed an array of tall and grave-looking men in white robes, and wearing on their foreheads the sacred ostrich feather, emblem of truth, and sign of the initiated priest. Next came a bevy of attendants, men and women, brilliantly attired, some carrying vessels of Phoenician glass that sparkled in the light; and one who bore on high and shook aloft the golden sistrum, with its bars and rings, emblem of Venus. Finally, borne in a litter on the shoulders of twelve Nubian slaves, appeared a woman, at the sight of whom my heart stood still and my breath failed me. She was dusky as the Nile at evening, and beautiful with a beauty that belongs to the morning of the world. Her eyes were long, black, and brilliant; and their gaze was royal. The outline of her smooth cheeks was oval, and her features were the features of the Pharaohs, but softened with all the loveliness of a woman. Above her low, broad forehead was placed the stately head-dress of an Egyptian princess; and, from her left temple, a long black braid, plaited with golden threads, hung down to her feet, as a sign of her royal line age. Her robe was purple, and of a tissue so delicate that the contours of her perfect form were discernible through its silky folds. Round her neck, and resting upon her bosom was a broad collar woven of pearls and precious stones; her arms were encircled by bracelets of massive gold. And in her girdle were woven turquoises from Serbal, talismans of good fortune. At her right hand crouched a monkey, sacred to Thoth, the god of her race; and on her left a white cat from Persia, in whose long silky fur the slender fingers the princess were hidden.

"When the bearers of the litter reached the center of the hall, beneath the illuminated semblance of the winged sun, they knelt and I slowly lowered their burden to the floor. Then, with a leisurely movement, the princess arose, and stood erect to her full and her eyes slowly themselves upon mine, remained opposite to her, in a vacant space alone; and a spell seemed to be upon me, so that I could move neither hand nor foot, nor remove my gaze from her transcendent countenance; yet it seemed to me a countenance that I had seen before, and had known well, and passionately loved. And it seemed to me that I was not myself, or that a truer self than I had hitherto known looked through my eyes and breathed through my nostrils.

"Then the princess spoke, in slow and measured tones, and in the clear tongue of ancient Egypt that I knew and remembered as my own.

"'Man,' she said, 'art thou he for whom I have waited?'

"And I answered her, 'I am Pantour, the son of Amosis.'

"And she said, 'Dost thou know me?'

"And I answered, 'Thou art Amunuhet the queen, the sister of Pharoah; thou art she who didst build the temple and the obelisk, and didst perform many mighty works.'

"And she said, 'Speak on, Pantour, and tell what thou knowest.'

"And I said, 'Queen, I loved thee; and thou didst deign to return my love. And our love was hidden, that none might know it. And in the midst of our love death came to thee. And when thy body was prepared for the embalmers, I stood beside thee, and there was none to see me.'

"And I put forth my hand and took thy heart out of thy bosom; because, I said, 'My heart is hers – let me, therefore, keep her heart in the stead of it. And I kept thy heart, and none knew what I had done. But when death overtook me also, I called my friend to me and charged him, saying: When I am dead, take thou my heart from my bosom and put in the place of it the heart of the Queen Amunuhet, whom I loved, but my heart thou shalt burn upon the altar of Osiris. And he swore to me to do as I had commanded. And in that same hour my spirit departed.'

"Then the queen answered, 'Thou hast said. Hear, now, what things have befallen me. For, when I entered into Kar-Neter, Osiris appeared to me, and mine eyes were dazzled, and my limbs were as if without life; neither could I speak, or eat food, or do battle with my enemies. But I prayed to the gods, and behold, my strength returned to me; and holding the sacred beetle above my head, I entered into Hades. Then did Typhon assail me with many monsters, and I fought sore combats with them; and I had been overcome, but that Nir gave me to eat of the tree of life, and the Divine Light instructed me. So I went on, and passed through many changes, and at last I entered once more into the body from which I had gone forth; and then, undergoing many trials and temptations, I sailed down the river that flows under the foundations of the world, and gained the Elysian fields. Then was I brought to the great judgment hall, where sat Osiris and the two and forty assessors, and to them I confessed both my evil and my good. But when they brought the scales of justice, with the ostrich feather of truth in the balance, and would have weighed my heart against the ostrich feather, behold the heart was gone out of my bosom. Then the judges took counsel together and said, "Thou shalt wait three thousand years, and half a thousand years, and he who took thy heart from thee shall come before thee; and if Jie will deliver it up to thee again, thou shalt enter into the bliss of Osiris.

"'Now, therefore, the time is come. Deliver back to me that which thou didst take from me; and when thou hast fulfilled thy course, and conquered Typhon, and overcome temptations, thou shalt afterward be united to me in the kingdom of Osiris, and the bliss of us twain shall be unto everlasting.'

"Thus spake the Queen Amunuhet; and when she had made an end of speaking, she sat on her throne, and waved her hand to the chief of priests, that he should take me, and lay me on the altar, and pluck her heart out of my breast. But then great fear came upon me, insomuch that I turned and fled away from before her. My limbs were as though sheathed in lead, and though I strove mightily, my steps were slow, for the air of the tomb had entered into my lungs, and all power of swiftness was gone from me. But the chief of the priests, and the other priests, and the attendants, pursued me; and though their steps also were slow, yet, by reason of the air that had entered the tomb from the outer world, they gathered ever new strength and swiftness ; so that it seemed as if I must be taken. Nevertheless, striving with all my might, I gained the upper platform where sat he who worked upon the windlass that lifted the stone from the entrance; and even then the hands of my pursuers were upon me. And he of the windlass arose, and loosed the check from the wheel, and the great stone slid down the incline toward its place. But I also plunged downward, and came in front of the stone as it descended, and was swept out before it, and the entrance was closed behind me; and I fell, and knew no more."

Here Carigliano paused, and bending forward as he sat, hid his face upon his knees. During several minutes there was silence; for he had spoken toward the close in a strain of exalted earnestness and passion; and the spell of his words was upon me. No doubt, the man must be mad; but his hallucination was so remarkable, and his expression of it so eloquent that, for the time being, I could not regain the equilibrium of my judgment.

"It was a narrow escape!" I said, at last. He sat erect, passed his hand over his forehead, and sighed. "It was a dastardly escape!" he replied; "and for these twenty years past I have repented it. I was found that evening by some wandering Arab, and taken back to Luxor. For some weeks I was ill with a fever; when I recovered, I tried in vain to find again the pictured stone; I have never set eyes upon it since. But, after a year of fruitless quest, Queen Amunuhet came to me one night in a dream, and told me that if, after waiting twenty years, I was prepared to make the restitution that she had demanded of me, the place of her tomb should be once more revealed to me, and I might enter in and deliver myself up to the altar. Tomorrow the period of trial will be fulfilled, and I shall be seen of men no more. You are the last to hear my voice, and to look upon my face. Henceforth, Pantour, the son of Amosis, belongs to the dead alone."

Soon after I returned to America, my friend Haymaker and I dined at Delmonico's; but I paid for the dinner.

"By the way," he exclaimed, as we sat over our coffee, "did you ever run across that fellow Carigliano?"

"Yes," I replied.

"Charming old maniac, isn't he?" continued my friend.

"He was a remarkable person, certainly."

"I think of running over to Egypt next winter, and I will make a point of looking him up again," said Haymaker, lighting a cigar.

"You won't find him," I answered. "The day after I last saw him he disappeared, and has never been seen or heard of since. But, from certain indications, it was thought he had wandered into the ruins of the tombs of the queens; probably he found his way into one of them and never got out again. He had related some of his history to me the day before; and certain hints that he let fall have made me suspect that he had a foreshadowing of what was to befall him."

"Poor fellow," said Haymaker. "What a pity! Romantic, too! Told you his story, did he? What was it?"

"It's eleven o'clock," said I; "I'm going to bed."

"Or you might write it out," continued my friend, as we put on our hats. "You're always writing things; and I dare say you might find somebody to print it."

A PROFESSOR OF EGYPTOLOGY

EGYPTOLOGY

GUY BOOTHBY

From seven o'clock in the evening until half past, that is to say for the half-hour preceding dinner, the Grand Hall of the Hotel Occidental, throughout the season, is practically a lounge, and is crowded with the most fashionable folk wintering in Cairo. The evening I am anxious to describe was certainly no exception to the rule. At the foot of the fine marble staircase – the pride of its owner – a well-known member of the French Ministry was chatting with an English Duchess whose pretty, but somewhat delicate, daughter was flirting mildly with one of the Sirdar's Bimbashis, on leave from the Soudan. On the right-hand lounge of the Hall an Italian Countess, whose antecedents were as doubtful as her diamonds, was apparently listening to a story a handsome Greek attaché was telling her; in reality, however, she was endeavouring to catch scraps of a conversation being carried on, a few feet away, between a witty Russian and an equally clever daughter of the United States. Almost every nationality was represented there, but unfortunately for our prestige, the majority were English. The scene was a brilliant one, and the sprinkling of military and diplomatic uniforms (there was a Reception at the Khedivial Palace later) lent an additional touch of colour to the picture. Taken altogether, and regarded from a political point of view, the gathering had a significance of its own.

At the end of the Hall, near the large glass doors, a handsome, elderly lady, with grey hair, was conversing with one of the leading English doctors of the place – a grey-haired, clever-looking man, who possessed the happy faculty of being able to impress everyone with whom he talked with the idea that he infinitely preferred his or her society to that of any other member of the world's population. They were discussing the question of the most suitable clothing for a Nile voyage, and as the lady's daughter, who was seated next her, had been conversant with her mother's ideas on the subject ever since their first visit to Egypt (as indeed had been the Doctor), she preferred to lie back on the divan and watch the people about her. She had large, dark, contemplative eyes. Like her mother she took life seriously, but in a somewhat different fashion.

One who has been bracketed third in the Mathematical Tripos can scarcely be expected to bestow very much thought on the comparative merits of Jger, as opposed to dresses of the Common or Garden flannel. From this, however, it must not be inferred that she was in any way a blue stocking, that is, of course, in the vulgar acceptation of the word. She was thorough in all she undertook, and for the reason that mathematics interested her very much the same way that Wagner, chess, and, shall we say, croquet, interest other people, she made it her hobby, and it must be confessed she certainly succeeded in it. At other times she rode, drove, played tennis and hockey, and looked upon her world with calm, observant eyes that were more disposed to find good than evil in it. Contradictions that we are, even to ourselves, it was only those who knew her intimately, and they were few and far between, who realised that, under that apparently sober, matter-of-fact personality, there existed a strong leaning towards the mysterious, or, more properly speaking, the occult. Possibly she herself would have been the first to deny this – but that I am right in my surmise this story will surely be sufficient proof.

Mrs Westmoreland and her daughter had left their comfortable Yorkshire home in September, and, after a little dawdling on the Continent, had reached Cairo in November – the best month to arrive, in my opinion, for then the rush has not set in, the hotel servants have not had sufficient time to become weary of their duties, and what is better still, all the best rooms have not been bespoken. It was now the middle of December, and the fashionable caravanserai, upon which they had for many years bestowed their patronage, was crowded from roof to cellar. Every day people were being turned away, and the manager's continual lament was that he had not another hundred rooms wherein to place more guests. He was a Swiss, and for that reason regarded hotel-keeping in the light of a profession.

On this particular evening Mrs Westmoreland and her daughter Cecilia had arranged to dine with Dr Forsyth – that is to say, they were to eat their meal at his table in order that they might meet a man of whom they had heard much, but whose acquaintance they had not as yet made.

The individual in question was a certain Professor Constanides – reputed one of the most advanced Egyptologists, and the author of several well-known works. Mrs Westmoreland was not of an exacting nature, and so long as she dined in agreeable company did not trouble herself very much whether it was with an English earl or a distinguished foreign savant.

"It really does not matter, my dear," she was wont to observe to her daughter. "So long as the cooking is good and the wine above reproach, there is absolutely nothing to choose between them. A Prime Minister and a country vicar are, after all, only men. Feed them well and they'll lie down and purr like tame cats. They don't want conversation." From this it will be seen that Mrs Westmoreland was well acquainted with her world. Whether Miss Cecilia shared her opinions is another matter. At any rate, she had been looking forward for nearly a fortnight to meeting Constanides, who was popularly supposed to possess an extraordinary intuitive knowledge – instinct, perhaps, it should be called – concerning the localities of tombs of the Pharaohs of the Eleventh, Twelfth and Thirteenth Dynasties.

"I am afraid Constanides is going to be late," said the Doctor, who had consulted his watch more than once. "I hope, in that case, as his friend and your host, you will permit me to offer you my apologies."

The Doctor at no time objected to the sound of his own voice, and on this occasion he was even less inclined to do so. Mrs Westmoreland was a widow with an ample income, and Cecilia, he felt sure, would marry ere long.

"He has still three minutes in which to put in an appearance," observed that young lady, quietly.

And then she added in the same tone, "Perhaps we ought to be thankful if he comes at all."

Both Mrs Westmoreland and her friend the Doctor regarded her with mildly reproachful eyes.

The former could not understand anyone refusing a dinner such as she felt sure the Doctor had arranged for them; while the latter found it impossible to imagine a man who would dare to disappoint the famous Dr Forsyth, who, having failed in Harley Street, was nevertheless coining a fortune in the land of the Pharaohs.

"My good friend Constanides will not disappoint us, I feel sure," he said, consulting his watch for the fourth time. "Possibly I am a little fast, at any rate I have never known him to be unpunctual. A remarkable – a very remarkable man is Constanides. I cannot remember ever to have met another like him. And such a scholar!"

Having thus bestowed his approval upon him the worthy Doctor pulled down his cuffs, straightened his tie, adjusted his pince-nez in his best professional manner, and looked round the hall as if searching for someone bold enough to contradict the assertion he had just made.

"You have, of course, read his Mythological Egypt," observed Miss Cecilia, demurely, speaking as if the matter were beyond doubt.

The Doctor looked a little confused.

"Ahem! Well, let me see," he stammered, trying to find a way out of the difficulty. "Well, to tell the truth, my dear young lady, I'm not quite sure that I have studied that particular work. As a matter of fact, you see, I have so little leisure at my disposal for any reading that is not intimately connected with my profession. That, of course, must necessarily come before everything else."

Miss Cecilia's mouth twitched as if she were endeavouring to keep back a smile. At the same moment the glass doors of the vestibule opened and a man entered. So remarkable was he that everyone turned to look at him – a fact which did not appear to disconcert him in the least.

He was tall, well shaped, and carried himself with the air of one accustomed to command. His face was oval, his eyes large and set somewhat wide apart. It was only when they were directed fairly at one that one became aware of the power they possessed. The cheekbones were a trifle high, and the forehead possibly retreated towards the jet-black hair more than is customary in Greeks. He wore neither beard nor moustache, thus enabling one to see the wide, firm mouth, the compression of the lips which spoke for the determination of their possessor. Those who had an eye for such things noted the fact that he was faultlessly dressed, while Miss Cecilia, who had the precious gift of observation largely developed, noted that, with the exception of a single ring and a magnificent pearl stud, the latter strangely set, he wore no jewellery of any sort. He looked about him for Dr Forsyth, and, when he had located him, hastened forward. "My dear friend," he said in English, which he spoke with scarcely a trace of foreign accent, "I must crave your pardon a thousand times if I have kept you waiting."

"On the contrary," replied the Doctor, effusively, "you are punctuality itself. Permit me to have the pleasure – the very great pleasure – of introducing you to my friends, Mrs Westmoreland and her daughter, Miss Cecilia, of whom you have often heard me speak." Professor Constanides bowed and expressed the pleasure he experienced in making their acquaintance. Though she could not have told you why, Miss Cecilia found herself undergoing very much the same sensation as she had done when she had passed up the Throne Room at her presentation. A moment later the gong sounded, and, with much rustling of skirts and fluttering of fans, a general movement was made towards the dining room.

As host, Dr Forsyth gave his arm to Mrs Westmoreland, Constanides following with Miss Cecilia. The latter was conscious of a vague feeling of irritation; she admired the man and his work, but she wished his name had been anything rather than what it was. (It should be here remarked that the last Constanides she had encountered had swindled her abominably in the matter of a turquoise brooch, and in consequence the name had been an offence to her ever since.) Dr Forsyth's table was situated at the further end, in the window, and from it a good view of the room could be obtained. The scene was an animated one, and one of the party, at least, I fancy, will never forget it – try how she may.

During the first two or three courses the conversation was practically limited to Cecilia and Constanides; the Doctor and Mrs Westmoreland being too busy to waste time on idle chatter.

Later, they became more amenable to the discipline of the table – or, in other words, they found time to pay attention to their neighbours.

Since then I have often wondered with what feelings Cecilia looks back upon that evening. In order, perhaps, to punish me for my curiosity, she has admitted to me since that she had never known, up to that time, what it was to converse with a really clever man. I submitted to the humiliation for the reason that we are, if not lovers, at least old friends, and, after all, Mrs Westmoreland's cook is one in a thousand.

From that evening forward, scarcely a day passed in which Constanides did not enjoy some portion of Miss Westmoreland's society. They met at the polo ground, drove in the Gezireh, shopped in the Muski, or listened to the band, over afternoon tea, on the balcony of Shepheard's Hotel. Constanides was always unobtrusive, always picturesque and invariably interesting. What was more to the point, he never failed to command attention whenever or wherever he might appear. In the Native Quarter he was apparently better known than in the European. Cecilia noticed that there he was treated with a deference such as one would only expect to be shown to a king. She marvelled, but said nothing. Personally, I can only wonder that her mother did not caution her before it was too late. Surely she must have seen how dangerous the intimacy was likely to become. It was old Colonel Bettenham who sounded the first note of warning. In some fashion or another he was connected with the Westmorelands, and therefore had more or less right to speak his mind.

"Who the man is, I am not in a position to say," he remarked to the mother; "but if I were in your place I should be very careful. Cairo at this time of year is full of adventurers."

"But, my dear Colonel," answered Mrs Westmoreland, "you surely do not mean to insinuate that the Professor is an adventurer. He was introduced to us by Dr Forsyth, and he has written so many clever books."

"Books, my dear madam, are not everything," the other replied judicially, and with that fine impartiality which marks a man who does not read. "As a matter of fact I am bound to confess that Phipps – one of my captains – wrote a novel some years ago, but only one. The mess pointed out to him that it wasn't good form, don't you know, so he never tried the experiment again. But as for this man, Constanides, as they call him, I should certainly be more than careful." I have been told since that this conversation worried poor Mrs Westmoreland more than she cared to admit, even to herself. To a very large extent she, like her daughter, had fallen under the spell of the Professor's fascination. Had she been asked, point blank, she would doubtless have declared that she preferred the Greek to the Englishman – though, of course, it would have seemed flat heresy to say so. And yet – well, doubtless you can understand what I mean without my explaining further. I am inclined to believe that I was the first to notice that there was serious trouble brewing. I could see a strained look in the girl's eyes for which I found if difficult to account. Then the truth dawned upon me, and I am ashamed to say that I began to watch her systematically. We have few secrets from each other now, and she has told me a good deal of what happened during that extraordinary time – for extraordinary it certainly was. Perhaps none of us realised what a unique drama we were watching – one of the strangest, I am tempted to believe, that this world of ours has ever seen. Christmas was just past and the New Year was fairly under way when the beginning of the end came. I think by that time even Mrs Westmoreland had arrived at some sort of knowledge of the case. But it was then too late to interfere. I am as sure that Cecilia was not in love with Constanides as I am of anything. She was merely fascinated by him, and to a degree that, happily for the peace of the world, is as rare as the reason for it is perplexing. To be precise, it was on Tuesday, January the 3rd, that the crisis came. On the evening of that day, accompanied by her daughter and escorted by Dr Forsyth, Mrs Westmoreland attended a reception at the palace of a certain Pasha, whose name I am obviously compelled to keep to myself. For the purposes of my story it is sufficient, however, that he is a man who prides himself on being up-to-date in most things, and for that and other reasons invitations to his receptions are eagerly sought after. In his drawing-room one may meet some of the most distinguished men in Europe, and on occasion it is even possible to obtain an insight into certain political intrigues that, to put it mildly, afford one an opportunity of reflecting on the instability of mundane affairs and of politics in particular.

The evening was well advanced before Constanides made his appearance. When he did, it was observed that he was more than usually quiet. Later, Cecilia permitted him to conduct her into the balcony, whence, since it was a perfect moonlight night, a fine view of the Nile could be obtained. Exactly what he said to her I have never been able to discover; I have, however, her mother's assurance that she was visibly agitated when she rejoined her. As a matter of fact, they returned to the hotel almost immediately, when Cecilia, pleading weariness, retired to her room.

And now this is the part of the story you will find as difficult to believe as I did. Yet I have indisputable evidence that it is true. It was nearly midnight and the large hotel was enjoying the only quiet it knows in the twenty-four hours. I have just said that Cecilia had retired, but in making that assertion I am not telling the exact truth, for though she had bade mother "Goodnight" and had gone to her room, it was not to rest. Regardless of the cold night air she had thrown open the window, and was standing looking out into the moonlit street. Of what she was thinking I do not know, nor can she remember. For my own part, however, I incline to the belief that she was in a semi-hypnotic condition and that for the time being her mind was a blank.

From this point I will let Cecilia tell the story herself.

How long I stood at the window I cannot say; it may have been only five minutes, it might have been an hour. Then, suddenly, an extraordinary thing happened. I knew that it was imprudent, I was aware that it was even wrong, but an overwhelming craving to go out seized me. I felt as if the house were stifling me, and that if I did not get out into the cool night air, and within a few minutes, I should die. Stranger still, I felt no desire to battle with the temptation. It was as if a will infinitely stronger than my own was dominating me and that I was powerless to resist. Scarcely conscious of what I was doing I changed my dress, and then, throwing on a cloak, switched off the electric light and stepped out into the corridor. The white-robed Arab servants were lying about on the floor as is their custom; they were all asleep. On the thick carpet of the great staircase my steps made no sound. The hall was in semi-darkness and the watchman must have been absent on his rounds, for there was no one there to spy upon me. Passing through the vestibule I turned the key of the front door. Still success attended me, for the lock shot back with scarcely a sound and I found myself in the street. Even then I had no thought of the folly of this escapade. I was merely conscious of the mysterious power that was dragging me on. Without hesitation I turned to the right and hastened along the pavement, faster I think than I had ever walked in my life. Under the trees it was comparatively dark, but out in the roadway it was well-nigh as bright as day. Once a carriage passed me and I could hear its occupants, who were French, conversing merrily – otherwise I seemed to have the city to myself. Later I heard a muezzin chanting his call to prayer from the minaret of some mosque in the neighbourhood, the cry being taken up and repeated from other mosques. Then at the corner of a street I stopped as if in obedience to a command. I can recall the fact that I was trembling, but for what reason I could not tell. I say this to show that while I was incapable of returning to the hotel, or of exercising my normal will power, I still possessed the faculty of observation.

I had scarcely reached the corner referred to, which, as a matter of fact, I believe I should recognise if I saw it again, when the door of a house opened and a man emerged. It was Professor Constanides, but his appearance at such a place and at such an hour, like everything else that happened that night, did not strike me as being in any way extraordinary.

"You have obeyed me," he said by way of greeting. "That is well. Now let us be going – the hour is late."

As he said it there came the rattle of wheels and a carriage drove swiftly round the corner and pulled up before us. My companion helped me into it and took his place beside me. Even then, unheard-of as my action was, I had no thought of resisting.

"What does it mean?" I asked. "Oh, tell me what it means? Why am I here?"

"You will soon know," was his reply, and his voice took a tone I had never noticed in it before. We had driven some considerable distance, in fact, I believe we had crossed the river, before either of us spoke again.

"Think," said my companion, "and tell me whether you can remember ever having driven with me before?"

"We have driven together many times lately," I replied. "Yesterday to the polo, and the day before to the Pyramids."

"Think again," he said, and as he did so he placed his hand on mine. It was as cold as ice.

However, I only shook my head.

"I cannot remember," I answered, and yet I seemed to be dimly conscious of something that was too intangible to be a recollection. He uttered a little sigh and once more we were silent. The horses must have been good ones for they whirled us along at a fast pace. I did not take much interest in the route we followed, but at last something attracted my attention and I knew that we were on the road to Gizeh. A few moments later the famous Museum, once the palace of the ex-Khedive Ismail, came into view. Almost immediately the carriage pulled up in the shadow of the Lebbek trees and my companion begged me to alight. I did so, whereupon he said something, in what I can only suppose was Arabic, to his coachman, who whipped up his horses and drove swiftly away.

"Come," he said, in the same tone of command as before, and then led the way towards the gates of the old palace. Dominated as my will was by his I could still notice how beautiful the building looked in the moonlight. In the daytime it presents a faded and unsubstantial appearance, but now, with its Oriental tracery, it was almost fairylike. The Professor halted at the gates and unlocked them. How he had admitted us, I cannot say. It suffices that, almost before I was aware of it, we had passed through the garden and were ascending the steps to the main entrance. The doors behind us, we entered the first room. It is only another point in this extraordinary adventure when I declare that even now I was not afraid; and yet to find oneself in such a place and at such an hour at any other time would probably have driven me beside myself with terror.

The moonlight streamed in upon us, revealing the ancient monuments and the other indescribable memorials of those long-dead ages. Once more my conductor uttered his command and we went on through the second room, passed the Skekh-El-Beled and the Seated Scribe. Room after room we traversed, and to do so it seemed to me that we ascended stairs innumerable. At last we came to one in which Constanides paused. It contained numerous mummy cases and was lighted by a skylight through which the rays of the moon streamed in. We were standing before one which I remembered to have remarked on the occasion of our last visit. I could distinguish the paintings upon it distinctly. Professor Constanides, with the deftness which showed his familiarity with the work, removed the lid and revealed to me the swathed-up figure within. The face was uncovered and was strangely well-preserved. I gazed down on it, and as I did so a sensation that I had never known before passed over me. My body seemed to be shrinking, my blood to be turning to ice.

For the first time I endeavoured to exert myself, to tear myself from the bonds that were holding me. But it was in vain. I was sinking – sinking – sinking – into I knew not what. Then the voice of the man who had brought me to the place sounded in my ears as if he were speaking from a long way off. After that a great light burst upon me, and it was as if I were walking in a dream; yet I knew it was too real, too true to life to be a mere creation of my fancy.

It was night and the heavens were studded with stars. In the distance a great army was encamped and at intervals the calls of the sentries reached me. Somehow I seemed to feel no wonderment at my position. Even my dress caused me no surprise. To my left, as I looked towards the river, was a large tent, before which armed men paced continually. I looked about me as if I expected to see someone, but there was no one.

"It is for the last time," I told myself. "Come what may, it shall be the last time!"

Still I waited, and as I did so I could hear the night wind sighing through the rushes on the river's bank. From the tent near me – for Usirtasen, son of Amenemhait – was then fighting against the Libyans and was commanding his army in person – came the sound of revelry. The air blew cold from the desert and I shivered, for I was but thinly clad. Then I hid myself in the shadow of a great rock that was near at hand. Presently I caught the sound of a footstep, and there came into view a tall man, walking carefully, as though he had no desire that the sentries on guard before the Royal tent should become aware of his presence in the neighbourhood. As I saw him I moved from where I was standing to meet him. He was none other than Sinfihit – younger son of

Amenemhait and brother of Usirtasen – who was at that moment conferring with his generals in the tent.

I can see him now as he came towards me, tall, handsome, and defiant in his bearing, as a man should be. He walked with the assured step of one who has been a soldier and trained to warlike exercises from his youth up. For a moment I regretted the news I had to tell him – but only for a moment. I could hear the voice of Usirtasen in the tent, and after that I had no thought for anyone else.

"Is it thou, Nofrit?" he asked as soon as he saw me.

"It is I!" I replied. "You are late, Sinfihit. You tarry too long over the wine cups."

"You wrong me, Nofrit," he answered, with all the fierceness for which he was celebrated. "I have drunk no wine this night. Had I not been kept by the Captain of the Guard I should have been here sooner. Thou art not angry with me, Nofrit?"

"Nay, that were presumption on my part, my lord," I answered. "Art thou not the King's son, Sinfihit?"

"And by the Holy Ones I swear that it were better for me if I were not," he replied. "Usirtasen, my brother, takes all and I am but the jackal that gathers up the scraps wheresoever he may find them." He paused for a moment. "However, all goes well with our plot. Let me but have time and I will yet be ruler of this land and of all the Land of Khem beside." He drew himself up to his full height and looked towards the sleeping camp. It was well known that between the brothers there was but little love, and still less trust.

"Peace, peace," I whispered, fearing lest his words might be overheard. "You must not talk so, my lord. Should you by chance be heard you know what the punishment would be!"

He laughed a short and bitter laugh. He was well aware that Usirtasen would show him no mercy. It was not the first time he had been suspected, and he was playing a desperate game. He came a step closer to me and took my hand in his. I would have withdrawn it – but he gave me no opportunity. Never was a man more in earnest than he was then.

"Nofrit," he said, and I could feel his breath upon my cheek, "what is my answer to be? The time for talking is past; now we must act. As thou knowest, I prefer deeds to words, and to-morrow my brother Usirtasen shall learn that I am as powerful as he."

Knowing what I knew I could have laughed him to scorn for his boastful speech. The time, however, was not yet ripe, so I held my peace. He was plotting against his brother, whom I loved, and it was his desire that I should help him. That, however, I would not do. "Listen," he said, drawing even closer to me, and speaking in a voice that showed me plainly how much in earnest he was, "thou knowest how much I love thee. Thou knowest that there is nought I would not do for thee or for thy sake. Be but faithful to me now and there is nothing thou shalt ask in vain of me hereafter. All is prepared, and ere the moon is gone I shall be Pharaoh and reign beside Amenemhait, my father."

"Are you so sure that your plans will not miscarry?" I asked, with what was almost a sneer at his recklessness – for recklessness it surely was to think that he could induce an army that had been admittedly successful to swerve in its allegiance to the general who had won its battles for it, and to desert in the face of the enemy. Moreover, I knew that he was wrong in believing that his father cared more for him than for Usirtasen, who had done so much for the kingdom, and who was beloved by high and low alike. But it was not in Sinfihit's nature to look upon the dark side of things. He had complete confidence in himself and in his power to bring his conspiracy against his father and brother to a successful issue. He revealed to me his plans, and, bold though they were, I could see that it was impossible that they could succeed. And in the event of his failing, what mercy could he hope to receive? I knew Usirtasen too well to think that he would show any. With all the eloquence I could command I implored him to abandon the attempt, or at least to delay it for a time. He seized my wrist and pulled me to him, peering fiercely into my face.

"Art playing me false?" he asked. "If it is so it were better that you should drown yourself in yonder river. Betray me and nothing shall save you – not even Pharaoh himself."

That he meant what he said I felt convinced. The man was desperate; he was staking all he had in the world upon the issue of his venture. I can say with truth that it was not my fault that we had been drawn together, and yet on this night of all others it seemed as if there were nothing left for me but to side with him or to bring about his downfall.

"Nofrit," he said, after a short pause, "is it nothing, thinkest thou, to be the wife of a Pharaoh? Is it not worth striving for, particularly when it can be so easily accomplished?"

I knew, however, that he was deluding himself with false hopes. What he had in his mind could never come to pass. I was like dry grass between two fires. All that was required was one small spark to bring about a conflagration in which I should be consumed.

"Harken to me, Nofrit," he continued. "You have means of learning Usirtasen's plans. Send me word to-morrow as to what is in his mind and the rest will be easy. Your reward shall be greater than you dream of."

Though I had no intention of doing what he asked, I knew that in his present humour it would be little short of madness to thwart him. I therefore temporised with him, and allowed him to suppose that I would do as he wished, and then, bidding him good-night, I sped away towards the hut where I was lodged. I had not been there many minutes when a messenger came to me from Usirtasen, summoning me to his presence. Though I could not understand what it meant I hastened to obey.

On arrival there I found him surrounded by the chief officers of his army. One glance at his face was sufficient to tell me that he was violently angry with someone, and I had the best of reasons for believing that someone was myself.

Alas! It was as I had expected. Sinfihit's plot had been discovered; he had been followed and watched, and my meeting with him that evening was known. I protested my innocence in vain. The evidence was too strong against me.

"Speak, girl, and tell what thou knowest," said Usirtasen, in a voice I had never heard him use before. "It is the only way by which thou canst save thyself. Look to it that thy story tallies with the tales of others!"

I trembled in every limb as I answered the questions he put to me. It was plain that he no longer trusted me, and that the favour I had once found in his eyes was gone, never to return. "It is well," he said when I had finished my story. "And now we will see thy partner – the man who would have put me – the Pharaoh who is to be – to the sword had I not been warned in time."

He made a sign to one of the officers who stood by, whereupon the latter left the tent, to return a few moments later with Sinfihit.

"Hail, brother!" said Usirtasen, mockingly, as he leaned back in his chair and looked at him through half-shut eyes. "You tarried but a short time over the wine cup this night. I fear it pleased thee but little. Forgive me; on another occasion better shall be found for thee lest thou shouldst deem us lacking in our hospitality."

"There were matters that needed my attention and I could not stay," Sinfihit replied, looking his brother in the face. "Thou wouldst not have me neglect my duties."

"Nay! Nay! Maybe they were matters that concerned our personal safety?" Usirtasen continued, still with the same gentleness. "Maybe you heard that there were those in our army who were not well disposed towards us? Give me their names, my brother, that due punishment may be meted out to them."

Before Sinfihit could reply, Usirtasen had sprung to his feet.

"Dog!" he cried, "darest thou prate to me of matters of importance when thou knowest thou hast been plotting against me and my father's throne. I have doubted thee these many months and now all is made clear. By the Gods, the Holy Ones, I swear that thou shalt die for this ere cock-crow.

It was at this moment that Sinfihit became aware of my presence. A little cry escaped him, and his face told me as plainly as any words could speak that he believed that I had betrayed him. He was about to speak, probably to denounce me, when the sound of voices reached us from outside.

Usirtasen bade the guards to ascertain what it meant, and presently a messenger entered the tent.

He was travel-stained and weary. Advancing towards where Usirtasen was seated, he knelt before him.

"Hail, Pharaoh," he said. "I come to three from the Palace of Titoui."

An anxious expression came over Usirtasen's face as he heard this. I also detected beads of perspiration on the brow of Sinfihit. A moment latter it was known to us that Amenemhait was dead, and, therefore, Usirtasen reigned in his stead. The news was so sudden, and the consequences so vast, that it was impossible to realise quite what it meant. I looked across at Sinfihit and his eyes met mine. He seemed to be making up his mind about something. Then with lightning speed he sprang upon me; a dagger gleamed in the air; I felt as if a hot iron had been thrust into my breast, and after that I remember no more.

As I felt myself falling I seemed to wake from my dream – if dream it were – to find myself standing in the Museum by the mummy case, and with Professor Constanides by my side.

"You have seen," he said. "You have looked back across the centuries to that day when, as Nofrit, I believed you had betrayed me, and killed you. After that I escaped from the camp and fled into Kaduma. There I died; but it was decreed that my soul should never know peace till we had met again and you had forgiven me. I have waited all these years, and see – we meet at last."

Strange to say, even then the situation did not strike me as being in any way improbable. Yet now, when I see it set down in black and white, I find myself wondering that I dare to ask anyone in their sober senses to believe it to be true. Was I in truth that same Nofrit who, four thousand years before, had been killed by Sinfihit, son of Amenemhait, because he believed that I had betrayed him? It seemed incredible, and yet, if it were a creation of my imagination, what did the dream mean? I fear it is a riddle of which I shall probably never know the answer. My failure to reply to his question seemed to cause him pain.

"Nofrit," he said, and his voice shook with emotion, "think what your forgiveness means to me. Without it I am lost both here and hereafter."

His voice was low and pleading and his face in the moonlight was like that of a man who knew the uttermost depths of despair.

"Forgive – forgive," he cried again, holding out his hands to me. "If you do not, I must go back to the sufferings which have been my portion since I did the deed which wrought my ruin."

I felt myself trembling like a leaf.

"If it is as you say, though I cannot believe it, I forgive you freely," I answered, in a voice that I scarcely recognised as my own.

For some moments he was silent, then he knelt before me and took my hand, which he raised to his lips. After that, rising, he laid his head upon the breast of the mummy before which we were standing. Looking down at it he addressed it thus:

"Rest, Sinfihit, son of Amenemhait – for that which was foretold for thee is now accomplished, and the punishment which was decreed is at an end. Henceforth thou mayest sleep in peace."

After that he replaced the lid of the coffin, and when this was done he turned to me.

"Let us be going," he said, and we went together through the rooms by the way we had come.

Together we left the building and passed through the gardens out into the road beyond. There we found the carriage waiting for us, and we took our places in it. Once more the horses sped along the silent road, carrying us swiftly back to Cairo. During the drive not a word was spoken by either of us. The only desire I had left was to get back to the hotel and lay my aching head upon my pillow. We crossed the bridge and entered the city. What the time was I had no idea, but I was conscious that the wind blew chill as if in anticipation of the dawn. At the same corner whence we had started, the coachman stopped his horses and I alighted, after which he drove away as if he had received his orders beforehand.

"Will you permit me to walk with you as far as your hotel?" said Constanides, with his customary politeness.

I tried to say something in reply, but my voice failed me. I would much rather have been alone, but as he would not allow this we set off together. At the corner of the street in which the hotel is situated we stopped.

"Here we must part," he said. Then, after a pause, he added, "And for ever. From this moment I shall never see your face again."

"You are leaving Cairo?" was the only thing I could say.

"Yes, I am leaving Cairo," he replied with peculiar emphasis. "My errand here is accomplished. You need have no fear that I shall ever trouble you again."

"I have no fear," I answered, though I am afraid it was only a half truth.

He looked earnestly into my face.

"Nofrit," he said, "for, say what you will, you are the Nofrit I would have made my Queen and have loved beyond all other women, never again will it be permitted you to look into the past as you did to-night. Had things been ordained otherwise we might have done great things together, but the gods willed that it should not be. Let it rest therefore. And now ¬– farewell! To-night I go to the rest for which I have so long been seeking."

Without another word he turned and left me. Then I went on to the hotel. How it came about I cannot say, but the door was open and I passed quickly in. Once more, to my joy, I found the watchman was absent from the hall. Trembling lest anyone might see me, I sped up the stairs and along the corridor, where the servants lay sleeping just as I had left them, and so to my room. Everything was exactly as I had left it, and there was nothing to show that my absence had been suspected. Again I went to the window, and, in a feeling of extraordinary agitation, looked out. Already there were signs of dawn in the sky. I sat down and tried to think over all that had happened to me that evening, endeavouring to convince myself, in the face of indisputable evidence, that it was not real and that I had only dreamt it. Yet it would not do! At last, worn out,

I retired to rest. As a rule I sleep soundly; it is scarcely, however, a matter for wonderment that I did not do so on this occasion.

Hour after hour I tumbled and tossed – thinking – thinking – thinking. When I rose and looked into the glass I scarcely recognised myself. Indeed, my mother commented on my fagged appearance when we met at the breakfast table.

"My dear child, you look as if you had been up all night," she said, and little did she guess, as she nibbled her toast, that there was a considerable amount of truth in her remark.

Later she went shopping with a lady staying in the hotel, while I went to my room to lie down.

When we met again at lunch it was easy to see that she had some news of importance to communicate.

"My dear Cecilia," she said, "I have just seen Dr Forsyth, and he has given me a terrible shock. I don't want to frighten you, my girl, but have you heard that Professor Constanides was found dead in bed this morning? It is a most terrible affair! He must have died during the night!"

I am not going to pretend that I had any reply ready to offer her at that moment.

THE BLOCK OF BRONZE

HERBERT CROTZER

"So you good people thought I gave you 'the truth, the whole truth, and nothing but the truth,' did you?"

"Well, yes," I replied; "we all noticed how your story coincided with what has been published concerning the operations, and we were especially struck with the way you seemed to cover all the details of the job; how anxious, in fact, you appeared to be to leave out no point or circumstance that would throw light on your subject."

"Just so," said my friend; "I noticed that you all seemed to take it in as gospel truth, but the fact is, Frank, the most remarkable thing that happened over there was omitted from my yarn altogether."

I gazed at the speaker in astonishment, but he pulled away at his disreputable old pipe as unconcernedly as if he had said the most natural thing in the world.

Edward Van Zant, the explorer, was my lifelong friend, college chum, and now my honoured guest.

At college, Ned went in for dead and hidden things, archaeology and all that; and after, absorbing all that the best schools of this and other countries could teach on those lines, he started in, digging here, prodding there, until he had punctured holes in the earth's crust in pretty much every country on the globe.

Now, after ten years of this sort of thing, he was back in his native city, with a hat full of medals and decorations, and his fame as an explorer and archaeologist established throughout civilization.

We had just returned from a dinner given in his honor by a local scientific body, and had adjourned to the library for a smoke and a chat before retiring.

Our talk, so far, had referred to his little speech concerning his latest most important discoveries in Egypt, and to the effect it had produced on his hearers.

That he should now acknowledge having intentionally omitted facts of importance bearing upon his work was, to put it mildly, an eye-opener, and I could only look the astonishment I felt.

After a few thoughtful puffs, Ned said: "Frank, what really did happen is so strange, so inconceivable, that were I to tell the story to the world, it would laugh at me, say I lied, or was crazy."

"See here," he exclaimed, throwing off coat and collar, and uncovering the upper portion of his brawny chest and shoulders; "here's a bit of evidence of the truth of my tale, that I always carry with me."

I looked, and on his throat, underneath the heavy beard, I beheld a lot of scars which, extending downward, spread out into rows that covered every inch almost of the body exposed to view. It looked as if some sharp-toothed instrument, like a rake, had gouged out the flesh, or as though the man had been seared by hot irons.

"Good heavens!" I cried. "What beast or thing did that?"

"Aye, you may well put it that way," replied Ned, resuming his garments and seat; "it was a Thing, the most horrible God ever allowed on his footstool."

"I told you this evening," he went on, "that I had set out to investigate a small pyramid which stood in the desert, a mile or two from the oasis that had been my base of operations while exploring in that part of Egypt. I explained how we spent weeks digging and sounding before success rewarded us; how we finally broke into the tomb underneath the pyramid, and discovered the mummies and the stores of jewels and ornaments, which proved that the bodies had lain there, undisturbed by mortal hand, since the days they were buried – six thousand years before. All these things occurred precisely as I stated. There was nothing here to conceal.'

"You also heard of the attempt made to steal some of our treasures from the building in which they were temporarily stored; how one of my men on guard at the time was murdered, and how I, while seeking traces of the murderer in the camp of a band of roving Arabs, was attacked in the tent of the sheik, and forced to kill that individual to save my own life. That part of the story was true enough, so far as it went, but the most important facts were omitted. What actually did occur was this: –

"After working for weeks on the job, and gaining nothing but hard labor for our pains, I got discouraged, and one evening I announced to the men that if the next day or two brought no better luck, I would abandon the undertaking. I also told them that, in order to be in good trim for what might be our last attempt, they should do no work next day, and suggested that they should go to headquarters at once and take a rest. They were glad enough to get a holiday, after working as they had done, and soon all hands were on their way to the oasis, where my party, with the exception of the native laborers, put up when off duty.

"I remained in camp, and early next morning made a tour of the diggings. I examined every hole and sounding, made careful measurements, and tried to think out some new plan of operation that would yield tangible results. Finally, I returned to my tent and was about to seat myself in front of it, when I happened to see far out on the desert what my field-glass showed me was a caravan. It was a small affair – a dozen camels, loaded, and as many horsemen. It was headed for the oasis, and would come no nearer to the pyramid.

"As I stood watching the travellers, a horseman, riding ahead, left the column, and followed closely by what seemed, at that distance, a child, also mounted, rode rapidly towards me, the rest continuing on their way. When they got within several rods of me the pair pulled up, and the man, dismounting, stood quietly while his little companion proceeded to the pyramid and passed behind it, out of sight, followed by the riderless horse. Then the stranger walked forward until but a few yards separated us, when he stopped, and instead of the usual salaam, made a profound bow. He uttered not a word, but stood with arms folded, as if waiting for me to address him. He was very tall, straight as a spear, and wore the ordinary long white garment of the desert tribes.

"Irritated by the man's silence, I finally cried out, in Arabic, 'Who are you, and what do you want?'

"At this, my visitor came up close to me, replying as he did so, 'Who I am matters little; what I want you will give me in return for services I shall render you.'

"I was astonished, as you may well suppose, but ere I could speak, he continued: 'I know you are Edward Van Zant, the explorer. I know what you expect to find here, and how you have worked, without avail, until you have become discouraged. How I know these things concerns me alone. What concerns you is the fact that I, and I alone, can show you how to enter the tomb, which is here, as you surmise, and I will do so, provided you give me my choice of what you may find in it.'

"Although amazed at the man's knowledge of me and my movements, and distrusting him instinctively, I determined to force his hand, if possible, and find out his demands and what he proposed to do.

"Inviting him to sit down on a block of stone at my side, I said, 'You seem to know so much, and to be so powerful, why haven't you opened this tomb yourself?'

"'Because,' he replied, 'to do so requires engineering skill and mechanical appliances, which it is impossible for me to obtain hereabouts.'

"'What do you require in payment for your services?' was my next query.

"'A mummy,' he replied.

"'A mummy!' I exclaimed; 'why, these are the things I am most anxious to find myself, and you may demand what is of the greatest value to me.'

"'Listen, said the man; 'you will find bodies of kings and queens who lived at a time of which man has no record. These shall be yours, together with all the jewels and ornaments buried with them. You will also discover a case in which is the body of a dwarf, an insignificant thing compared to all the other treasures. This case and contents are all I ask, and I swear there is nothing in them that would be of value to you. As a guarantee that I am not trifling or trying to deceive you, take these;' saying which, he drew out a small pouch, from which he poured into my hands a dozen or so of the finest diamonds I ever saw. 'If I fail you in any way, ' he continued, 'or you do not find everything as I say, these shall be yours.'

"To be brief, I agreed to the proposal, the Arab accepting my verbal promise to live up to the contract.

"'Now,' said he, when the preliminaries were settled – and here is where the incomprehensible part of the affair begins – 'I will fulfil my part of the agreement.'

"With this he gave a shrill whistle, following upon which the little fellow came out from behind the pyramid, and, with the other horse by his side, rode up to us and dismounted. Making a low bow to me, he stepped in front of the other and gazed, without a word, into his face, as if awaiting a command.

"I now saw that, instead of being a child, the newcomer was a dwarf, twenty years old, or thereabouts. He was a handsome, dark-eyed little fellow, with a red fez and zouave-like outfit that became him well. That he was uncommonly active and powerful, I had reason to thank my stars later on.

"At a word, in some strange dialect, the dwarf detached from the Arab's saddle and handed him a scimitar, the hilt and scabbard of which were covered with some scaly material that I afterward found to be the skin of a snake.

"Another word or two, in the same unknown tongue, and the little man drew back and faced the big one. As he did so, I caught a look of aversion on his face, and his eyes gleamed as if with hatred or defiance. The Arab noticed the look and returned it with an ugly scowl and a growl that sounded like a threat.

"Arising from his seat, he unsheathed the blade, and the next moment the dwarf seemed to be standing in the midst of a rain of fire. The Arab was laying about him with the weapon, and such sword play, I'm free to say, I never saw before, and never will see again while I life.

"The exhibition ceased as suddenly as it began. The dwarf stood with arms folded, and a queer, far-away look in his eyes. The Arab gazed at him a moment, and then, tearing the covering from the hilt, held that part of the scimitar close to his face.

"The hilt was of gold, beautifully chased and set with gems. On the end was an immense diamond that blazed in the sunlight like flame, and this was waved slowly before the dwarf's eyes until the lids dropped and he seemingly slept.

"As the Arab sheathed the sword and replaced the covering on the hilt, he said, 'Ali grows rebellious and objects to serving me; he must be disciplined.' Then, producing a sheet of paper and pencil, he laid them on the stone he had vacated, and, stepping in front of his subject, he gave what seemed to be a command in a loud, imperious tone, and in the same outlandish tongue he had used before.

"In a few moments the dwarf made reply in a muffled voice that sounded as if it came from underground.

"Then, as though interpreting, the Arab said, 'He tells me a great rock closes the entrance to the tunnel leading to the tomb, but he has passed through it.'

"For the next few minutes not a word was spoken. Then came a little cry from the dwarf, followed by a few sentences in a broken, gasping voice, as of one utterly exhausted. At another command, he staggered to the stone, and, seizing the pencil, he rapidly laid off on the paper what looked like the ground plan of a building. A lot of writing followed, and when this was completed the Arab handed me what turned out to be an accurate plan of the tomb and tunnel, with full directions for entering them.

"As Ali finished, he fell over in a dead faint; but a few drops from a vial, which the Arab held to his lips, soon restored him. Then the strange pair mounted and set off towards the oasis, and that was the last I saw of them for some days.

"In the evening I rode back to camp, where I learned that the newcomers had pitched their tents on the outskirts of the oasis, and seemed a quiet, well-disposed lot.

"I told my associates that the sheik had visited me and given me certain directions for finding and entering the tomb, for which, if they proved correct, he was to receive an ordinary mummy, in case any such were found.

"Not until we broke into the tomb and laid profane hands upon its contents, did the sheik put in an appearance at the workings.

"On that momentous day he came, bright and early, accompanied by four of his people, big, solemn-looking fellows. Seeing me out, he obtained permission to enter the tomb with me, and while there, no movement of ours, as we opened sarcophagi and took out mummies, jewels, and what not, escaped his watchful eye.

"For a long time there was no sign of the wooden case, but when most of the things had been removed he called attention to a crack in the wall in front of him. A few blows of a pick disclosed a niche, the front of which had been walled up. Within stood upright a covered box, and in this we found, as the Arab foretold, the body of a dwarf. It was that of a man with immensely broad shoulders, and arms reaching nearly to the knees. The face was hideous, and a ferocious smile had drawn the thin lips apart, disclosing teeth sharp, and gleaming like those of a beast.

"Strange to say, the body was not swathed in bandages, as mummies always are, but clothed in a loose garment of some peculiar stuff that bore our rough handling without a break.

"Great bunches of muscle covered the frame, and nowhere was there an opening or, in fact, any indication that an internal organ had been removed, as is always done in the case of mummies.

"The body, with its stiffened limbs, was like that of one in a cataleptic fit or trance, and represented, as I supposed, some strange and wonderful process of embalming, of which this was the only specimen in existence.

"The head rested on an oblong block, covered with a piece of the same material of which the garment was made, and on this odd pillow the Arab's eyes were fastened with the most intense eagerness. Before I could lay a hand on it, he had replaced the lid of the box, saying as he did so, 'I suppose I may take this now? You have seen how insignificant it is, and I desire to get it to my tent at once.'

"Reluctantly I gave my consent, and his own men carried the case to the surface and placed it in the cart I loaned him to convey his prize to camp.

"An hour or two after they left, we found in the niche, under some rubbish, what I took to be a block of bronze. I was about twice the size of a common brick, quite heavy, and on every side it was inlaid with gold in strange designs. I sent it up to be put with the other stuff in the storeroom, and shortly afterward was told that the sheik was above, asking to see me privately. When, at my request, he joined me in the tomb, he was greatly excited, and his first words were, "I have lost a small bronze block belonging to that case; have it seen it about here?'

"'My friend,' I said, 'in return for your services I agreed to give you a certain case and contents. Have I fulfilled my promise?' He replied, 'Yes, but' – 'All bronze blocks,' I put in, 'and everything else, outside the case, belong to me and I shall keep them.'

"At this the sheik said not another word, but, with a murderous scowl on his face, turned and left the pit.

"Upon quitting work for the day, I went to the storeroom and hid the block in a corner, under a pile of tools. Later, when my assistants had gone back to headquarters, and the laborers had settled down for the night, I called in Sam, my African servant, and one of the native laborers, an intelligent, trustworthy Arab, and arranged with them for guarding the storehouse during the night. I was to take the first and longest watch, Sam the next, and the native the last, which would end when the camp was astir in the morning.

"This plan was carried out, and nothing occurred while either myself or Sam was on duty. When the Arab took his post, I examined the building inside and out, but found the block in place and everything in proper condition.

"Upon resuming my bunk, where I had slept like a top through Sam's watch, I found that sleep had deserted me, and for more than an hour I tossed about, unable to close my eyes. At last I dropped off into a doze, from which, a few minutes later, I awoke with a start. Something had disturbed me, I knew not what, but a faint echo seemed to ring in my ears, as of a voice calling for help.

"Jumping up, I made for the storehouse at the top of my speed.

"The moon had not yet gone down, so that objects near by were fairly visible.

"When standing close to the building, I saw what brought me up standing.

"The door stood wide open, and some one was moving about inside!

"The Arab was nowhere in sight.

"Approaching close to the opening, I called out the man's name. There was no reply, and the noise within ceased.

"As I stood there, peering into the dark room, there was a sudden scrambling, a horrible, snarling cry, and out of the doorway came something on all fours which, leaping past me like a flash, was out of sight almost before I could move.

"Recovering my wits, which, I confess, were scared out of me for the moment, I was inside the room and at the hiding place with a lantern in short order.

"The block was gone!

"A hasty examination showed that nothing else was disturbed, and that the door had been forced by pressure from without; the broken lock, and screws torn from the wood, indicating that extraordinary force had been applied.

"Outside, lying on his back, close to the building, I found the watchman. The poor fellow was dead. His neck was broken, his face distorted with fear and horror, and upon his throat were deep scratches, from which the blood was still flowing.

"Arousing the camp, I had the body taken to the hospital tent, and explained to the men that their comrade had been murdered by a burglar who failed to secure anything of value.

"What it was that did the deed, I could not imagine, but I felt assured that the sheik was the responsible party, and determined to visit him at an early hour.

"Soon after sunrise, I was standing in front of my tent, when, to my surprise, Ali, the dwarf, rode up at a furious gallop. Without dismounting or uttering a word, he thrust into my hand a folded paper and, turning, was off again like a shot. The paper contained these words:

The sheik sleeps, and I have stolen away. He has sworn you shall die as did your guard. If you are brave, come to his tent at midnight with axe and knife. The guards will sleep, and I will help you. The block is –

"Here the note broke off abruptly, as though the writer had been interrupted, and just what he meant by that reference to the block I'd have given something to know.

"That evening I went back to headquarters with the rest, leaving the storehouse in charge of an assistant and armed guards.

"I believed that Ali's note was written in good faith, and determined to act as he advised, but alone, and without the knowledge of any of my people.

"Shortly before midnight I was in the vicinity of the sheik's tent, which stood near the edge of the oasis, its entrance facing the desert.

"As I cautiously approached the door, the moonlight enabled me to see, stretched on the ground in front of it, the body of a man, his hands clasping a long gun. Already one of Ali's statements was verified. The guard slept, and soundly too, I could see that.

"Just then the sheik's voice rang out in a sort of wild chant, and I prepared for action.

"Securing the broad-bladed hatchet I had brought with me, to my wrist, by means of a leather loop on the handle, and carrying a stout hunting knife in the other hand, I stepped over the sleeper and peered into the tent. A tall screen in front of the door cut off my view completely. Then I crawled through the opening and stood behind the screen. Cutting a slit in this with my knife, I could see that rugs and skins covered the ground, and screens stood at the sides, and at the opposite end of the tent, which was large and oblong in shape. In the center was a table, draped in black, and in front of this, with his back towards me, stood the Arab.

"He wore a black robe that reached from his neck to his heels, and in his right hand was a short, black rod, which waved back and forth in unison with the chant.

"On the table I could see the bronze block, and beside it lay the beautiful scimitar, its hilt glittering in the rays of the lamp that hung from the top of the tent.

"Neither Ali nor the case was in sight, but I felt confident that the dwarf was near, ready to lend a hand, if necessary.

"With weapons ready for instant use, I moved towards the table, and my hand was already on the block before the Arab knew I was there.

"A startled cry fell from his lips as he saw me. His hand flew to the sword, and, quicker than I can tell it, he aimed a blow which, had it reached me, would have split me to the shoulders.

"A leap aside, however, saved me, and before he could straighten himself, I dropped the hatchet and sent in a right-hander that nearly lifted him off his feet. He recovered himself, though, like a born prize-fighter, and, with blood streaming from his nose and mouth, and a hellish fire blazing in his eyes, he sprang at me again.

"But just then a gleam of light flashed by me and I heard a dull, crunching sound. The Arab's rush was suddenly checked. His sword wavered an instant, and then fell to the ground. The hand that held it dropped and closed convulsively upon something that protruded from his breast. It was instantly withdrawn, and with it, the fingers already stiffening around the haft, came a long, broad-bladed knife, dripping with blood. A dark stream followed and flowed over the long robe.

"The Arab swayed to and fro several times; then, with a gurgling, choking cry, he fell to the ground, dead!

"As if in response to the cry, and before I could turn to see where the knife came from, I heard a savage snarl, and something sprang upon me from behind. A pair of long, brown arms were clasped round my neck, and instantly my clothing was being torn to shreds, and my flesh gashed by fingers that were more like claws of steel.

"So sudden and fierce was the attack that I staggered forward and would have fallen, had not my assailant's backward tug kept me on my feet.

"My throat seemed to be the point aimed at, and in its mad efforts to reach this, the beast, or whatever it was, soon had my shoulders laid bare and channels dug into my flesh, from which the blood ran in streams.

"I am a powerful man, as you know, Frank, but in the grasp of this fiend I was as helpless as a child. Try as I might, I could not shake him off, and my utmost exertions failed to prevent his inhuman gouging and tearing.

"I had dropped my knife when first attacked, and all I could do was hold my head down to protect my throat, and make an occasional futile stroke with the hatchet.

"Soon I began to grow week from loss of blood.

"I wondered vaguely what had become of Ali, and, in a voice scarcely audible, I called upon him for help.

"As I did so, my head went back with a jerk, and the sharp claws sank into my throat.

"Death in a frightful form was very close to me when Ali's shout of encouragement reached my ears, and I felt, rather than heard, quick blows falling upon the body of my assailant.

"The pressure on my throat relaxed, the terrible arms dropped by my shoulders, and I was free!

"I fell against the table, gasping for breath, but still conscious that another struggle was going on near me, and that Ali might be needing help, as I had.

"Pulling myself together, I turned to take a hand, when, as I am a living man, Frank, I found myself gazing upon the mummy we had resurrected!

"There was no mistaking that stumpy, powerful body, or those features, now distorted with rage, and more horrible than ever.

"Just now it was facing me, making short, savage rushes at Ali, who, knife in hand, eluded the attacks with wonderful agility, driving the blade into the Thing at its every attempt to reach him.

"Stiff with horror and unable to stir, I watched the fight until Ali, in avoiding a vicious rush, slipped and, ere he could recover himself, was in the clutches of the monster.

"With one long arm it hugged the little fellow close to its body, and the free hand was already at his throat before the power to move returned to me.

"Then, staggering forward, I raised the heavy hatchet and, with all the strength in me, I brought it down squarely upon the top of the ugly head.

"I heard the crash and saw the blade eat its way through the skull to the neck – and then I fainted.

"The next thing I knew, I was lying on a pile of rugs, and Ali was busy patching me up. So potent were his remedies and treatment that, in a little while, I was on my feet nearly as strong as ever, and feeling only a trifling pain from my injuries.

"'Where is the mummy?' was my first query.

"'I chopped the accursed thing up, and my men are now burning it,' Ali replied.

"'You and I, this night,' he went on, 'rid the world of two monsters. How the sheik put life into the Thing, I know not. He had strange powers. He knew yon tomb existed, and that in it was the body of one who, ages ago, had been a high priest and mighty magician. He knew that with the priest were buried his profoundest secrets – those by which he controlled the elements, and even life itself.

"'He knew, moreover, by what dread means the priest had preserved his trance-like existence through all these centuries, and had acquired the formula by which life could be restored to the body.

"'Many of his mysteries he learned through me by various unholy methods, one of which you witnessed; but his prying into things forbidden was hateful to me, and I often refused to aid him, until beaten into submission.

"'The sheik was aware that the priest's secrets were contained in a bronze casket, and this, he believed, was in the case with the body. In the thing under the priest's head he was sure he beheld the object of his search, and when he found this to be nothing but a block of wood, he was mad with rage and disappointment. He knew, then, that the casket must be in your possession, and your refusal to give it to him did not tend to lessen his anger. So furious, indeed, was he, that he beat me cruelly, and swore he would get the casket if he had to kill you all.

"'I then swore I would kill him for beating me.

"'At night the miracle was performed that let loose the evil one, whose first act was to murder your guard and bring back the box.

"'This night he would have opened it and disclosed its mysteries to the sheik, who, once master of them, would have made the other his slave, else taken his life for good.

"'Here is the casket,' continued Ali, handing me what I had hitherto thought to be a block of bronze; 'take it, but never dream of looking inside. The contents would make one, able to secure and use them, the most powerful of all created beings; but woe to him who would handle them, or even attempt to open the casket, without proper knowledge. This knowledge is now lost forever, and I would bury the unholy thing where none would ever find it, were I not sure it would be safe with you.

"'Take this, also, as a token of my regard and slight return for saving my life,' and he put into my hand the magnificent scimitar, sheathed, and in its snakeskin covering.

"'The sheik,' he went on, ignoring my objections to receiving so valuable a gift, 'claimed to be my father. He lied; but as I am recognised as his son by my tribe, I shall succeed him, and all his possessions are mine.'

"Here I endeavoured to force upon him the diamonds left by the sheik as a pledge; but Ali refused them, saying, that as the sheik had broken his agreement, the jewels were rightfully mind.

"As to the death of the sheik, that had been explained, he said, to his people as the result of an attempt of the Arab's to murder me; and having been a cruel task-master, his death caused joy rather than grief.

"Already the body was being prepared for removal, and in a few hours, the boy explained, the would start for home.

"Where that home was, or how it was reached, however, Ali obstinately refused to tell me, and from the moment when I rode away from the door of his tent, where he stood motionless, watching me until he faded out of sight, I have never seen nor heard from this savior of my life.

"My wounds I had no occasion to exhibit, and so easily accounted for as the result of my fight with the Arab, my version of which was the more readily accepted as that night the strangers disappeared, leaving no trace behind them.

"Thanks to Ali's ointment, my injuries soon healed, and to this day, Frank, you are the only one to whom I have ever told their history.

"Do you wonder at my silence?"

THE STORY OF
BAELBROW

E. AND H. HERON

It is a matter for regret that so many of Mr Flaxman Low's reminiscences should deal with the darker episodes of his career. Yet this is almost unavoidable, as the more purely scientific and less strongly marked cases would not, perhaps, contain the same elements of interest for the general public however valuable and instructive they might be to the expert student. It has also been considered better to choose the completer cases, those that ended in something like satisfactory proof, rather than the many instances where the thread broke abruptly amongst surmisings, which it was never possible to subject to convincing tests.

North of a low-lying strip of promontory of Bael Ness thrusts a blunt nose into the sea. On the ness, backed by pinewoods, stands a square, comfortable stone mansion, known to the countryside as Baelbrow. It has faced the east winds for close upon three hundred years, and during the whole period has been the home of the Swaffam family, who were never in any wise put out of conceit of their ancestral dwelling by the fact that it had always been haunted. Indeed, the Swaffams were proud of the Baelbrow Ghost, which enjoyed a wide notoriety, and no one dreamt of complaining of its behaviour until Professor Jungvort, of Nuremburg, laid information against it, and sent an urgent appeal for help to Mr Flaxman Low.

The Professor, who was well acquainted with Mr Low, detailed the circumstances of his tenancy of Baelbrow, and the unpleasant events that had followed thereupon.

It appeared that Mr Swaffam, senior, who spent a large portion of his time abroad, had offered to lend his house to the Professor for the summer season. When the Jungvorts arrived at Baelbrow, they were charmed with the place. The prospect, though not very varied, was at least extensive, and the air exhilarating. Also the Professor's daughter enjoyed frequent visits from her betrothed – Harold Swaffam – and the Professor was delightfully employed in overhauling the Swaffam library.

The Jungvorts had been duly told of the ghost, which lent distinction to the old house, but never in any way interfered with the comfort of the inmates. For some time they found this description to be strictly true, but with the beginning of October came a change. Up to this time and as far back as the Swaffam annals reached, the ghost had been a shadow, a rustle, a passing sigh – nothing definite or troublesome. But early in October strange things began to occur, and the terror culminated when a housemaid was found dead in a corridor three weeks later. Upon this the Professor felt that it was time to send for Flaxman Low.

Mr Low arrived upon a chilly evening when the house was already beginning to blur in the purple twilight, and the resinous scent of the pines came sweetly on the land breeze. Jungvort welcomed him in the spacious, firelit hall. He was a stout German with a quantity of white hair, round eyes emphasized by spectacles, and a kindly, dreamy face. His life-study was philology, and his two relaxations: chess and the smoking of a big Bismarck-bowled meerschaum.

"Now, Professor," said Mr Low when they had settled themselves in the smoking room, "how did it all begin?"

"I will tell you," replied Jungvort, thrusting out his chin, and tapping his broad chest, and speaking as if an unwarrantable liberty had been taken with him. "First of all, it has shown itself to me!"

Mr Flaxman Low smiled and assured him that nothing could be more satisfactory.

"But not at all satisfactory!" exclaimed the Professor, "I was sitting here alone, it might have been midnight – when I hear something come creeping like a little dog with its nails, tick-tick, upon the oak flooring of the hall. I whistle, for I think it is the little 'Rags' of my daughter, and afterwards opened the door, and I saw" – he hesitated and looked hard at Low through his spectacles, "something that was just disappearing into the passage which connects the two wings of the house. It was a figure, not unlike the human figure, but narrow and straight. I fancied I saw a bunch of black hair, and a flutter of something detached, which may have been a handkerchief. I was overcome by a feeling of repulsion. I heard a few, clicking steps, then it stopped, as I thought, at the museum door. Come, I will show you the spot."

The Professor conducted Mr Low into the hall. The main staircase, dark and massive, yawned above them, and directly behind it ran the passage referred to by the Professor. It was over twenty feet long, and about midway led past a deep arch containing a door reached by two steps. Jungvort explained that this door formed the entrance to a large room called the Museum, in which Mr Swaffam senior, who was something of a dilettante, stored the various curios he picked up during his excursions abroad. The Professor went on to say that he immediately followed the figure, which he believed had gone into the museum, but he found nothing there except the cases containing Swaffam's treasures.

"I mentioned my experience to no one. I concluded that I had seen the ghost. But two days after, one of the female servants coming through the passage in the dark, declared that a man leapt out at her from the embrasure of the Museum door, but she released herself and ran screaming into the servants' hall. We at once made a search but found nothing to substantiate her story.

"I took no notice of this, though it coincided pretty well my own experience. The week after, my daughter Lena came down late one night for a book. As she was about to cross the hall, something leapt upon her from behind. Women are of little use in serious investigations – she fainted! Since then she has been ill and the doctor says 'Run down.'" Here the Professor spread out his hands. "So she leaves for a change tomorrow. Since then other members of the household have been attacked in much the same manner, with always the same result, they faint and are weak and useless when they recover.

"But, last Wednesday, the affair became a tragedy. By that time the servants had refused to come through the passage except in a crowd of three or four – most of them preferring to go round by the terrace to reach this part of the house. But one maid, named Eliza Freeman, said she was not afraid of the Baelbrow Ghost, and undertook to put out the lights in the hall one night. When she had done, and was returning through the passage past the Museum door, she appears to have been attacked, or at any rate frightened. In the grey of the morning they found her lying beside the steps dead. There was a little blood upon her sleeve but no mark upon her body except a small raised pustule under the ear. The doctor said the girl was extraordinarily anæmic, and that she probably died from fright, her heart being weak. I was surprised at this, for she had always seemed to be a particularly strong and active young woman."

"Can I see Miss Jungvort tomorrow before she goes?" asked Low, as the Professor signified he had nothing more to tell.

The Professor was rather unwilling that his daughter should be questioned, but he at last gave his permission, and next morning Low had a short talk with the girl before she left the house. He found her a very pretty girl, though listless and startlingly pale, and with a frightened stare in her light brown eyes. Mr Low asked if she could describe her assailant.

"No," she answered, "I could not see him, for he was behind me. I only saw a dark, bony hand, with shining nails, and a bandaged arm pass just under my eyes before I fainted."

"Bandaged arm? I have heard nothing of this."

"Tut-tut, mere fancy!" put in the Professor impatiently.

"I saw the bandages on the arm," repeated the girl, turning her head wearily away, "and I smelt the antiseptics it was dressed with."

"You have hurt your neck," remarked Mr Low, who noticed a small circular patch of pink under her ear.

She flushed and paled, raising her hand to her neck with a nervous jerk, as she said in a low voice:

"It has almost killed me. Before he touched me, I knew he was there! I felt it!"

When they left her the Professor apologised for the unreliability of her evidence, and pointed out the discrepancy between her statement and his own.

"She says she sees nothing but an arm, yet I tell you it had no arms! Preposterous! Conceive a wounded man entering this house to frighten the young women! I do not know what to make of it! Is it a man, or is it the Baelbrow Ghost?"

During the afternoon when Mr Low and the Professor returned from a stroll on the shore, they found a dark-browed young man with a bull neck, and strongly marked features, standing sullenly before the hall fire. The Professor presented him to Mr Low as Harold Swaffam. Swaffam seemed to be about thirty, but was already known as a far-seeing and successful member of the Stock Exchange.

"I am pleased to meet you, Mr Low," he began, with a keen glance, "though you don't look sufficiently high- strung for one of your profession."

Mr Low merely bowed.

"Come, you don't defend your craft against my insinuations?" went on Swaffam. "And so you have come to rout out our poor old ghost from Baelbrow? You forget that he is an heirloom, a family possession! What's this about his having turned rabid, eh, Professor?" he ended, wheeling round upon Jungvort in his brusque way.

The Professor told the story over again. It was plain that he stood rather in awe of his prospective son-in-law.

"I heard much the same from Lena, whom I met at the station," said Swaffam. "It is my opinion that the women in this house are suffering from an epidemic of hysteria. You agree with me, Mr Low?"

"Possibly. Though hysteria could hardly account for Freeman's death."

"I can't say as to that until I have looked further into the particulars. I have not been idle since I arrived. I have examined the Museum. No one has entered it from the outside, and there is no other way of entrance except through the passage. The flooring is laid, I happen to know, on a thick layer of concrete. And there the case for the ghost stands at present." After a few moments of dogged reflection, he swung round on Mr Low, in a manner that seemed peculiar to him when about to address any person. "What do you say to this plan, Mr Low? I propose to drive the Professor over to Ferryvale, to stop there for a day or two at the hotel, and I will also dispose of the servants who still remain in the house for, say, forty-eight hours. Meanwhile you and I can try to go further into the secret of the ghost's new pranks?"

Flaxman Low replied that this scheme exactly met his views. But the Professor protested against being sent away. Harold Swaffam however was a man who liked to arrange things in his own fashion, and within forty-five minutes he and Jungvort departed in the dogcart.

The evening was lowering, and Baelbrow, like all houses built in exposed situations, was extremely susceptible to the changes of the weather. Therefore, before many hours were over, the place was full of creaking noises as the screaming gale battered at the shuttered windows, and the tree-branches tapped and groaned against walls.

Harold Swaffam, on his way back, was caught in the storm and drenched to the skin. It was, therefore, settled that after he had changed his clothes he should have a couple of hours' rest on the smoking-room sofa, while Mr Low kept watch in the hall.

The early part of the night passed over uneventfully. A light burned faintly in the great wainscotted hall, but the passage was dark. There was nothing to be heard but the wild moan and whistle of the wind coming in from the sea, and the squalls of rain dashing against the windows. As the hours advanced, Mr Low lit a lantern that lay at hand, and, carrying it along the passage, tried the Museum door. It yielded, and the wind came muttering through to meet him. He looked round at the shutters and behind the big cases which held Mr Swaffam's treasures, to make sure that the room contained no living occupant but himself.

Suddenly he fancied he heard a scraping noise behind him, and turned round, hut discovered nothing to account for it. Finally, he laid the lantern on a bench so that its light should fall through the door into the passage, and returned again to the hall, where he put out the lamp, and then once more took up his station by the closed door of the smoking-room.

A long hour passed, during which the wind continued to roar down the wide hall chimney, and the old boards creaked as if furtive footsteps were gathering from every corner of the house. But Flaxman Low heeded none of these; he was waiting for a certain sound.

After a while, he heard it – the cautious scraping of wood on wood. He leant forward to watch the Museum door. Click, click came the curious dog-like tread upon the tiled floor of the Museum till the thing, whatever it was, paused and listened behind the open door. The wind lulled at the moment, and Low listened also, but no further sound was to be heard, only slowly across the broad ray of light falling through the door grew a stealthy shadow.

Again the wind rose, and blew in heavy gusts about the house, till even the flame in the lantern flickered, but when it steadied once more, Flaxman Low saw that the silent form had passed through the door, and was now on the steps outside. He could just make out a dim shadow in the dark angle of the embrasure.

Presently, from the shapeless shadow came a sound Mr Low was not prepared to hear. The thing sniffed the air with the strong, audible inspiration of a bear, or some large animal. At the same moment, carried on the draughts of the hall, a faint, unfamiliar odour reached his nostrils. Lena Jungvort's words flashed back upon him – this, then, was the creature with the bandaged arm!

Again, as the storm shrieked and shook the windows, a darkness passed across the light. The thing had sprung out from the angle of the door, and Flaxman Low knew that it was making its way towards him through the illusive blackness of the hall. He hesitated for a second; then he opened the smoking-room door.

Harold Swaffam sat up on the sofa, dazed with sleep.

"What has happened? Has it come?"

Low told him what he had just seen. Swaffam listened half-smilingly.

"What do you make of it now?" he said.

"I must ask you to defer that question for a little," replied Low.

"Then you mean me to suppose that you have a theory to fit all these incongruous items?"

"I have a theory, which may be modified by further knowledge," said Low. "Meantime, am I right in concluding from the name of this house that it was built on a barrow or burying-place"

"You are right, though that has nothing to do with the latest freaks of our ghost," returned Swaffam decidedly.

"I also gather that Mr Swaffam has lately sent home one of the many cases now lying in the Museum?" went on Mr Low.

"He sent one, certainly, last September."

"And you have opened it," asserted Low.

"Yes; though I flattered myself I had left no trace of my handiwork."

"I have not examined the cases," said Low. "I inferred that you had done so from other facts."

"Now, one thing more," went on Swaffam, still smiling. "Do you imagine there is any danger – I mean to men like ourselves? Hysterical women cannot be taken into serious account."

"Certainly; the gravest danger to any person who moves about this part of the house alone after dark," replied Low.

Harold Swaffam leant back and crossed his legs.

"To go back to the beginning of our conversation, Mr Low, may I remind you of the various conflicting particulars you will have to reconcile before you can present any decent theory to the world?"

"I am quite aware of that."

"First of all, our original ghost was a mere misty presence, rather guessed at from vague sounds and shadows – now we have something that is tangible, and that can, as we have proof, kill with fright. Next Jungvort declares the thing was a narrow, long and distinctly armless object, while Miss Jungvort has not only seen the arm and hand of a human being, but saw them clearly enough to tell us that the nails were gleaming and the arm bandaged. She also felt its strength. Jungvort, on the other hand, maintained that it clicked along like a dog – you bear out this description with the additional information that it sniffs like a wild beast. Now what can this thing be? It is capable of being seen, smelt, and felt, yet it hides itself successfully in a room where there is no cavity or space sufficient to afford covert to a cat! You still tell me that you believe that you can explain?"

"Most certainly," replied Flaxman Low with conviction.

"I have not the slightest intention or desire to be rude, but as a mere matter of common sense, I must express my opinion plainly. I believe the whole thing to be the result of excited imaginations, and I am about to prove it. Do you think there is any further danger to-night?"

"Very great danger to-night," replied Low.

"Very well as I said, I am going to prove it. I will ask you to allow, me to lock you up in one of the distant rooms, where I can get no help from you, and I will pass the remainder of the night walking about the passage and hall in the dark. That should give proof one way or the other."

"You can do so if you wish, but I must at least beg to be allowed to look on. I will leave the house and watch what goes on from the window in the passage, which I saw opposite the Museum door. You cannot, in all fairness, refuse to let me be a witness."

"I cannot, of course," returned Swaffam. "Still, the night is too bad to turn a dog out into, and I warn you that I shall lock you out."

"That will not matter. Lend me a macintosh, and leave the lantern lit in the Museum, where I placed it."

Swaffam agreed to this. Mr Low gives a graphic account of what followed. He left the house and was duly locked out, and after groping his way round the house, found himself at length outside the window of the passage, which was almost opposite to the door of the Museum. The door was still ajar and a thin band of light cut out into the gloom. Further down the hall gaped black and void. Low, sheltering himself as well as he could from the rain, waited for Swaffam's appearance. Was the terrible yellow watcher balancing itself upon its lean legs in the dim corner opposite, ready to spring out with its deadly strength upon the passer-by?

Presently Low heard a door bang inside the house, and the next moment Swaffam appeared with a candle in his hand, an isolated spread of weak rays against the vast darkness behind. He advanced steadily down the passage, his dark face grim and set, and as he came Mr Low experienced that tingling sensation, which is so often the forerunner of some strange experience.

Swaffam passed on towards the other end of the passage. There was a quick vibration of the Museum door as a lean shape with a shrunken head leapt out into the passage after him. Then all together came a hoarse shout, the noise of a fall and utter darkness.

In an instant, Mr Low had broken the glass, opened the window, and swung himself into the passage. There he lit a match and as it flared he saw by its dim light a picture painted for a second upon the obscurity beyond.

Swaffam's big figure lay with outstretched arms, face downwards, and as Low looked a crouching shape extricated itself from the fallen man, raising a narrow vicious head from his shoulder.

The match spluttered feebly and went out, and Low heard a flying step click on the boards, before he could find the candle Swaffam had dropped. Lighting it, he stooped over Swaffam and turned him on his back. The man's strong colour had gone, and the wax-white face looked whiter still against the blackness of hair and brows, and upon his neck under the ear, was a little raised pustule from which a thin line of blood was streaked up to the angle of his cheekbone.

Some instinctive feeling prompted Low to glance up at this moment. Half extended from the Museum doorway were a face and bony neck – a high-nosed, dull-eyed, malignant face, the eye-sockets hollow, and the darkened teeth showing. Low plunged his hand into his pocket, and a shot rang out in the echoing passage-way and hall. The wind sighed through the broken panes, a ribbon of stuff fluttered along the polished flooring, and that was all, as Flaxman Low half dragged, half carried Swaffam into the smoking-room.

It was some time before Swaffam recovered consciousness. He listened to Low's story of how he had found him with a red angry gleam in his sombre eyes.

"The ghost has scored off me," he said with an odd, sullen laugh, "but now I fancy it's my turn! But before we adjourn to the Museum to examine the place, I will ask you to let me hear your notion of things. You have been right in saying there was real danger. For myself I can only tell you that I felt something spring upon me, and I knew no more. Had this not happened I am afraid I should never have asked you a second time what your idea of the matter might be," he ended with a sort of sulky frankness.

"There are two main indications," replied Low. "This strip of yellow bandage, which I have just now picked up from the passage floor, and the mark on your neck."

"What's that you say?" Swaffam rose quickly and examined his neck in a small glass beside the mantelshelf.

"Connect those two, and I think I call leave you to work it out for yourself," said Low.

"Pray let us have your theory in full," requested Swaffam shortly.

"Very well," answered Low good-humouredly – he thought Swaffam's annoyance natural under the circumstances – "The long, narrow figure which seemed to the Professor to be armless is developed on the next occasion. For Miss Jungvort sees a bandaged arm and a dark hand with gleaming – which means, of course, gilded – nails. The clicking sound of the footstep coincides with these particulars, for we know that sandals made of strips of leather are not uncommon in company with gilt nails and bandages. Old and dry leather would naturally click upon your polished floors."

"Bravo, Mr Low! So you mean to say that this house is haunted by a mummy!"

"That is my idea, and all I have seen confirms me in my opinion"

"To do you justice, you held this theory before to-night – before, in fact, you had seen anything for yourself. You gathered that my father had sent home a mummy, and you went on to conclude that I had opened the case."

"Yes. I imagine you took off most of, or rather all, the outer bandages, thus leaving the limbs free, wrapped only in the inner bandages which were swathed round each separate limb. I fancy this mummy was preserved by the Theban method with aromatic spices which left the skin olive-coloured, dry and flexible, like tanned leather, the features remaining distinct, and the hair, teeth and eyebrows perfect."

"So far, good," said Swaffam. "But now, how about the intermittent vitality? The pustule on the neck of those whom it attacks? And where is our old Baelbrow ghost to come in?"

Swaffam tried to speak in a rallying tone, but his excitement and lowering temper were visible enough, in spite of the attempts he made to suppress them.

"To begin at the beginning," said Flaxman Low, "everybody who, in a rational and honest manner, investigates the phenomena of spiritism will, sooner or later, meet in them some perplexing element, which is not to be explained by any of the ordinary theories. For reasons into which I need not now enter, this present case appears to me to be one of these. I am led to believe that the ghost which has for so many years given dim and vague manifestations of its existence in this house is a vampire."

Swaffam threw back his head with an incredulous gesture.

"We no longer live in the middle ages, Mr Low! And besides how could a vampire come here?" he said scoffingly.

"It is held by some authorities on these subjects that under certain conditions a vampire may be self-created. You tell me that this house is built upon an ancient barrow, in fact, on a spot where we might naturally expect to find such an elemental psychic germ. In those dead human systems were contained all the seeds for good and evil. The power which causes these psychic seeds or germs to grow is thought, and from being long dwelt on and indulged, a thought might finally gain a mysterious vitality, which could go increasing more and more by attracting to itself suitable and appropriate elements from its environment. For a long period this germ remained a helpless intelligence, awaiting the opportunity to assume some material form, by means of which to carry out its desires. The invisible is the real; the material only subserves its manifestation. The impalpable reality already existed, when you provided for it a physical medium for action by unwrapping the mummy's form. Now, we can only judge of the nature of the germ by its manifestation through matter. Here we have every indication of a vampire intelligence touching into life and energy the dead human frame. Hence the mark on the neck of its victims, and their bloodless and anæmic condition. For a vampire, as you know, sucks blood."

Swaffam rose, and took up the lamp.

"Now, for proof," he said bluntly. "Wait a second, Mr Low. You say you fired at this appearance?" And he took up the pistol which Low had laid down on the table.

"Yes, I aimed at a small portion of its foot which I saw on the step."

Without more words, and with the pistol still in his hand, Swaffam led the way to the Museum.

The wind howled round the house, and the darkness, which precedes the dawn, lay upon the world, when the two men looked upon one of the strangest sights it has ever been given to men to shudder at.

Half in and half out of an oblong wooden box in a corner of the great room, lay a lean shape in its rotten yellow bandages, the scraggy neck surmounted by a mop of frizzled hair. The toe strap of a sandal and a portion of the right foot had been shot away.

Swaffam, with a working face, gazed down at it, then seizing it by its tearing bandages, he flung it into the box, where if fell into life-like posture, its wide, moist-lipped mouth gaping up at them.

For a moment Swaffam stood over the thing; then with a curse he raised the revolver and shot into the grinning face again and again with a deliberate vindictiveness. Finally he rammed the thing down into the box, and clubbing the weapon, smashed the head into fragments with a vicious energy that coloured the whole horrible scene with a suggestion of murder done.

Then, turning to Low, he said:

"Help me to fasten the cover on it."

"Are you going to bury it?"

"No, we must rid the earth of it," he answered savagely. "I'll put it into the old canoe and burn it."

The rain had ceased when in the daybreak they carried the old canoe down to the shore. In it they placed the mummy case with its ghastly occupant, and piled faggots about it. The sail was raised and the pile lighted, and Low and Swaffam watched it creep out on the ebb-tide, at first a twinkling spark, then a flare of waving fire, until far out to sea the history of that dead thing ended 3000 years after the priests of Amen had laid it to rest in its appointed pyramid.

THE VANISHED MUMMY

CHARLES BUMP

In the detective headquarters in the Courthouse they have mistakenly built up a very high notion of my sleuth qualities. Personally I have always felt that such help as I have been able to render them in two or three different cases was most largely due to luck, and only in a small degree to the exercise of logic and common sense in making deductions of subsequently proven importance from apparently trivial facts. Nevertheless, the good fortune that attended me in those cases fixed my reputation with them as the Sherlock Holmes of Balti – more, while the generosity with which I permitted them to take all the glory of solving the mysteries made me solid and caused them to consult me the more frequently in hours of perplexity. At the same time, I confess it, the love of the game made me eager to be in it and I not only installed a 'phone in my apartment in the Arundel, but I was always careful, in absenting myself from my office or my flat, to leave word where I would most likely be found during the next few hours. In this way the puzzled Vidocqs were usually able to reach me when my help was needed.

I was whiling away a rainy Saturday afternoon at the Maryland a few weeks ago when I saw Borland making signs to me from the passageway behind the boxes on the right of the theatre. Lieutenant Amers' redcoated British band, of which I had grown very fond, was rendering the final crashing bars of the overture to "Wilhelm Tell," and, with my passionate love for music, I was loth to leave until the programme was completed. But Borland was a detective who never came for me unless there was an interesting mystery to offer and I left my seat at once and joined him in the lobby.

"Which way, Borland?" I asked.

"Woman's College, sir," he answered, just as briefly.

I gave an exclamation of surprise. An institution attended by hundreds of girls from the best families of America was not the place one would expect a mystery of crime.

"Very curious case, sir. Mummy of an Egyptian princess stolen."

"Odd affair," I remarked. "Gives promise of being most unusual. Any clue?"

"Not a shred, sir."

On our way out to the College on a Roland-Park car, Borland gave me a recital of such facts as he had learned. The mummy had been secured in Egypt with much difficulty by President Goucher and was one of the prized possessions of the College museum. Partly divested of its wrappings of fine linen turned brown with the centuries, the body of this daughter of the Pharaohs had been exhibited in a glass case on the second floor of Goucher Hall, while nearby had been placed the case in which it had rested for ages, a case of wood painted with figures and hieroglyphics that told the rank and virtues of the little lady.

The night before at 6 o'clock the mummy had been in its place. In the morning when the janitor's wife was sweeping she discovered the glass lid prized open and the mummy gone. The night watch- man saw nothing, heard nothing.

"And what are your theories?" I asked Borland, as we passed along Twenty-third street.

"That it was taken to be sold at a good figure to some other museum; that it was taken to be sold back to the College; that it was a students' prank; or that it was done by girls being initiated into one of the College secret societies."

When I had been introduced to and cordially welcomed by a trio of anxious College officials, the dean hastened to assure me of their desire to avoid publicity and notoriety.

"Have you questioned any of the girls today?" I asked.

"No," replied the dean; "it being Saturday, there have been few of them here, and we have sent for none, so that the loss might be kept secret until we determine on the motive."

A close examination of the empty glass case and its surroundings was fruitless. Nor did questioning of the janitor and his wife elicit anything new.

"You cleaned very thoroughly," I said to the woman. "What did you do with the sweepings?"

"They're in a box in the basement, sir."

At my request the box was brought up. It was a soap box almost full. "Are these only the sweepings of today?" I asked. The janitor spoke up. "I emptied all the others yesterday, sir," he declared. With this assurance, I plunged my hands into the pile and began a minute and careful search of it, dumping handful after handful on news- papers spread over a table in Dr. Goucher's office. Borland kept the others in conversation, and this fortunately enabled me to make a couple of finds unnoticed by them.

At the end of ten minutes I had reached the bottom of the box. Turning then to the dean, I said:

"How many Canadian students have you here?"

"Canadians? Oh, two Miss Carothers and Miss Anstey,"

"And may I see them?"

"I cannot see...," began the dean warmly.

I hastened to assure him I had no idea of suspecting them. "Nevertheless," I added, "I should like to question them. I have a theory that one or the other may help me.

The dean was mollified. "Miss Carothers has been absent sick for several days. Miss Anstey you can see. She is a charming girl. Her father is one of the leading Methodist divines of Canada, and an old friend of Dr. Goucher and myself. She does not live in the College homes, but with a lady around the corner on Charles street, who is also an old family friend. I will send you there. She may not be at home just now, but you can try."

The janitor's wife spoke up, "Miss Anstey was here an hour or so ago, sir.

She was upstairs for a few minutes, and then went out and got in an auto with a young gentleman."

"I will go around to her home at any rate," I said.

"You have very little hope of finding the mummy, have you not, Mr. McIver?" asked the dean, anxiously.

"On the contrary," I replied confidently. "I expect to bring back the Egyptian princess in an hour or two."

He accepted my boast dubiously. "Whatever you do," he urged, "use no questionable methods, for the sake of the College. If you find the thief, let me decide whether to prosecute him. If you can get back the mummy without injury, I would prefer to hush up the affair."

I promised him I would. "I consider this a very unusual case," I said, "and I believe you will be satisfied with my disposition of it." With this I left him.

Borland and the College professor who accompanied us were both eager to know what clue I had, but I stood them off as we walked round to the Charles street dwelling.

Miss Anstey was out, as I had anticipated, but we were graciously re-received by Mrs. Eden, her hostess. It was a home of culture and refinement, and the large parlor abounded in paintings, art objects and other curios evidently picked up in foreign travel. "I expect Ethel home soon," said the sweet-faced and sweet-voiced old lady. "She went motoring this afternoon with a friend, and she said she would be home to supper."

"We called to ask," I remarked, "whether she had not lost this bit of jewelry." And to the surprise of Dorland and the professor I produced a pin I had found in the sweepings of Goucher Hall, a tiny enameled maple leaf, set around with pearls.

"Yes, that is Ethel's!" exclaimed Mrs. Eden. "I don't think she lost it, how- ever, for she had recently loaned it to a friend." She smiled. "You know, young girls nowadays have a great habit of exchanging tokens like this with young men. It was not so in my day."

"And if I be not rude," I continued, "may I not know the name of this young man?"

"Why, certainly," replied the lady. "He is Mr. Raymond Harding."

"You mean," I inquired, "the son of Mr. Harding, the bank president?" The Hardings, as everybody knows, are among the best-known millionaire families in Baltimore society.

"The same," replied Mrs. Eden. "Miss Anstey and he have been friends for a couple of years. I am sure both will be grateful to you for finding this pin. Now that I recall it, it may be that they have already had words about it being lost. He was here last evening and they were both rather excited. At breakfast Ethel complained of having a headache and looked as though she had been crying. They called each other up several times by 'phone during the morning, but Ethel told me nothing, and I thought it tactful to say nothing to her. When he came this afternoon I told her she looked so pale she ought to rest, but she laughed me off."

"We will come again after they have returned," I said to Mrs. Eden as I rose to go. "Perhaps, as you say, I may be able to straighten out the little trouble. Meanwhile, I would suggest that you say nothing to them."

It had grown dark when we stepped outside. Dorland gripped my hand warmly. "McIver," he exclaimed, "you're a wonder! I see the whole case now. Gee, but its a rum affair!"

The professor was mystified. "I don't quite see, gentlemen, how the whole affair is settled. Where is the mummy? And who was the thief?"

"The mummy, professor," I remarked, oracularly, "is most probably in the automobile of Mr. Raymond Harding."

"You don't mean that he is the thief?"

"I believe he took the mummy. I believe he dropped the pin in doing it. This also fell out of his auto cap." I produced a gilt paper initial "H," such as hatters put in headwear for their customers. It was my second find in the sweepings.

"But the motive, man, the motive!" persisted the professor. "Why should a millionaire's son break into a Woman's College building to steal a mummy? It sounds ridiculous."

"That, sir, is the part I want Miss Anstey to explain. It is the only element of doubt in a perfectly plain chain of circumstances. Raymond Harding I know slightly, and he has a certain reputation for reckless pranks, although he's not a bad fellow."

"But surely you don't suspect Ethel Anstey. Why, man, she's a –"

The mournful notes of a Gabriel's horn down at Twenty-second street betokened the approach of an auto, and interrupted the professor's eulogium of one who was manifestly a favorite pupil. "Quick!" I exclaimed; "saunter to the corner." A big touring car came up Charles street and stopped in front of the Eden home. A slender young chap stepped out and aided a young lady to descend. They stood for a minute on the curb beside the machine undecided, as I figured out, whether the mummy would be safe there if left alone and then both passed into the house.

The three of us with one accord moved down the pavement. "Look on the rear seat, Borland," I said, as the headquarters man ran to the auto. A great part of my confidence in my well- developed solution of the mystery would have gone to smash if the mummy had not been there. But Borland gave a little cry of triumph. "It's here, all right," he called, "wrapped up in a rubber blanket." We tried to lift the bundle, but the petrified daughter of the Pharaohs was heavier than he had calculated. "Be careful, Mr. Borland," the professor entreated; "don't smash her."

"Now for the young man," said Borland, jumping down to the curb.

"No," said I. "I have a better plan. Can you run an auto?"

Borland could.

"And have you a key to Goucher Hall?" I asked the professor.

The professor had.

"Then you two quietly take the mummy back to her box while I go in and question Miss Anstey."

They got off without fuss, and when I had seen them turn the corner I rang the bell and asked for Miss Anstey. In placing my hat on the hallrack I moved Harding's cap to another peg and observed, as I had thought, that the "H" had parted company with the other gilt initials.

I felt unfeignedly sorry for the girl when she came into the parlor a few minutes later. She had fine regular features, and with her limpid blue eyes was unquestionably pretty when the flush of youth and vivacity had full play. But that day there were dark circles under her eyes, her lids were suspiciously red and there was a pallid hue in her cheeks that was accentuated by the dark blue silk suit she wore. A novice at reading character could have told she had been spending hours in worry and tears.

"You wished to see me?" she said, inquiringly, as she slowly advanced to where I had risen to meet her.

"To return this," I answered. And I held out the maple leaf pin to her.

She grew, if possible, more white and sought the help of the piano to support herself.

"I– I– It is not – Where did you get it?" she said, with several gulps to keep down the sobs.

"It was found in Goucher Hall near the mummy case."

She stepped back uncertainly. Then she pulled herself together.

"You are a detective?"

I winced. "No," I said; "I am a friend of the College and of Mr. Harding's."

At the mention of his name she broke down completely and, sinking on the stool, leaned her head and began to cry. "Oh, Raymond!" I heard her say. "It means disgrace. It means the penitentiary." Her form shook violently with her emotion. It was more than I could stand.

"Listen, Miss Anstey," I said, and I laid my hand lightly on her shoulder. "It means nothing of the kind. You have my word as a gentleman that no one shall know the story save the two or three who already know it."

She lifted her tear-stained face and studied me earnestly. "It was a mad prank," she sobbed. "I am to blame. I ought to be punished. It started as a joke. I had no idea he'd do it."

"Call Raymond down."

206

She went out into the hallway and a whistled signal brought Harding to us. When he entered the parlor his surprise at seeing me was great.

"He knows about the mummy," said the girl faintly.

Harding stepped away from us both. "He knows?"

"Yes, he wants to help us."

"I want to get you out of a nasty scrape, Raymond," I remarked.

The boy eyed me intently. Then he put out his hand and gripped mine. "Thank you, McIver," he said, simply. And the three of us sitting down, the boy and the girl told me the whole truth about the kidnapping of the Egyptian princess. Each supplied parts of the narrative. Raymond, I learned, had prized open the case on a visit to the College museum on Friday afternoon and had then secreted himself in the building. When the watchman was in a remote corner, it had taken but a minute to lift the mummy, carry it downstairs, unlock the north door and slip out to where he had left his auto. "Then he came here to show it to me," said Miss Anstey. "And then I went to take it back," pursued the boy. "And, Lord, McIver, I found the watchman had locked the door. Ever since then we've been in an awful fright. I didn't know what to do with the bloody thing."

"What on earth made you take it?" I asked.

The boy turned a troubled eye on the girl. "I did it on a dare," he said after a pause.

A rosy flush had replaced her pallor. "That isn't the whole truth, Mr. McIver," she said. "There was a wager, and a lot of teasing, and talk about a kiss. It sounds so silly now, but it was all in fun. I didn't expect him to do it. And, oh! How sorry I am!"

"The question is, McIver," said the boy, "how on earth am I to get it back."

"That's the easiest part," I said. "In fact, it is already back." I paused to enjoy their pleased surprise. "And if I mistake not here are the two gentlemen that did it." The doorbell had rung and I stepped out to admit Dorland and the professor.

The next fifteen minutes was a medley of questions, of explanations, of promises to keep mum and of expressions of heartfelt thanks from the young couple. The professor was the only one who thought it incumbent to scold them for a silly prank and to point out the serious danger in which they had been involved. It sobered them, and at the same time it made them realize what a tremendous service I had done them.

One point puzzled Dorland. When we had left the house and parted from the professor, he asked me:

"How on earth did you know that pin was Miss Anstey's?"

"Had it been a thistle design," I said, "I should have begun a search for that 'bonnie sweet lass', the Maid o' Dundee."

"I don't exactly see," he ejaculated.

"The maple leaf, my son, is the national emblem of Canada."

"Ah," said Dorland, "that's what you get by book-larnin'."

"Yes," I admitted; "it helps some."

THE DEATH-BRIDAL OF NITOCRIS

GEORGE GRIFFITHS

The City of a Hundred Kings, vast and sombre, stretched away into the dim, soft distance of the moonlit night to right and left and far behind him. In front lay the broad, smooth, silver-gleaming Nile, then approaching its full flood-time, and looking like a wide, shining road out of the shadows through the light and into the shadows again—symbol of the visible present coming invisibly out of the domains of the past, and fading away into the still more hazy domain of the unknown future. Symbol, too, in its countless ripples under the fresh north wind, of the generations of Man drifting endlessly down the Stream of Time.

He was standing in the dark shadows of a huge pylon at one end of the broad white terrace of the palace of Pepi in Memphis – he, Ma-Rimon, Priest of Amen-Ra and Initiate of the Higher Mysteries.

Nitocris was standing beside him with her hands clasped behind her and her head slightly thrown back, and as she gazed out over the river the moonlight fell full on the white loveliness of her face and into the dark depths of her eyes, where it seemed to lose itself in the dusk that lay deep down in them, a dusk like the shadow of a soul in sorrow.

He looked upon her face, and saw in it a beauty and a mystery deeper even than the beauty and the mystery of the Egyptian night as it was in those old days – the face of a fair woman, a riddle of the gods which men might go mad in seeking to read aright, and yet never learn the true meaning of it.

The silence between them had been long and yet so solemn in its wordless meaning that he had not dared to break it. Then at length she spoke, moving only her lips, her body still motionless and her eyes still gazing at the stars, or into the depths beyond them.

"Can it be true, Ma-Rimon? Can the gods indeed have permitted such a thing to be? Can the All-Father have given His Chief Minister to be the instrument of such a foul crime and monstrous impiety as this?"

And he replied, slowly and sadly:

"Yes, it is true, Nitocris, true that thou art now Queen in the land by the will of the great Ramesses; and true also it is that the shade of Nefer is now waiting in the halls of Amenti till his murderers shall be sent by the hand of a just vengeance into the presence of the Divine Assessors."

"Ah yes, vengeance," she replied, turning towards him with a gasp in her voice, "that must come; but whose hand shall cast the spear or draw the bow? We claim kinship with the gods, but we are not the gods, and what mortal hand could avenge a crime like this?"

"A woman's hand is soft and a woman's lips are sweet, yet what so cruel or so merciless in all the world as a woman? As there is nothing more like Heaven than a woman's love, so there is nothing more like Hell than a woman's hate. So saith the Ancient Wisdom, O Nitocris; and therefore, as thou hast loved Nefer the Prince, so shalt thou also hate Menkau-Ra and Anemen-Ha, his murderers and the destroyers of his promised happiness."

She shivered as he spoke, not with cold, for the breath of that perfect night was well nigh as soft as her touch and as warm as her own breath. She turned swiftly and laid her hand on his shoulder. Her touch was as light as the falling of the rose-leaves in the gardens of Sais, yet he trembled under it, and his face, which had been as pale as her own before, flushed darkly red as she looked into his eyes.

"You – yes, you, Ma-Rimon, you too love me, do you not – truly? The stars are the eyes of the gods: they are looking on you. Tell me, do you love me? Does your blood throb in your veins when I touch you? Does your heart beat quicker when you come near me? Are your ears keener for my voice than for that of any other woman – tell me?"

His hands went up and clasped hers as they lay on his shoulders. He took her right hand and pressed it to his heart, and laid her left hand on his cheek. Then he let them fall. He stepped back, bowed his head, and said:

"The Queen is answered!"

"Not the Queen, but the woman, Ma-Rimon, and as a woman loves to be answered. And now the woman shall speak. Nefer is dead, yet is not Nefer re-incarnated in another form, another man of another build, but yet Nefer that was – and is beside me now?"

She whispered these words very softly and very distinctly, and as the words came rippling out from between her half-smiling lips, she took half a pace forward and looked up into his face.

"Not dead – Nefer – I!" he exclaimed, starting back. "Have not the Paraschites done their work on his body? Is not his mummy even now resting in the City of the Dead? How can it be? Surely, Nitocris, thou art dreaming."

"And hast thou, a priest and sage, standing on the threshold of the Holy Mysteries, hast thou not learned the law which tells thee how, with the permission of the Divine Assessors, the souls of the dead may come back from the halls of Amenti to do their bidding in other mortal shapes? And what if they should have ordained that his soul should have thus returned?

"Thou, who art so like him that while he was yet alive mortal eyes could scarce distinguish the one from the other. May it not be that the gods, who foresee all things, made thee in the same image, perchance to this very end?"

"No, the riddle is too deep for me, even as that other riddle which I read in thy eyes, O Queen!"

"Let thy love help thee to read it, then!" she replied, coming to him and putting her hands on his shoulders again. "Tell me now, Ma-Rimon, what wouldst thou do if thy soul were now waiting in the land of Aalu and the soul of Nefer was listening to me with thine ears, and looking at me with thine eyes?"

"And if thou –"

"Yes, and if I too believed that this were so?"

He saw the sweet, red, smiling lips coming nearer to him, and felt the soft breath on his bare throat. He saw the deep eyes melting into tenderness as the moonlight shone upon them, and in the pale olive cheeks a faint flush swiftly deepened.

"Nefer or Ma-Rimon, I am mortal," he said, swiftly catching her wrists and drawing her towards him. "I am flesh and blood. I am man, and thou art woman – and I love thee! I love thee! Ah, how sweet thy kisses are! Now let the gods bless or curse, for never could they take away what thou hast given – and for it I will give thee all. All that has been, and is, and might have been! Priest and sage, Initiate of the Mysteries, what are they to me now! O Nitocris, my queen and my love! Sooner would I live through one year of bliss with thee than an eternity in the Peace of the Gods itself!"

The words of blasphemy came hot and fast between his kisses, and she heard them unresisting in his arms, giving him back kiss for kiss, and looking into his eyes under the dark lashes which half-hid hers; and so Ma-Rimon, the youthful Initiate of the Holy Mysteries, became in that moment a man, and so he began to learn the long lesson which teaches to what heights and depths a woman who has loved and hated can rise and fall for the sake of her love and her hate.

"And now, my Nefer," she went on, throwing her clinging arms round his neck again, "now, good-night! Go and dream of me as I will dream of thee, and remember that, though mortals may plan, the gods decide. We may try to paint the picture, but the outline is drawn by their hands and may not be changed by ours. But, so far as this matter is concerned, I swear by the Veil of Isis, by these sacred kisses of ours, and by the Uraeus Crown of the Three Kingdoms, that, rather than be sold as a priceless chattel to grace the triumph of Menkau-Ra, I will give myself, as others did in the old days, to be the bride of Father Nile. Remember that, and remember, too, that, whatever the outward seeming of things may be, I am thine and thou art mine, as it was, and is, and shall be, until the Peace of all Things shall come."

- 2 -

Then the dream-vision changed from moonlight to sunlight, from night to morning; for it was the dawn of the day that was to see, as all men believed, the gorgeous ceremony of the nuptials of the daughter of Ramesses with Menkau-Ra, the Mohar, chief of the House of War and mightiest of all the warriors of the Land of Khem, now that Ramesses had passed from the black banks of the Nile to the shores of Amenti, and his mummy was waiting the summons of the High Gods which should recall it to life in the fulness of time and the dawn of the Everlasting Peace.

Never had even the Land of Khem seen a fairer dawn. The East shone in silver, blushed into amethyst, and flamed in gold as the Restorer of all things rose bright and glorious in sudden splendour over the City of the White Wall. Standing on the flat roof of the temple of Ptah, he looked about him in the first flush of this morning which had just dawned, big with fate, not only for him and his beloved, but also for the Land of Khem, and perchance for the world.

The great river was spreading its annual blessings over the land. The waters were broadening out into wide shining sheets, and the slow, soft music of their rippling was stealing along the great water-walls of the temples and palaces which formed the river-front of Memphis. Only a week ago the victorious armies of Khem had brought their spoils and their prisoners across the eastern frontier. There had been fruit, bread, and flesh, and wine for the poor, and banquets of royal lavishness for those who could claim right of entry into the sacred circle which enclosed the Throne, the Temple, and the camp of the victorious warrior.

For days he had heard the name of Menkau-Ra the Conqueror shouted up to the heavens by the crowds that had thronged the streets and the market-places, and, mingled with it, he had also heard the name of the girl-queen whose arms had been about his neck, and whose lips he had kissed the night before, and he knew that even now the people were asking why the Conqueror should not wed the daughter of Ramesses, and become the father of a line of even greater and yet mightier Pharaohs.

He had heard their cries calmly and without anger, for he knew that one stolen hour of sweet intercourse with her meant much more than the Conqueror himself could win – something that could not be taken by force, or even through the will of the dead king. Her soul was his, and he knew well that the man to whom she had not given her soul would never be permitted to lay a loving hand on her body.

"Ah yes, there he comes, I suppose," he went on, still talking aloud to himself, as a shrill musical peal of silver trumpets broke out from the direction of the barracks to the north of the palace. "Alas! Were I but truly Nefer! That golden-crowned murderer – for sure I am that he killed him – he would not now be making ready for his triumph at the head of his victorious troops through the streets and squares of Memphis. If that were so, how glad a day this would be for Egypt and for us!"

But, as the Divine Assessors willed it, there was no triumph that day in Memphis. The sun had hardly risen to a level with the topmost wall of the Rameseum before messengers were sent out from the palace bearing the tidings that Nitocris the Queen had been stricken with a sudden malady, and that all festivities were to be deferred till the next day at the earliest.

That night, when the moon was sinking low down in the west towards the dark hills of the Libyan Desert, and the Isis Star was glowing palely like an expiring lamp hung high above the brightening eastern earth-line, he saw her muffled form gliding ghost-like towards him as he stood waiting for her on the terrace. She was clad like the meanest of her serving-maids, just as a common slave-wench who had stolen out to meet a lover of her own sort might have been. When she came within a pace of him, he held his arms out. She put hers out too, and for a moment they looked in silence into each other's eyes, and then she, seeing that the kiss which she expected did not come, parted her lips and said smilingly:

"You need not fear to kiss them, dearest, they have not yet been polluted by the lips of Menkau-Ra, although all the city has been hailing him as the betrothed of Nitocris."

Then he smiled too, and their lips met in such a long, silent kiss as only lovers give and take.

"Thy words are almost as sweet as thy kisses are, O Nitocris!" he said, "for I would sooner see thee – yes, I would sooner see thee in the hands of the Paraschites – this lovely body of thine dead – knowing that thy soul was waiting for mine on the shores of Amenti, than I would know that those sweet lips had been defiled by the touch of such as he; and yet surely thou hast spoken with him. Did he not claim the fulfilment of the promise of the great king?"

"Ah yes," she replied softly, as she slipped out of his arms, "but it is one thing to claim and another to get. Yes, I have spoken with him. I have promised all, and given nothing. I have not even yielded my hand to his lips, for I told him in answer to all the entreaties of his love – and of a truth I tell thee that he loves me very dearly, for that great, strong frame of his shook like a bulrush in the wind under the breath of my lightest words – that, until the last vows had made us man and wife, I would be his queen and he should be my subject and my slave, even as he was of the great Ramesses; and with this he was fain to be content, thinking, no doubt, how soon he would be my lord and master, and I his – his queen and plaything, bound by the law that may not be broken, to submit to every varying whim and humour of his passion."

"Thy master, Nitocris! Thine! Such shame could never be. Rather would the High Gods permit Death to be the Master of Life, or Night to be Lord of Day. Is there no other way?"

"Yes, there is another way, and only one to save me, Nefer – if truly the soul of my beloved is looking out of thine eyes into mine," she whispered, coming close to him and laying her hands lightly upon his shoulders, "there is another way, but it is the way that leads through the mystery of the things that are into the deeper mystery of the things that are to be – the way of death and vengeance. Tell me, my beloved, hast thou the courage to tread it with me?"

The lovely face, the pleading lips, the searching eyes were close to his. He could feel the soft contact of her body, even her fluttering heartbeats answering his. It was the moment of the supreme test, the parting of the ways – to the heights whose pinnacles reach to the heaven of Perfect Knowledge, or to the abysses whose lowest depths are the roof of hell; for there is but one heaven and one hell, and their names are Knowledge and Ignorance.

There lay the fulfilment of his vows, the renunciation of the lower life with all its potent witcheries of the senses, with all its exquisite delights and glittering prizes, fame and honours, power and wealth, and, dearest of all, the love of woman.

Here, clasped in his arms, stood Nitocris, her hands still resting lightly on his shoulders, her head lying on his breast, her eyes upturned, the star-beams swimming in their luminous depths.

"Nefer, beloved, answer me!"

The stars grew dim, and the solid floor of the terrace shook under his feet. He bent his head and laid his lips upon hers.

"Thou art answered, O Nitocris – even unto death and the life beyond!"

Her lips returned his kisses – kisses that were curses – and then for many minutes they conversed in hurried whispers. At last she slipped out of his arms and left him, his lips burning from the clinging touch of hers, and his heart cold with a fear that was greater than the fear of death.

He clasped his hands to his temples and looked up at the coldly shining Isis Star, and through the silence there came to his soul in the speech that is never heard by the ears of flesh the fateful words:

"Once only is it given to mortals to look into the eyes of Isis. He who looks and turns his gaze aside has found and lost."

- 3 -

The day of the bridal of Nitocris the Queen with Menkau-Ra the Conqueror had come and gone in a blaze of golden splendour. In all the Upper and Lower Lands no head was held so proudly as the head of Menkau-Ra, no heart beat so high as his that day, nor did any cheek bloom so sweetly, or any eyes shine so brightly as the cheeks and the eyes of Nitocris – so strange are the workings of a woman's heart, and so far are its mysteries past finding out.

And now the bridal feast was spread in the great banqueting hall which Pepi the Wise had made deep down in the foundations of his palace below the waters of the Nile at flood-time, and at midnight the waters would be at the full. It was here that Nitocris had sat at the betrothal feast with Nefer but a few hours before his death, for here he had drunk from the poisoned cup which Anemen-Ha the High Priest had prepared, and here only would Nitocris meet her guests.

The great hall shone with the light of a thousand golden lamps, which shed their radiance and the perfume from the scented oils in which were dissolved the most precious gums of the distant East.

The long tables, spread with snowy linen and loaded with vessels of gold and silver and glass of many hues and curious forms, flashed and glittered in the glow of the thousand flames. The vineyards of Cos and Sais had yielded their oldest and sweetest wines, red and purple and golden. The choicest meats and the rarest fruits that ripened under the glowing suns of Khem – all was there that could make glad the heart of man and fill his soul with contentment.

At the centre of the table, which stood on a raised platform in front of the great black pedestal of the Colossus of Pepi, Nitocris the Queen sat in her chair of ivory and gold, clad in almost transparent robes of the finest silk of Cos, shining with gems, and crowned with the Uraeus Snake, and the double diadem of the Two Lands.

On her right sat Menkau-Ra, crowned and robed in royal vesture, and on her left Anemen-Ha in his priestly garments of snowy linen. At the other tables sat their friends and kindred, the families of the Mohar and the High Priest, the chief officers of the victorious army and all the proud hierarchy of the Temple of Ptah, for was not this the triumph of Anemen-Ha no less than of Menkau-Ra?

Only Ma-Rimon was absent. He had disappeared from the temple early in the morning, and no one had given a thought to his going, for one base-born, even though of royal blood, had no place at the bridal feast of the Queen and her chosen consort.

The libations had been poured out to the Lords and Ladies of Heaven—to Ptah the Beginner, and Ra the Lord of Day, to Sechet the Lady of Love and War, and Necheb the Bringer of Victory; and when the slaves had carried round the viands till all were satisfied, the guests were crowned with garlands, and the jars of the oldest and choicest wines were broached. The feast was ended, and the revel was about to begin.

The last half of the last hour of the night was well-nigh spent, and while the guests were waiting for the signal from the royal table, the Queen rose in her place, and, in the silence that greeted her, her voice sounded sweetly as she spoke and said:

"O my guests – ye who are the holiest and the bravest in the Land of Khem, though our hearts are joyful, and our souls refreshed with wine and good cheer, let us not forget the pious customs and wise ways of our ancestors, for it is fitting that in such hours as this our hearts should be turned from pride by the remembrance that we live ever in the presence of death, and that this world is but the threshold of the next. Ill, too, would it become me to forget, in the midst of my present happiness, to pay the honour due to him who might have shared this crown with me; wherefore let the noble dead be brought into our midst, so that the soul of Nefer, looking down from the flowery fields of Aalu, may see that in the hour of our joy we do not forget the sorrow of his untimely death."

Then she clapped her hands, and Menkau-Ra and Anemen-Ha shifted in their seats, and looked at each other with eyes of evil meaning as six slaves appeared at the lower end of the hall, bearing upon their shoulders the mummy-case of Nefer, the dead Prince, beloved of Nitocris. Now low, sad music sounded from a hidden source, and to the cadence of this the slaves marched slowly round the tables, followed by the eyes of the silenced and sobered guests. Then they stopped in front of the Queen's seat, and she said:

"Let the case be set up against the central pillar yonder, and let the face of the Prince be uncovered, that I may look upon him who was to have been my lord."

"But if I may speak, Royal Egypt," said Anemen-Ha, the chief of the House of Ptah, leaning towards her, "that would be beyond the law of the gods and the customs of the land. To look on the face of the dead were defilement for thee and us."

"Yet this once it shall be done, O Priest of the Father of the Gods," answered Nitocris, turning and looking into his eyes, "for last night I had a vision, and I saw the soul of Nefer come back to his mummy, here in this hall, at my bridal feast, and his eyes opened, and his lips spoke, and made plain to me many things that I greatly longed to know. But why shouldst thou turn pale and tremble, thou the holiest man in the land? What hast thou to fear, even if my vision came true? And thou, too, Menkau-Ra the Mighty, hast thou slain thy thousands, and yet fearest to look upon the face of one dead man? See, see!" and she pointed her finger at the face of the mummy. "By the power of the just and merciful gods, my vision shall be made very truth indeed! Look, Anemen-Ha, Priest of the God who is King of Gods! Look, Menkau-Ra, thou who wouldst reign in the place of Nefer. Behold, he has come back from the bosom of Osiris to greet thee!"

With eyes fixed and ears sharpened by such terror as only the sin-steeped soul can know, they saw the waxen eyelids of the mummy slowly rise, the dim, glazed eyes look out from underneath them, the dry, black lips move, and heard a thin, harsh voice say through the awful silence:

"Greeting, Nitocris, my Queen – greeting from the gloom of Amenthes, where I have waited too long for those who ere now should have stood with me in the Halls of Doom and the presence of the Assessors! Say now, thou who sittest feasting between my murderers, how much longer must I wait for thee and them?"

"Not long, O Nefer, my beloved, not long! Tarry yet a little while, O outraged soul, in the shape that once was thine, and thou shalt see thyself avenged. Lo, I hear the wings of Kefa, Goddess of the Flood-time, rustling in the silence of the midnight skies. She herself shall pour out a libation to thine injured shade!

"Nay, nay, my lords, and you good friends of those who did my own true lord to death, sit still, and drain a farewell cup with me, your Queen. It is too late to fly, for every way is closed. The High Gods have spoken, and I will do their bidding!" Then, extending her white, jewelled arms toward the mummy, she cried in a deeper, harsher tone: "O Nefer, my Prince and my love! There lives no man in Khem who shall take thy place beside me, or usurp the throne that should have been thine. I have sinned, but I repent me of the wrong. Lo, now I come and bring thee a goodly sacrifice to cheer thine angry heart – my lord, my love, I come!"

Held by the triple spell of guilt and fear and wonder, they listened to these terrible words in silence, white horror sitting on their blanching cheeks and brows.

As she ceased she raised her arms above her head, a golden cup full-crowned between her glittering hands. A moment she held it aloft, then dashed it to the floor, and cried in a voice that rang like the laughter of devils through the awful silence:

"Come, Kefa, come, and bear me to my lord!"

The goddess answered in a mighty rush and roar of waters, long pent and swiftly loosed. Then above the tumult rose the hoarse shouts of men and the shrill screams of women, and the crash and clash of tables overturned; then came the swirl and bubbling hiss of a flood that gleamed darkly under the golden lamps and swiftly rose towards them, bearing upon its surface white arms with outstretched hands gripping at the empty air, and gauzy robes which half hid gleaming limbs, white faces with wildly-staring eyes, and teeth that grinned between tight-drawn lips so lately smiling; strong swimmers fighting for another moment's breath, and one by one dragged down by many hidden hands: then the sharp hiss of swift-quenched flames, then darkness, and the stifling of sobbing groans into silence, and after that only the sibilant undertone of waters rushing swiftly past smooth walls through utter night.

CONTRIBUTORS

JOHN J. JOHNSTON is Vice-Chair of the Egypt Exploration Society. He is currently undertaking research on Ptolemaic mortuary beliefs and practices for his PhD at UCL, although his research interests encompass the reception of ancient Egypt in popular culture, sexuality in the ancient world and the history of Egyptology. He has lectured extensively on all of these topics throughout the UK and abroad and has contributed to the DVD/BD releases of two gloriously restored Hammer mummy films. In addition writing to a number of reception-based articles, he is co-editor of *Narratives of Egypt and the Ancient Near East: Literary Linguistic Approaches* (Peeters, 2011) and A *Good Scribe and an Exceedingly Wise Man: studies in honour of W.J. Tait* (Golden House, In press) and the author of the introduction to *The Book of the Dead* (Jurassic London, 2013).

JARED SHURIN has edited or co-edited anthologies of original fiction in conjunction with not-for-profit partners such as English PEN, Tate Britain and the Royal Observatory. In 2013, he was selected as one of the *Guardian*/Hospital Club's top 10 "Pioneers and Innovators" in publishing. He has won the British Fantasy Award for Non-Fiction twice, and his work has been a finalist for the Hugo, Shirley Jackson, BFS and BSFA awards.

GAREN EWING is the creator of the Adventures of Julius Chancer, with *The Rainbow Orchid* being named one of *The Observer*'s best graphic novels of 2012. Other work includes illustrations for books, magazines, websites, DVDs, and even a Royal Mail stamp. He lives in Sussex with his wife and two children.

THE EGYPT EXPLORATION SOCIETY

The Egypt Exploration Society was founded in 1882 by the writer Amelia Edwards, who had become captivated by Egypt and its history during a lengthy sojourn there in the winter of 1873-4. The visit, however, left her deeply troubled by the deterioration of many of the ancient sites and, together with a group of like-minded scholars and other interested individuals, she created the Society in order to fully explore and document the archaeological remains as a means of creating a lasting record of the country's ancient past.

Over the course of more than a century, the EES has explored hundreds of sites in Egypt, excavating not only tombs and temples but also entire towns and cities. Millions of the objects most threatened by treasure hunters have been excavated on behalf of the Society by some of the great names of Egyptology, resulting in substantial quantities of scientifically excavated artefacts entering many of the great museum collections in Egypt and throughout the world, where they continue to attract the attention academics and the public, alike.

Part of the EES' mission is to generate enthusiasm for Egypt's past and to raise awareness of the importance of protecting its sites, through continuing excavation, publication, and education. The EES relies almost entirely on public support to fund its work and needs your help, through subscriptions and donations, to ensure that it continues to fulfil its mission at a time when Egypt's heritage is no less threatened than it was at the time of the Society's conception.

To learn more about the work of the EES or to become a member visit their website at http://www.ees.ac.uk/

The Egypt Exploration Society is a Company limited by guarantee and registered in England No. 25816. Registered charity No.212384.

ACKNOWLEDGEMENTS

In addition to the countless writers, actors, directors, and crews, whose inspired work has strengthened my love of mummy fiction in all its forms, I would like to thank the Director and Board of Trustees of the Egypt Exploration Society for their support in producing *Unearthed* and *The Book of the Dead*, John Cunningham for his continuing patience with my numerous Egyptological and cultural obsessions, and Jared Shurin for making such a grisly business such extraordinary fun. - *John J. Johnston*

I would also like to thank the support of the Egypt Exploration Society, who have been a terrific partner in this endeavour. Also Anne Perry and Garen Ewing for their support, knowledge and patience (all of which were tested at the last minute). And, of course, John J. Johnston, who has the ability to bring make the driest and dustiest topics not just interesting, but fun. - *Jared Shurin*